THE MYSTERY OF THE MISSING HEIRESS

MISSING HEIRESS

GRAVESYDE PRIORY MYSTERY, #2

PATRICIA RICE

PLEASE JOIN MY READER LIST

Please consider joining my newsletter for exclusive content and news of upcoming releases. Be the first to know about special sales, freebies, stories from my writer life, and other fun information. You'll even receive a thank-you gift. Join me on my writing adventures!

To Join, Please Visit —
https://www.subscribepage.com/ricehr

ONE

APRIL 25, 1815, TUESDAY

JOHN CECIL DE SACKVILLE LOCATED THE BUTTONS OF HIS trousers and stumbled back up the muddy hill strewn with blue flowers. He wasn't much on botanicals and couldn't name them. Ale now—the tavern last night had a damned fine ale. His aching head was proof. Jack de Sack had an excellent head for alcohol, but he'd been felled by last night's barrel.

He probably shouldn't have celebrated so heartily on St. George's Day, but if he were to die with Wellington, he wanted to say farewell properly. Except, then he'd needed a hair of the dog that bit him the next day after he realized he'd have to make a substantial detour to rural outposts with an aching head. Now it was Tuesday, and he was lost. Civilian life took some adjustment, but he'd be a soldier again once he finished a few errands.

Having watered the hedgerow with this morning's partaking, Jack contemplated his very rural surroundings. If the recipients of the package he carried had oddly retired to the country when they should be in London, it was his responsibility to track them down. After all these years, he should at least have the courtesy to deliver it personally and explain the delay.

According to his directions, there ought to be a village nearby, although Gravesyde Priory seemed an ominous destination. Still, manors did not exist without villages, although he couldn't discern even a puff of smoke on the horizon.

A brook babbled between the dirt lane he traversed and abandoned fields. After the neat spring crops and paved roadways he'd passed on his way from the city, he wondered if he'd taken a wrong turn into an uninhabited farm.

He ran his hand over his cropped brown hair, swung a proper curly-brimmed beaver on top of it, and hoped his great coat protected his new civilian attire. He didn't want to ruin a lady's warm memory because the bearer was a wastrel.

Before untying his horse from the shrubbery, he checked his Hessians for mud—and spied a polished boot poking from blooming nettles beneath the hedgerow.

Jack's head wasn't so muddled as to not recognize Hoby's expensive new design. Those boots cost enough to feed a family of four—lousy for long horse rides but designed to impress ladies. *What the devil?*

In no particular hurry and always ready for a challenge, Jack unsheathed his sword from the saddle and hacked away at the brambles.

His gorge rose as the branches fell aside, and he discerned the owner of the boots. He'd seen dead bodies in his career. One did not fight Napoleon and spend years in India without viewing corpses. Sometimes, they were even men he knew. But they were usually soldiers who tempted death—not foppish nobles who sauntered city streets in fancy boots.

"Bastard." Jack stopped hacking and planted his sword in the muddy ground as he studied a face he hadn't seen since his frivolous youth. A dozen years ago, he'd considered him a friend. Ten years ago he would have cut off the fellow's head, if he had not been on the wrong side of the Channel at the time.

A dozen years and a bloody great hole in his head hadn't improved Culpepper's once handsome phiz.

Jack rolled his eyes skyward, but the Man above seldom provided answers.

He could leave the bastard here for the beasts of the field to gnaw on, save everyone a lot of trouble. Ten years ago, he probably would have.

He'd learned a little more respect for the law since his rakehell youth, not much, but some.

Why was an impoverished dandy on this road to nowhere? Even if Culpepper had changed his colors and finally left London to apologize to the lady whose happiness he'd destroyed, he'd missed the main highway. As far as Jack was aware, Elspeth still resided in Newchurch, well north of here. Besides, apologizing to everyone Culpepper had offended would probably take until Doomsday.

It seemed unlikely that the bastard would be on any such mission. Even so, Jack couldn't leave his corpse for the buzzards.

In disgust, he sheathed his sword. Malaria had weakened him, but he'd spent these past months rebuilding his strength. He tested it now, dragging the fop's body from the mud and tossing him over the saddle with more difficulty than he liked.

Good old Beans didn't do more than flinch at the stench of death. Jack petted the gelding, and in resignation, proceeded down the lane on foot. Fine gift he brought for poor Miss Knightley, a lady he'd last seen in the worst of circumstances. She'd think him cursed.

The guardian of his late friend's infant had been a bookish creature. Jack wasn't in the least surprised to learn she remained unmarried. He was rather surprised, however, to discover she'd leased her wealthy family's townhome and absconded to rural nonentity. He'd hoped to be on his way to Wellington by now, not traipsing about the Midlands.

Miss Knightley's lawyers had given him directions to this outpost of bloody rural Worcestershire. He hoped they hadn't misled him.

After hours of walking a corpse along the designated farm road, accompanied by swooping raptors and ravens, and meeting no one, Jack was ready to stop at the first tavern he found.

He owed Henry Owen a lot, but if the man hadn't been dead these six years or more, he'd have started counting the debt in reverse in recompense for this miserable jaunt. Maybe this suffering was the cost of not carrying out his duty sooner. He understood debts and finance in terms of money, not in personal obligation.

By the time he came across what appeared to be a newly repaired drive with a faded, overgrown sign indicating it belonged to his destination of Wycliffe Manor, he was in no humor for riding up with his ghoulish burden and setting off a household of shrieking females. Besides, the drive led up a bloody great hill with no manor in sight, and his boots had worn through. The village would be closer to the road. A village should have a physician or vicar or someone to handle this situation.

He told himself this lie until the first dilapidated chimneys came into sight.

KEEPING HER HEAD DOWN, AS A GOOD SERVANT SHOULD, LADY Elspeth Villiers carried her employer's market basket and stayed one foot behind the unsuspecting Miss Knightley. She desperately wished to keep the position of cook for Wycliffe Manor, but the kitchen staff recognized she wasn't one of them. She feared the disruption she caused by the basic breach of upstairs/downstairs rules would soon reach her employer's ears. It had been easy enough the first few weeks after the deaths of the manor's caretakers when all had been confusion. But now, settling into routine. . .

She really should confide in Miss Knightley. Her employer —and distant cousin—was a few years younger than herself but seemed knowledgeable and understanding. Living with the motley household of barely related family, she had to be. Surely her cousin wouldn't mind discovering one more of her family hidden in the kitchen—but then, she most likely would not allow Elsa to continue cooking.

As she was debating, a dusty gentleman in an expensive greatcoat and top hat, leading a magnificent gelding, walked down the lane. *Beans?* Was that Jack's Beanstalk?

Was that Jack? The hat concealed much of his face but the chestnut lock falling on his brow. . .

Oh, dear Lord in Heaven, what have I done to offend thee?

Elsa ducked her head and hid behind her employer. Miss Knightley was slender and Elsa most certainly was not, but her cousin's broad-brimmed bonnet could hide an elephant, and no one noticed servants.

The stench reached them first as the gentleman approached. Elsa held her nose, gagging. That's when she noticed the buzzards lazily looping overhead. She'd grown up in rural Staffordshire. She knew buzzards.

The gentleman halted a good distance away. "I'm sorry, my ladies. I will not come closer. Is there someone in authority with whom I might speak?"

Jack, that was definitely John Cecil de Sackville. He was *alive?* She could scarcely breathe for the rush of confusing emotion. He was alive and leading a *corpse?*

Undeterred by the horrid sight—and smell—Miss Knightley gestured toward the blacksmith's abandoned stable

PATRICIA RICE

half-hidden behind what must once have been a tavern. "You'll want to speak with Captain Huntley at the manor, but I do not advise going further with your burden. The stable is empty and has a door. Do you know how to find Wycliffe Manor?"

"I was heading that way when I encountered. . ." Even from a distance, his grimace was visible. "I apologize again and will not offend you with my company."

Studying him from beneath her lashes, Elsa decided the boy she'd once known had grown into a strikingly handsome man, although his cheekbones cut a little more sharply than they ought. Had he been ill? Injured? Unlike Captain Huntley, he seemed to have all his parts.

"We'll see you at the manor and exchange introductions then. I'll tell the captain to expect you." With the quiet dignity she'd employed to turn around a derelict household, Miss Knightley aimed for the manor footpath.

In the dilapidated cottages of Gravesyde, curtains dropped back. The village had very few inhabitants, most of them elderly. The gossip wouldn't fly far.

Elsa's tongue had turned to stone. She couldn't let Jack see her. She'd finally found a haven and didn't wish to leave. She simply could not go home, but if he told anyone he'd seen her. . . No, she did not dare speak to him, no matter how much she longed to.

But she whispered a quiet prayer of gratitude that her childhood friend had survived the war, even if he hadn't bothered to write, the ingrate.

The Honorable John de Sackville had always been a wild card, but he'd still, in his own way, been honorable. And an honorable man couldn't be trusted to conceal her whereabouts.

Had he killed a man? It had to have been in self-defense. Which meant. . . Elsa refused to consider what that might mean. Only, Gravesyde Priory was well off the highway from

6

London to Birmingham. Generally, travelers on this lane were headed for Wycliffe Manor. Jack had no reason to do so, did he?

The walking path to the manor cut over a babbling brook, up a hill, and through a forest of pines. The ground was covered in spring blossoms. Normally, she would have lingered to pick a bouquet of bluebells and campion to brighten her rooms in the cellar. Not today.

"I'll take the basket around to the kitchen," she murmured, hiding her agitation as they reached the upper drive.

"We should talk, Mrs. Evans," Miss Knightley said before Elsa could escape. "I hope you know you are safe here."

Elsa bobbed a curtsey. "Yes, miss."

CLARISSA KNIGHTLEY WATCHED HER EDUCATED, ARISTOCRATIC cook rush off to the servant's entrance of the manor in the rear and shook her head. Even had the cook's speech and mannerisms not given her away, the Reid family traits were revealing—blond hair, blue eyes, widow's peak, the odd ear lobes, dimples, and the wayward thumb.

She glanced at her hand, but her glove hid her thumb's backward tilt. She could be describing herself, except, the earl's descendants came in different sizes. She was average height and on the skinny side. Mrs. Evans was about the same height but possessed the bosom and plump curves men appreciated.

She had hoped the woman she knew as Lara Evans would eventually feel comfortable enough to speak up, but Wycliffe Manor. . . Clare sighed and hurried up the steps to the aging, carved front doors. The grim walls of the former priory were all that remained after the first earl had rebuilt it into a manor house. The stone gargoyles and turrets were foreboding even during the light of day. Add *another dead body. . .* They'd already buried an elderly butler, housekeeper, and a scoundrel who'd attempted murder to steal a valuable pharmacopeia.

They would need a chapel, a vicar, and a larger graveyard if any more corpses turned up. She couldn't blame poor Mrs. Evans for hiding in the kitchen. Wycliffe Manor would never be a luxurious country estate, and who would want to claim a seriously flawed family such as theirs?

At least, she did not think this visitor was family. As far as they were aware, no more males, other than her nephew, hung from the Reid family tree, and no descendant of the Earl of Wycliffe had brown hair. The family traits were distinctive, and the visitor did not possess them.

She detected a hint of soldier in the way the stranger carried himself, which made her want to run and hide.

But she was learning to be brave these days. The months she'd spent in Egypt with her sister and Bea's soldier husband were a distant memory, even if those last fateful days of terror would never fade.

Inside, she handed over her coat and hat to their illustrious new butler, Quincy, a massive door guardian who'd once been a prizefighter. "Where is Captain Huntley? We are about to have a visitor with a most unpleasant problem."

"He's just come out of the cellar to wash for dinner, miss. Shall I send Adam to let him know you wish to speak with him?"

That meant Hunt was bathing. He'd spent these last weeks preparing the crypt beneath the great hall for the new coal gas retort. Engineers simply were not gentlemen, she was learning. That didn't mean her overactive imagination didn't conjure a brief image of the strapping captain naked in a tub. That unsteadied her nerves more than the encounter with the stranger and his corpse.

"If you will, please. What about Arnaud or Walker? Are

they about? I do not think I should be the one to interview this visitor." She might *want* to hear the visitor's story, but she wasn't about to decide what to do with a dead body.

Her gothic novels didn't need to be that realistic. Which reminded her of the letter in her hand. Or guilt did. She was hiding from Aunt Martha so she might finish her novel in peace. Why had her aunt tracked her down?

"I'll have Adam send them to the captain's study, miss. Will there be anything else?" The butler hid any evidence of interest behind his smashed nose and stoic demeanor.

"Have Marie prepare a guest room for a gentleman, please." Clutching her unopened letter, she hurried up the marble stairs to the family floor. They needed to hire a house-keeper. She had no interest in running a place this large on her own.

Flinging her outer garments over a chair, she hastily popped the seal on her letter. Aunt Martha was a busybody married to her father's brother. Six years ago, after Clare's sister and her soldier husband, Henry Owen, had perished in Egypt, leaving their infant child behind, their aunt and uncle had declined to take on Oliver, citing age and illness. More like, lack of funds for a nursemaid and a disinclination to deal with children they'd never had. The Owen family had been equally disinclined to take on an infant. Which had left Clare, at the tender age of nineteen, the guardianship of her nephew.

Clare scanned the letter, skipping over the scolding for not telling her dearest relation, who only had Clare's best interest in mind, that she was renting her lovely townhouse while absconding to rural nonentity. In the final paragraph, there it was. *I have spoken with the Owens. They are equally concerned that Oliver is not in school. It is time he started making the connections necessary for families of our stature. Please let us know where you have enrolled him and when he will begin. The Owens are considering speaking with their solicitor about your guardianship.*

9

Clare swallowed hard. There it was, the sword of Damocles that perpetually hung over her. She'd been resentful when both families had insisted that she take responsibility for her sister's infant, but she'd understood. She'd been Oliver's nursemaid since birth, and he was attached to her. But, at nineteen, she'd still stupidly held out hopes of marrying. Her limited funds had not stretched to infant caretakers.

Now, she was glad she'd become Oliver's guardian. Nannies and governesses would not have understood her nephew's brilliance or oddities. Neither would Aunt Martha.

Hearing footsteps in the hall, she shoved the letter into her pocket. A moment later, Meera arrived with an arm full of clothes. They'd been best friends for years, even though Meera's Jewish-Hindu family were apothecaries, and Meera had been trained as one. Clare didn't know what she'd do without her.

Her friend was another reason Aunt Martha disapproved of Clare's eccentric London household. Heaven forfend that her aunt take it in her head to visit Wycliffe Manor!

Meera performed a grand curtsey in her new gown, and Clare studied the effect. "It is lovely! Our little seamstress has outdone herself. Turn about, let me see."

Dark-haired, round, and short, Meera spun about in her spangled India muslin. The high waist and fuller skirt hid the slight swell of the child she carried. The peach-colored crossover handkerchief bodice emphasized her splendid bosom. "It feels decadent."

"Walker's eyes will fall out of his sockets. I wish I possessed half your beauty." Clare opened her armoire to choose a dinner gown. The long-abandoned manor needed too much work to indulge funds in ladies' maids. She and Meera did for each other.

"You are beautiful in a different way," Meera assured her. "I am earthy. Your golden coloring is celestial. Besides, the captain is captivated even when you're wearing mobcaps and aprons. What are you frowning about?"

"Mysteries. While I love writing them, I am growing a little weary of dead bodies on the doorstep. If I do not mistake, we will have a guest at dinner tonight." Their visitor was more important than fretting over what she couldn't control.

"Dead bodies?" Having grown up as a physician's assistant, Meera was not in the least squeamish. She helped Clare unfasten her walking gown.

"Very dead, buzzards overhead and all. Unpleasant dinner conversation, so I will have to pry the story from Hunt later. I fear if he has to act as magistrate, he will take the next ship back to the Americas. He likes hammering things, but not gavels, I think."

"Would you go the Americas with him?" Meera asked, troubled.

"No, which is half our problem. His home is there. Mine is here. Or at least, mine is in London and partially here. Oliver needs to grow up in familiar surroundings. He's lost too much as it is."

"If he is destined to go off to school, would it make a difference where you live?" Meera buttoned the back of Clare's ice-blue sarcenet dinner gown. The fashion was several years old, but Clare preferred sleeves to the current strapless fashion. Lavender, her very young but talented seamstress cousin, had trimmed it with tulle so it almost seemed strapless.

The effect was wasted once she flung a shawl over her shoulders. The sixteenth-century manor wasn't exactly warm, even on a lovely April evening.

Clare sighed. "Since I have never been to school, I am no expert. I simply know he does not mix well with people. I fear I coddle him."

"I fear we're too far from civilization to find the tutor you

11

seek. He will have to attend school sometime." Meera pulled the pins from Clare's fine hair and brushed it out.

"He is doing better with all these men around. It's early days yet. We've only been here a little over a month. He's like a little sponge and has learned a great deal already. But that also means we should limit the people who stay to ones of good character."

"Except your entire family owns a share in this ramshackle abode, as your great-aunt calls it. They can't all be as refined as you." Meera began wrapping Clare's hair into ringlets and pinning them.

Clare laughed. "If I am the scale we measure by, then we could invite the entire village. This is a ridiculous discussion. There is a dead man in the blacksmith's stable. His killer might be coming to dinner. Perhaps we should dine up here."

Meera laughed loud and hearty.

Clare managed a wan smile in acknowledgment of the jest. She was already itching to run downstairs to see what their visitor had to say and resenting that the men would hear the tale first.

TWO

Captain Alastair Huntley, retired U.S. Army Corps of Engineers, did not want to hear the stranger's tale. He wanted his dinner and to talk with Clare.

Given that the visitor sat across the desk from him in his expensively tailored attire, looking solemn, he didn't seem to have a choice. Besides, Hunt's artist cousin, Arnaud Lavigne, waited, arms crossed and frowning, to hear the tale. Having barely survived a revolution, Arnaud did not take corpses lightly. Next to him, Walker, Hunt's stoic friend and African steward, merely observed.

Hunt propped his bad leg on a stool and poured brandy from the manor's fine cellar. His cousin had once said that their great-aunt, the French viscountess, most likely had it smuggled from her home and sold it to finance her needs. It was probably worth a fortune if Hunt meant to deal in illegal trade. Instead, he offered a snifter to the stranger, who accepted it gratefully. Arnaud and Walker declined.

Introductions had been exchanged, but being a newly arrived American, Hunt had no idea who the Honorable John de Sackville might be. The man wore several days' scruff on his jaw, but his brown hair had been recently barbered. The clothes were more expensive than Hunt's own wool and homespun. Given that the nobility didn't seem to pay for anything, Hunt didn't count that in their guest's favor.

"And you recognize this. . . person. . . you've left in a stable?" Hunt asked, settling his thoughts with a sip of brandy.

"The Dishonorable Basil Culpepper," the visitor acknowledged. "Younger son of a baronet and a wealthy Cit. His parents aren't bad people, and I hate to be the one who must notify them." De Sackville sipped his brandy gloomily.

"Better you than me, if they know you. I don't suppose they live nearby so we might deliver his remains?" Hunt had just buried three people in the manor's graveyard—none of them family. The village had only an abandoned chapel, no cemetery, and certainly no mortician. They would need an ice house if they were to become a morgue.

"The baronet and his wife will be in London this time of year." Their guest took another sip to fortify his courage and added, "Culpepper was murdered, a bullet straight through his skull. His horse was gone, so I assume thieves."

Hunt muttered imprecations under his breath. "We have no sheriff and no physician and no thieves of which I'm aware. As has been brought to my attention, this manor is an exclave of Shropshire, but unless Mr. Culpepper was killed on our doorstep, he probably died in Worcestershire. I am not familiar enough with legal proceedings to know on whom to call."

"Henri will confirm it when he returns." Arnaud stretched his long legs across the carpet. "To confuse matters, Birmingham is in Warwickshire, but it is closer than Worcester. Whether insane British law allows them to take interest in our problem is another matter entirely."

Provoking more problems than they resolved, England's ancient legal jurisdictions had given Hunt headaches since his arrival. "Henri is due back tomorrow, isn't he?"

Henri was Arnaud's younger brother. He'd set himself up as an itinerant peddler since losing their home in France to revolutionaries, but he knew everyone from the highest to the lowest.

"He is, and since there is little we can do tonight, Mr. de Sackville needs a chance to prepare for dinner." Walker pulled the rope beside his chair.

To his credit, the Honorable de Sackville hadn't blinked an eye at being introduced to an African steward, a French émigré, or a one-eyed American who looked the part of pirate. Hunt was inclined to accept their noble guest's character based on that alone.

The footman arrived to lead their guest upstairs. Hunt had no idea what arrangements Clare had made, but he was sure she had. His co-general in this mad household portrayed a demure lady well, but she wielded authority in every soft word—one of many reasons he worshipped her, when they weren't squabbling.

"Who tells the cook that dinner needs to be set back half an hour?" Hunt's knee was gradually strengthening, but that didn't mean he wouldn't play cripple if it got him out of unpleasant tasks. This demented manor had far too many stairs.

"I'll go. Mrs. Evans lets me taste test, and I'm famished." Arnaud hauled himself up. "If I didn't need to marry an heiress to support my general uselessness, I'd court the cook and never go hungry again." He strode out.

Since Arnaud had been starved for years as a prisoner in France and while hiding in England, he was a skeleton wearing gentleman's clothes. Once taller and broader than Hunt, he had a lot of eating to catch up on.

Without being asked, Walker rose. "I'll take a couple of stable hands and the cart and fetch the corpse. If he's a gentleman, we can't leave him rotting in a barn for the rats. They left the community coffin in our woodshed, didn't they?"

15

The village was so poor that they had a reusable coffin for laying out the dead and carrying them to the grave. Corpses were buried in only a shroud. Hunt grimaced. "It should still be there. We need a carpenter to help rebuild the cottages and for tasks like this."

"Pretty sure coffins don't come under the maintenance trust. Go over those numbers I left on your desk. Your gas lighting will put us over budget for the month." Walker ambled out.

They needed income. Hunt understood the warning. The old earl had wanted his estate maintained after his death and had left funds to do so. He hadn't cared if the inhabitants could clothe themselves. Or bury their dead, for all that mattered. The estate lawyers allowed the trust to feed the staff and call it maintenance. Family and guests benefitted from the largesse. But once the wine cellar was emptied, they'd have to buy their own.

The village's ownership and maintenance was another problem entirely, the one lawyers were currently debating. If only Clare's theory about the earl concealing family jewels on the property could be proved. . . But the codes Arnaud had discovered in family portraits were meaningless.

Walker had written the budget numbers large so Hunt didn't have to strain his one eye to read them in the lamplight. The rooms along this corridor had no windows. He made a few notes and pushed the purchase of some larger items to May.

Setting the books aside, Hunt finished his brandy while studying the family tree tapestry the last viscountess had embroidered. She'd left off the banker, Bosworth, because he was illegitimate, but she'd known about him. The natural son of the late viscount, the banker at least had a blood claim to the manor. Hunt's mother had only marriage lines to shield her legitimacy, despite the viscountess's dalliance with Arnaud's family.

Life was complicated. Basing inheritance on blood or family or title was arbitrary at best. Land should go to the people best able to care for it. That probably wasn't him, but it wasn't the banker either. The earl had no descendants capable of improving his once immense estates.

Instead, the heirs were dozens of females without the education, funds, or ability to restore this ancient edifice or the lands around it. Over the last decades, all the earl's great wealth had been whistled away by husbands and sons on their own interests. Understandable, but Hunt shook his head at the waste.

Bosworth the Bastard had apparently nursed dreams of claiming the land and manor, by hook or by crook, but he'd inherited no fortunes. And what did bankers know of farming or servants or keeping a sixteenth-century manor from moldering away? The man didn't even have a wife to help him.

A man needed a managing wife with domestic skills to run a household the size of this one—a sensible, intelligent woman like Clare. Like a sensible, intelligent woman, she might flee to the comfort of her city townhome at the first opportunity. Hunt couldn't blame her. Despite his growing affection for the meddling female, he was one eye blink from fleeing to Philadelphia. Or maybe, one corpse away.

Why was a noble dandy traveling in rural nowhere, and who would put a hole in his nob?

Jack had left his batman in India. He hadn't planned on remaining in England long enough to hire a valet. So he shaved as carefully as he could manage, eyed the hair dangling on his brow with disfavor, and shrugged. He wasn't here to court Miss Knightley, just deliver a long overdue package.

He dug his evening jacket out of his valise, and a maid scurried off to press it. She returned as he finished his hasty ablutions. The servants probably couldn't have their dinners until he'd had his, and the maid was ready to speed him on. Running on someone else's time was just one of many reasons he'd never settle into domesticity.

It hadn't worked well in the military, either, but it was the only profession he knew.

Using water to brush his hair back with a comb, he called himself ready. The return journey to the ground floor appeared simple enough—down the corridor to the marble stairs and ask a footman.

At the bottom of the stairs, a lanky young man in a new uniform coat, worn breeches, and darned stockings directed him to a small parlor where the family gathered. Jack would deliver the package this evening, leave Culpepper's remains in the captain's capable hands, and be gone on the morrow.

No one announced his entrance, but he didn't think too many guests turned up for dinner. He assumed, when the room's inhabitants watched his entrance, that they knew who he was. Despite the glorified surroundings of velvet draperies, coffered ceilings, and ostentatious oils larger than a poor man's walls, the company seemed to be an interesting collection one wouldn't normally find in London's rarefied spheres.

His host, in his black eyepatch, had donned what looked suspiciously like a uniform coat stripped of insignia. Captain Hunt offered an introduction to the slender blond lady Jack had met in the village. Without the enormous bonnet concealing them, her big blue eyes threw him back in time.

"Miss Knightley, of course! It's been years, but I remember you and your lovely sister gracing our company in Egypt." She'd been young and shy then. Wariness wrinkled her brow now. After the violent riot she'd suffered, he understood. Women had no place in backward foreign lands.

She curtsied. "Lt. de Sackville, this is quite a surprise. I'm glad to see the Army has treated you so well."

"Just a plain mister, not an officer any longer. I sold my colors and joined the East India Company after your departure. I'm not well suited to regimented behavior, I fear." He produced the wrapped package from his pocket. "And this is evidence of my inability to do anything properly. Owen asked me to deliver this to his son. I understand he's in your care these days?"

Looking surprised, Miss Knightley didn't accept the package but glanced around. "He's here about somewhere. Look for shoes beneath the draperies."

Of course, the infant he vaguely remembered must now be what, seven or so? Jack studied the wall of draperies. They were more faded and shabby than he'd first noticed, as if they'd hung there for a century. Probably had. He located a pair of dusty knees in the far corner, and his lips turned upward. "Ah, our lad is unsocial, is he? Shall I introduce myself?"

"He'll be out for dinner. Give him time to adjust to a stranger in our midst. Do you have any idea what Owen might have sent? His belongings were shipped to us after his death. I had not thought he owned more." She spoke softly, lingering near the captain and keeping a distance from Jack.

"I was told they were personal items. I assume a pocket watch and such that he had on him when he fell ill. They were packaged up when they were given to me as messenger." Jack shrugged uncomfortably. "I was headed home. He knew he was dying. I assume he thought I'd be better than the mail."

"But you didn't go home," the captain added.

Jack winced, hearing the disapproval. "The offer in India was lucrative. I'm a bit of a gadabout, I fear, not much for settling down. I completely forgot about the package until I boxed up my belongings to return home."

19

"And are you returning home for good?" Miss Knightley asked without censor.

Jack had to shove his hand in his pocket to prevent running it through his hair. "Well, truth to tell, I'm only here to sign up again. I'll pop in on the pater, but there's naught else to hold me here."

Visiting his father would mean visiting his childhood home and memories he'd prefer to forget. He was hoping to go in without warning, avoid the neighbors, and ride out again before anyone knew he had returned. In truth, there was no one at home a gallivant like him needed to see.

Suffering a sudden chill, he took a hurried gulp of very fine brandy. Thankfully, dinner was called, and the party filtered into the dining room in no particular order. Without formality, everyone settled into their favorite seats. Jack chose an empty one next to the boy and Miss Knightley, across from the African steward and a brown-skinned woman he could swear was Indian. He greeted her in Hindu.

She flashed him a white smile with a crooked front tooth. "I can return the greeting, sir, but that would be the limit of my skill. My mother died when I was quite young, and my father was English. We have not been formally introduced. I am Meera Abrams."

"Sorry, everyone, this is the Honorable John de Sackville." Miss Knightley gestured at the table. "Mr. de Sackville, I believe you have met Monsieur Lavigne and Mr. Walker."

The skeletal Frenchman sat at the far end of the table, next to empty chairs, where he commanded an entire platter of bread for himself. Jack wanted to know his story. Well, he also wanted to know about an African who spoke and dressed better than his employer, but he'd lived in Egypt and India and could deduce most of it.

His hostess continued speaking. "Meera is our resident apothecary and my closest companion. Next to Meera is Lavender Marlowe, our talented seamstress and great-granddaughter of the late Earl of Wycliffe. And this, of course, is Oliver Owen, my nephew."

The luscious Miss Marlowe flapped long lashes and offered an adolescent smile that would someday slay dragons. Jack considered himself well beyond the wiles of children but offered the impish miss a smile anyway.

But it was the solemn, suspicious boy next to him who commanded his attention. He remembered Henry Owen as big, boisterous, and always ready for adventure. His son more resembled Miss Knightley, small, blond, and wary. The Egyptian bomb and ensuing riot had exploded their lives and damaged the pair without actual physical injury.

"Master Oliver, pleased to meet you." Jack offered his hand to the boy. "I knew your father."

Big blue eyes much like his aunt's watched him with distrust. "He's dead."

"Yes, I'm afraid so. I think he was grieving your mother when he died of malaria. I've had malaria. It makes you so sick, you want to die." He probably shouldn't say this to a child, but he had no experience with children.

The boy's bottom lip stuck out as he considered this. "I have Aunt Clare. Papa needed Mama."

Jack glanced over the boy's head. Miss Knightley wiped away a tear. Uncomfortably warm, he returned to his bowl.

The lady took over the difficult discussion. "You are absolutely correct, Oliver. And your mama needed him. So now they're together and happy, and I have you, which makes me very, very happy." She hugged his frail shoulders.

Oliver squirmed but didn't protest. He simply dug into his soup.

At Miss Knightley's nod, Jack wriggled the palm-sized package out of his tightly tailored coat and set it on the table next to the boy's bowl. "I must apologize, Master Oliver. Your father gave me this before he died and asked that I deliver it to you personally. But I went to India instead."

The boy frowned at the package or the soup, it was hard to say. He didn't reach for it, as Jack had expected.

"Could be dragon eggs," the captain suggested casually, between spoons of soup.

"More likely calcified fruit cake," the steward offered without looking up.

"Diamonds and gold," Lavigne offered from the other end.

Miss Marlowe offered, "Pocket watch," which was what Jack had assumed. Apparently, exhaustion was catching up with him because he was feeling a little muzzy.

"Incense," Meera offered. "Do they have incense in Egypt?"

"Sand," the boy offered in disgruntlement. "They have sand and bugs."

"And beautiful objects that are even older than sand and bugs." He might not be much use in a family setting, but Jack knew how to keep up his end of a conversation. He produced an alabaster scarab he used as a watch fob. "This is the kind of bug they must have had before Jesus was born."

The boy's eyes widened as he examined the bug, then glanced at the package. "Dragon eggs."

Jack had no notion what dragon eggs might be, but he nodded in agreement. "Maybe. I make no promises."

All the occupants of the table watched while pretending to butter bread and eat their soup.

Reluctantly, Oliver picked at the package wrappings. It crumbled in his fingers, which seemed to amuse him. He took his time crumbling the paper rather than unwrap the string.

"The worms crawled out, the worms crawled in," Jack murmured, repeating an old nursery rhyme.

"Then she unto the parson said, Shall I be so when I am dead," Oliver solemnly intoned the next grim line. And finally, he ripped off the string.

A dusty handful of crystalized rocks fell out.

"Dragon eggs!" Oliver crowed.

Startled, Jack lifted an unpolished brownish crystal. *What the hell?* He studied the remainder of the unappealing dull stones scattered across the cloth. "Garnet," he said, handing the rock to Miss Knightley. Then, carefully picking through the pile, continued, "Turquoise, amethyst, malachite, and gold." He held up a larger chunk. "Unprocessed, none of it looks like much. Processed, I'd say Owen's dragon eggs are a tidy hoard."

Aware that everyone stared, he shrugged. "My task in India was to uncover precious stones. I'm quite good at it. Apparently, Owen wasn't half bad either."

THREE

As the staff ran up and down stairs, gossip filtered to the kitchen. Kneading the dough for tomorrow's bread, Elsa only half paid attention until she thought she heard the name *Culpepper*. Telling herself she misheard, she continued her task.

But even the memory of that name chilled her. Combining it with the arrival of Jack. . . If she were superstitious, she'd say it was time to move on.

Except. . . *she belonged here*. She felt it deep down in her bones. She couldn't run and hide again. According to the documents she'd received, as a great-granddaughter of the last earl of Wycliffe, she had as much right to live here as anyone above stairs. She simply didn't want her presence known.

So, after setting the loaves aside to rise, she took her dinner to the broad kitchen table and sat down, as had become their routine after an evening's work. She sipped and nibbled and listened. Her accent worked against her. The gossip would close up if she spoke.

"He's an explorer from furrin parts," simple Betsy said

with enthusiasm. As a local, and the first maid hired, she assumed priority.

"Quincy says he brung pirate's gold." Marie, one of the chambermaids whose grandparents lived in the village, took second in command. She managed to canoodle tittle-tattle from the otherwise stoic butler.

Elsa listened with half an ear while planning what she needed to prepare for the next day's meals. Gossip below stairs was as boring as any at home. Basic facts became buried under wild speculation with one storyteller attempting to outdo the other. She gathered that Jack had arrived from wherever he'd been and carried something valuable. Good for him. His family's wealth had been lost over the years, until his father was barely able to maintain the family estate. As the younger son, Jack had to make his way in the world. She hoped he'd come home a wealthy nabob.

It wasn't until Adam hurried down to eat that the news turned dark. The footman took a seat next to Ned, the deaf-mute, and announced, "They say above that the body had a bloody great hole in its skull."

A young stable hand nodded eagerly. "We peeked. He's a right rotter. Gotta put him in soon."

Elsa's stomach churned, and she pushed up from the table. "That's enough, gentlemen. Show respect for the dead and for the company. We should all say a prayer for the poor man, dying unknown and alone."

"Not unknown, ma'am," Adam said eagerly. "I heard them say his name was Culpepper, that the gentleman knows him."

At this verification of her fear, Elsa's head spun, and she grabbed the table for support.

Culpepper. If Jack knew him, then it had to be the same Culpepper, the man who had destroyed her life. Did Jack know that? He'd been fighting Napoleon at the time. Surely Jack had not. . .?

No, he wouldn't, not any more than her own stepfather would. Or anyone else, for all that mattered. Culpepper had trotted off, safe to ruin as many women as he liked, while she was relegated to rural spinsterdom in shame.

And now the dandy was dead. Agitated, she wanted to see that for herself, to know for certain she'd never cross his path again. Maybe stab a kitchen knife through his non-existent heart. . .

Excusing herself, she picked up a bin of peelings for the chickens and carried it up the cellar stairs to the stable yard as she did most evenings. April nights were still cool, but she didn't notice. Humiliation heated her as she hurried past the neat parterres of herbs and vegetables to the newly installed fence containing the latest batch of chicks. Scattering the peels, she studied the dark yard, but the stable hands were in the kitchen, eating. Gripping the now-empty bucket, she darted toward the gravel drive.

Surely they had not left the body in the stable for the horses to smell, even if the stalls contained only a pony and a couple of hacks. Jack's Beanstalk would be in there too.

She took a chance and checked the door on the woodshed. It was unlocked and unlit. Stupid of her not to bring a lantern.

The stench hit her first. How long had the perfumed dandy been left lying in a ditch? She suffered a moment's unseemly triumph that the rotten apple had fallen where it belonged. She'd pray for her soul later. Right now, vengefulness reined. Had it not been for the wicked. . . rotter. . . she'd be happily married now, living in a vicarage, baking for a family and the parishioners.

Without a light, she could only grope in the dark. The lid was down on the coffin. It wasn't as if she could see his face anyway. This had been a stupid. . . hateful. . . thing to do.

She simply needed to know that he was dead and gone and would haunt her no more. She would have that on the morrow when they buried him.

Scolding herself for the same kind of impulsive stupidity that had caused her troubles in the first place, she tugged her shawl tighter and hurried back to the manor.

Miss Knightley paced the neat paths of the apothecary's herb garden. Elsa faltered, but her cousin had already seen her.

"Ah, Mrs. Evans, perhaps you can distract me from my too-vivid fears. Would you have a cup of tea with me?" She gestured toward the manor's rear door, not the kitchen steps.

Heart stammering in terror, Elsa obediently fell in step, leaving the scrap bucket outside.

CLARE KEPT TEA LEAVES AND A POT IN THE SMALL SITTING ROOM she used when she was writing but wanted to be accessible to the household. She hadn't told anyone, other than Meera, that she was writing gothic novels. No one had ever asked what she scribbled.

Despite Hunt's tentative expression of courtship and her interest in being courted, she would have to return to London and society in the autumn. Aunt Martha and Uncle George would take Oliver away if Clare didn't provide a tutor soon, and that couldn't be done in rural nowhere. If they learned about her scandalous novel writing, even a tutor might not be sufficient. Only, writing would pay for a tutor—caught between a rock and a hard place.

The steaming kettle over the fire added comfort on cool nights. She made the tea while the nervous cook wandered the room, reading the titles on the bookshelves.

No cook raised in domestic service would ever do such a thing. Only an educated female accustomed to entire rooms with books would be comfortable surveying shelves while her employer made the tea.

Mrs. Evans woke to her duty a moment later, taking the

cups and setting them on the writing desk, waiting until Clare took the chair at the desk before perching on one across from her. Like a good servant, she did not speak unless spoken to.

"We should meet like this once a week to discuss menus and what the kitchen needs," Clare suggested after a soothing sip of Darjeeling. It had been a long evening of anxious discussion over Oliver's unexpected inheritance. Her nephew had gone to bed in the midst of it, taking his *dragon eggs* with him.

She was terrified he would lose them but couldn't bear to take away the only gift he'd ever receive from his late father.

"I should be happy to do so," the cook said, looking relieved. "It's been such a hurly-burly these past weeks, I've simply thrown together whatever I could find. I'd be much happier with a plan."

Definitely educated speech and someone accustomed to giving orders, not taking them. Clare toyed with her cup handle, searching for words. Until she'd come to the manor, she'd had to deal with nothing more complicated than a dying mother. Her London servants had been with her since childhood.

The manor and its inhabitants presented a challenge to her limited domestic skills and hermit tendencies.

"We are all grateful that you have so excellently stepped into Mrs. Gaither's shoes." Clare sighed, spun the cup around, and simply came out with it. "As a member of the family, you are entitled to choose any chamber you wish, even if it's in the cellar. If you wish to be a cook, none among us will object, I promise. But I know so little of my extended family, I do wish to know you."

The cook's cup rattled on the saucer, and she hastily set it back on the desk. Ducking her mob-capped head, she studied her hands. "I am sure I do not know what you mean."

"Don't be ridiculous," Clare said more sharply than she intended because she was tired. "You are older than I am. You must know the family traits. Hold up your hand with your fingers outstretched."

Blue eyes just like Clare's seemed honestly bewildered as she did as told. The thumb extended backward. Clare held up her hand to show a similar feature.

"Widow's peak, dimples, coloring, we're nearly identical. I think the earl married a cousin and all his descendants look like them. Have you seen the portraits in the gallery?" Clare returned to sipping her tea.

"Identical?" The woman calling herself Lara Evans glanced down at her abundant curves. "I am pure peasant, as I've been told on many occasions. I am a cook, nothing more."

Clare almost snorted up her tea. "What does that make me, scarecrow? My sister Bea was twice my size and far sturdier. She'd have made a good farmhand. However unfair it might be, we can't disguise that we were raised with education, etiquette, and expectations that *peasants*, as you call yourself, can't afford."

Mrs. Evans held her cup with her pinky extended and hid her blush behind it. "I did not mean to offend. I enjoy good food and learned to cook so I didn't have to suffer burned mutton and inedible vegetables. The kitchen is where I am happiest. If you believe I am a disruption in the kitchen, then I will find another position."

"No, you won't." Clare gestured impatiently. "Had you arrived now, instead of amid turmoil, I would have interviewed you, as would any normal household. Only a nodcock would believe you were brought up in domestic service. And yes, I understand you are causing a bit of consternation below, and I simply do not care. You are a superb cook and appear to operate the kitchen with efficiency. I'd hate to lose you. But the fact remains, you belong upstairs, at the table, and not serving it."

Her obstinate cousin shook her head. "No. I have no facility for dealing with society. I was raised by servants, and

I am most comfortable in their company. I would be a disaster at your dinner table. The kitchen is my home." A hint of humor lit her eyes. "Although the stove is an abomination."

Clare had to chuckle. "Most of the manor is an abomination. We'll add *stove* to the very long list of improvements needed. The previous caretakers never lived elsewhere and were content to leave the manor as they knew it. Even though they're gone, I can make no promises. With mortgages and lawsuits hovering our heads, I do not know how long any of us will remain here. But we are trying to make changes while we can. Will you not at least give me your name so I know where you fit on the family tree?"

"I can stay in the kitchen?" she asked warily.

"If you are indeed a shareholder in the manor, and I must assume you have read the captain's documents for you to have found us, then you may stay anywhere you choose. But to verify your claim, you *do* need to provide the estate solicitors with your birth registry and presumably your parents' marriage papers." Family traits did not impress lawyers, or they'd have noticed the banker's relationship long ago.

Her cousin nodded, threaded her fingers in her lap, and took a deep breath. "I am Elspeth Laurel Villiers. My mother was Elena, nee Hardwick. My grandmother was Eleanor, nee Reid, the earl's third child."

Clare sat back, sipped her tea, and did a mental review of the family tree tapestry and the gallery of family portraits. "Your grandmother wore the ruby and diamond necklace for her presentation. You should peruse the gallery sometime and see how much you look like her."

"It is difficult enough to fit in below as it is," Elspeth Villiers murmured. "I could not trespass above. Let me be Lara Evans, please."

"I will never understand people if I live to be a hundred. It is very hard to know I have a cousin and can't speak with her except over menus. How do you know no one will come looking for you?" Clare's active imagination noted her newly discovered cousin's twitch. There was more here than met the eye.

"They won't," the cook said firmly. "My father and stepfather are deceased. My mother is in London being courted by a marquess. A twenty-seven-year-old spinster daughter is an embarrassment when one is pretending to be forty. Now that my stepbrother is married and off my father's estate, there is no one but me and my father's heir, who has his own estate in Suffolk. Everyone has grander places to be than rural Shropshire."

"Not all families are warm and welcoming." Clare set down her cup and waited until Miss Elspeth Villiers looked up. "You are welcome here. This is your home as much as it is anyone's, which is to say, not a lot." She smiled. "You should be included in family discussions of how to deal with our next disaster. I don't think the staff will like being surprised to discover you are one of us. They will resent being taken for fools."

Her cousin's face fell. "Then I shall have to leave."

"Don't be ridiculous. If, for whatever reason, you feel safe here, and you are determined to work in that medieval torture chamber called a kitchen, then we simply tell them you are family, you are in charge of the kitchen, and there's an end on it."

"You can't give them my name!"

Ah, so she was right—there was more to the story. She would have to look closer at the family tree. Clare nodded in agreement. "We will simply tell them we have discovered Lara Evans is our cousin, and you have elected to be in charge of the kitchen. I will support you."

Miss Villiers looked doubtful. "I suppose they have to listen to you."

"Precisely, if they wish to keep their positions. And when you are ready to tell us who you fear, we are here to help in any way necessary. But it takes time to trust, I understand. Let's start now." She rose and held out her hand as a merchant might do.

Miss Villiers rose, regarded her extended hand with hesitation, then took it. "Thank you for being so understanding. I promise, I will cause you no further trouble."

Clare highly doubted that. The lady had been in the shed with the dead body. She hoped the carcass didn't end up being carved into stew.

FOUR

DONNING HIS GREAT COAT AGAINST A DAMP APRIL WIND, HUNT joined Walker and their unexpected guest the next morning in visiting the shed where the body was laid out.

"You're looking a bit peaked, my friend," he told Mr. de Sackville, who did indeed sport dark circles and a pinched expression, as if battling demons. "Would you rather not do this?"

De Sackville shook his head grimly. "I'm the one who knows him. I did not think to rifle his pockets. I assumed thieves already had."

"Meera has examined him." Walker strode ahead wearing Hunt's military duster, which hung to his ankles. "She reports a contusion on the back of the skull that might be from a fall or a club. The bullet was close range. She believes he was knocked unconscious before he was shot. She didn't touch his clothing."

"Meera?" de Sackville asked. "Mrs. Abrams? A *lady* examined him?"

"Apothecary, remember." Hunt winced at the thought, too, but he also cringed at the idea of women bearing children. Women were stronger than men knew, and it was probably best that men not speak about what they didn't understand.

The stench had not improved overnight. Holding their noses, they lifted the coffin lid. De Sackville appeared too ill to touch his friend's corpse. Hunt and Walker left the nobleman swaying in the doorway. Each took a side and worked their way through pockets and seams and the places a man might hide his valuables. Expensive tailoring for the outerwear, Hunt noted, but the linen was worn, and the cuffs had been turned. Either a pinchpenny or his clothiers had cut off his credit.

"Pocket watch gone, but the chain and fob are still here, along with his signet ring and empty purse. A few shillings sewn into his hem where a thief might not find them." Hunt twisted off a boot and a piece of paper fell out.

"Those boots cost two pounds new," de Sackville muttered. "They're worth more than Culpepper is. Don't waste them with burial."

Hunt snorted and glanced at his guest. The former lieutenant looked yellow around the edges, so he ignored the crudity. Soldiers had to be pragmatic, and he was right, boots like this might last a few hundred miles of marching. Someone should have use of them.

He opened the paper to a hastily scribbled note. Unable to make out the scrawl with one eye in this dim light, he handed it to their guest and helped Walker remove the other boot. No message there but a few more coins.

"*Damn.*" De Sackville glared at the worn piece of paper. "Bloody damn hell."

"As Clare would say, that is blasphemy for which you can be arrested." Holding the boots in distaste, Hunt waited for their guest to explain.

"Why the devil can't they leave her alone? I'll have to ride out—" The noble Jack de Sackville crumpled to his knees, heaved up his breakfast, and fell flat, moaning.

Stoic Walker rescued the paper before it blew away, shoving it in his pocket before helping Hunt lift their barely conscious guest. Walker had been at Hunt's side since childhood, suffering school and war with him. Except from Hunt, he'd never received the recognition reserved for white men, despite his many talents.

"A soldier should hold up better than this." Hunt shifted his unwieldy burden and aimed for the house.

"We no longer have a crazy housekeeper to poison him," Walker mused. "Besides, he ate the same things we did."

Hunt glanced down at their now unconscious guest. "He's burning up. If he's contagious, we can't let Meera near him. We'd better carry him upstairs and avoid the infirmary." Where the pregnant apothecary reigned.

Foolish of him to believe they could bypass the women. Hunt swore the house had eyes. Meera was already in the corridor, and Clare rushing from her small sitting room, by the time they hauled de Sackville inside.

"Couldn't handle the sight?" Meera asked skeptically as they tried to pass her. Before they could escape, she pressed a brown palm to their guest's forehead and studied his eyes. "Fever. Jaundice."

"Malaria," Clare recalled. "He said he was recovering from malaria. It recurs."

Hunt thought a few swear words but refrained from uttering them. After years of living with men, he had a lot of bad habits to suppress if he wanted the ladies to remain. And he and Walker very much wanted these sweet-smelling, hard-headed females to remain. "Not contagious?" he verified.

"Not contagious," Meera confirmed. "He'll be more comfortable in his own bed. I'll be up shortly. If it survived the madman, I have some cinchona bark that is said to be efficacious mixed in wine. Open his window. Try to keep him cool." She vanished into her bottle-lined infirmary.

Hunt had to admire the little apothecary's determined bravado. Shortly after her arrival here, her inventory had been destroyed by a thieving scoundrel in search of her pharmacopeia. She'd been steadily gathering and drying and accumulating what she could ever since. Some of her medicines had been in tins, unharmed. He hoped the bark had survived. It wouldn't be easily acquired.

Arnaud loped down the corridor at some unseen signal passed along to the gallery, where he worked on the family portraits. His cousin took their guest's weight from Hunt, who had only just started managing the stairs on his bad knee. The young footman, more of a height with Arnaud, ran up offering to take Walker's place.

"I feel less of an invalid if you give it up, too, old man." Hunt stepped back and waited for his friend to do the same. Walker grimaced but handed over the patient. He was, after all, more slender accountant than strongman, and de Sackville wasn't small.

They waited for ladylike Clare to flutter after the patient to see to his comfort. Instead, she waited. "Well, gentlemen? I assume you learned something? It's written all over your faces that you're just waiting for me to leave."

Hunt bit back a laugh. Little over a month ago, she had been terrified of her own shadow. Give her a little security, and she out-generaled Wellington—one of the many reasons he needed her to stay and share the burden of their mutual inheritance.

"Hand over the note that sent our guest into the vapors," Hunt ordered.

An astute observer, Walker already had his hand in his pocket.

After donning her spectacles, Clare took the folded paper by a corner and shook it out. It was little more than a scrap torn from the bottom of an invoice and scribbled on the back. *"Meet me at the tavern in Newchurch with the barouche. Have fresh horses at Greene's Inn."*

"Are we on the road to Newchurch? Might we find friends or family there?" Hunt asked, reasonably enough, he thought.

"I am not positive. . ." Clare's big blue eyes grew wide in alarm. "Where is Lavender? She's more familiar with those parts."

In a flurry of muslin and ribbons, and a cloud of his grandmother's mysterious jasmine scent, she hurried toward the gallery at the front of the house. Swearing, Hunt limped after her, admiring the way her dangling curls swayed with her hips. Walker, sensibly, headed for the library where maps might be found. As Americans, they didn't have familiarity with English villages.

A lover of fashion and animals, seventeen-year-old Lavender Marlowe had industriously set up sewing tables in the long, window-lined gallery. The earls had most likely used the chamber as a ballroom and a place to walk in colder months. The talented adolescent had turned a portion into a tailoring and dressmaker shop using local seamstresses, while giving her active puppy a large playground.

As the result of a dalliance between one of the earl's grandsons and a maid, Lavender was family, but under English law, not a legitimate heir, like Bosworth. But she had nowhere else to go, and Clare had insisted she stay. She'd quickly proved her worth.

Hunt had used the trust fund to buy fabric to create uniforms for the servants. Somehow, the earl's devious great-granddaughter was persuading the cloth merchants to throw in laces and ribbons and bits of scrap material that she used to update the ladies' gowns.

"Lavender." Clare waved the note. "Isn't Newchurch north of Birmingham?"

No longer striving to fit in by looking like the fashion

plate she'd first appeared when she arrived, Miss Marlowe wore her blond hair stacked loosely on her head, with strands tumbling as they willed. She took pins from her mouth and frowned. "Quite some distance north, near Cheshire. Why?"

"And Green's Inn?"

"On the road to Liverpool. Very respectable establishment, or so I've heard. My boarding school was not far from there. Some of the students lived in Scotland and traveled by yacht to Liverpool. The inn was a resting place before they reached the school."

"*Scotland*, that's what I thought. I knew I'd heard of it." Clare whipped around and handed the scrap back. "A closed barouche, a clandestine meeting, fresh horses for a quick journey. . . Someone is planning an elopement. But without the messenger. . ."

Lavender looked fascinated, but she had wisely learned to listen instead of speak.

"We need our guest's knowledge." Hunt folded the paper and returned it to his pocket. "Given his reaction, he seemed to have reached the same conclusion as you, except it appears he may know who is involved. He was rather effusive in his condemnation."

"There are no dates." Clare crinkled her pretty nose. "Henri might know how to find Newchurch, but we have no notion of when they'll be waiting. Although eloping is such a havey-cavey way of doing things, perhaps we're saving some poor lady from a bad mistake."

"Eloping means no wedding gown." Lavender couldn't contain herself any longer. "Who would *do* that?"

Clare shook her ribbons. "Desperate people do desperate things. Running away is how you got here, is it not? Perhaps this lady has no one to turn to."

Hunt didn't want to be desperate, but he despaired of ever accomplishing anything in this household. He led Clare back to the hall, laying out the problem away from the child.

"We need to notify *someone* of the man's demise. Other than de Sackville's identification, we have no direction." He was an engineer, not a man who craved the power of local magistrate or arbiter of justice. He'd buried many a soldier along the road, but this wasn't war.

Done with depositing the patient in bed, Arnaud heard this last as he traversed the stairs. "Henri travels these roads. Unless they're returning soldiers, thieves around here do not normally have pistols. He's fought off a few carrying knives, but they were near the city. It's not as if crowds of wealthy victims ride through this tiny corner of nowhere."

Clare looked alarmed, presumably that Henri traveled dangerous byways. Hunt could have told her that his cousin carried both pistol and sword, but the lady feared weaponry.

"Perhaps Henri can tell us more. In the meantime, I need to call in the gravediggers." Hating this part of his duty, Hunt reluctantly turned away from the winsome woman who held his interest too much for their own good.

They'd agreed that kisses were much too distracting and dangerous until the disposal of the manor was decided on. If they had to return to their respective homes. . . then they had no future together.

The scent of jasmine wafted around him, almost in sorrow.

IN FEVERED DREAMS, JACK SAW CULPEPPER'S LAUGHING VISAGE explode in blood. A boy with ruby eggs raced away, into the arms of a pleasingly plump young lady who offered chocolate biscuits. Gunfire and waltzes danced around a series of young women whose faces he couldn't recall but whose bodies his remembered.

Moaning in more than one kind of fever, he calmed under a cool hand and sipped bitter liquid thirstily. *He needed to ride out tonight. Napoleon awaited.*

"He's sweating cobs," a familiar lilting accent whispered above him. He tossed and turned, trying to find the speaker. Sweat poured down his brow, and he wiped it impatiently.

"The fever has broken," an unfamiliar female said briskly. "If you'll hold the cloth on his forehead, I'll fetch more water."

Water. Water would be good. Was he back in the Sahara?

"Ow bist thee, Jack?" the familiar accent whispered. "You canna possibly return from India and sniff me out when naught knows my whereabouts."

She smelled of home. He lay still, letting the cool cloth ease his head, attempting to gather his wits. It was dark, he could tell that much. Violets, he decided, she smelled of violets and lilacs and new spring fields. And cake. Very definitely cake. His mouth watered.

"How long?" he muttered, trying to determine when and where he was.

Her chuckle was low and melodious, even though the reply dropped the familiar accent. "So many ways that could be interpreted, Jack."

"You're not here," he decided. "I'm dreaming. Why now?"

"As a figment of your imagination, I can answer any way I like, can't I? You're delirious. Even I heard about it below. I don't want you to die now after fearing your demise all these years."

He knew that voice. When had he heard it last? Or had he dreamed it? Maybe angels appeared in his fevered dreams.

"Does heaven smell of jasmine and cake?" he murmured senselessly.

"I like that question. Roses, I should think. Shouldn't heaven smell of roses and chocolate cake?"

"And sound like home," he said emphatically.

She chuckled again. "Ah, you dimmy-simmy dolt, you were always that faddy, off on hops and girds, pitherin' about when you should be home with your old da."

Oh damn, angels wanted him to go home. He'd meant to this time. If he meant to die on the battlefield, he should at least say his farewells.

Angels shouldn't talk like a Shropshire field hand.

"You meant to go home, didn't you, Jack? He wants to see you." The voice was fainter.

"I will," he promised. "Don't go."

"Go on to bed." The brisk voice returned. "The hungry hordes will be demanding food in a few hours. Thank you for the sandwiches."

"I should have thought of water, sorry." A rustle and a soft footstep, and the angel was gone.

Leaving Jack to ponder jasmine and cake and a dialect he hadn't heard since leaving home.

By morning, he felt weak as a kitten, but his mind was no longer a muddle. He remembered Culpepper's body, the note concealed in expensive boots, and a voice that sounded like home.

Elspeth. Who was guarding the heiress these days?

41

FIVE

Since her discussion with their new cook two days ago, Clare had done some research in the earl's library and the viscountess's diaries. The family histories were old, but her *Debrett's Peerage* had provided. Mrs. Evans/Miss Villiers had failed to mention that her family favored marriage into the nobility. Her grandmother had married Lord Hardwick, and her mother had married a Lord Villiers, both earls.

Their cook wasn't a Miss Villiers but *Lady Elspeth*.

Clare refused to summon a lady as if she were a common servant. But if she didn't, her reclusive cousin would never emerge from the kitchen. She hadn't talked to Elspeth/Lara since yesterday morning when Clare had announced to the staff that the cook was family. She thought that had gone reasonably well, but it had apparently made no difference to an earl's daughter who preferred to be a cook.

She hadn't seen the lady since yesterday, when she and several of the family had paid their respects at poor Mr. Culpepper's graveside. Mr. de Sackville had been too ill to attend, but at least the poor soul hadn't been buried unmourned, exactly. Lady Elsa had left quickly, without speaking to anyone.

But a family meeting could no longer be delayed. The day after the funeral, Clare set her jaw and went in search of her elusive cousin. Generally, she preferred to be courteous and not trespass on the staff's limited privacy by entering the kitchen, but that was just an excuse, she realized, as she descended to the landing to the cacophony of pots clanging and banging. One of the women screeched and another shouted for the burn unguent. A heavy pan hit the tile floor with a loud clang, and she nearly fled back up the stairs. The clamor reminded her too sharply of the Egyptian riot that had blown her life apart.

She refused to live in fear any longer.

Forcing herself not to flee at another shout and bang, Clare waited on the landing with a clear view of the kitchen. Eventually, she was noticed and silence descended. Elspeth finally glanced up.

"Captain Huntley would like a brief family meeting, if you can spare us some time, Mrs. Evans." She supposed using an alias protected her cousin's close family, as she protected hers by using a pseudonym for her novels.

Elspeth looked vexed but rallied quickly. "Betsy, stir the onions and add the potatoes in a few minutes. Marie, you may reshape the dough into the pans and put the loaves into the oven once it heats."

Both Betsy and Marie were meant to be upstairs maids, but with limited staff, everyone performed any function needed—just as the upstairs inhabitants did. Food came before dusting.

Elspeth took off her apron, hastily washed her hands, and tucked her hair beneath her cap before joining Clare on the stairs. "Is it really important enough to delay lunch?"

"They just cleaned up breakfast. No one will starve. You

haven't been properly introduced, so we cannot go on without you." Clare hurried back upstairs.

At the top, she halted and turned around so quickly that Elspeth nearly plowed into her. "Are you as uncomfortable above stairs as I am below?"

Her cousin's oblong eyes had enviably long, dark lashes that gave her more expression than Clare's pale coloring. The lady blinked in surprise. "You are uncomfortable in the kitchen? Why?"

Clare accepted that non-answer as a no and relieved that her cousin wasn't uncomfortable, aimed for the library again. "I still have difficulty with loud noises, strange men, and too many people in a confined space. Kitchens—let us just say I am not familiar with the territory."

"The chaos can be disconcerting, I suppose. Some day we should learn each other's stories. Kitchens make me feel safe. I spent half my childhood in ours." Nervously, Elsa adjusted the white scarf over her black bodice.

"Perhaps the day will come when we have leisure to converse, but restoring this manor to serviceable with limited staff is such a large undertaking—" Taking a breath, Clare pushed open the library door.

The men were already there, gathered around the various artifacts of interest that tended to accumulate on the library table. Oliver had even added his dragon hoard, Clare noted in relief.

Arnaud and Henri Lavigne were not technically the earl's family, but they were Hunt's, and their knowledge was valuable. Clare beamed as she noticed the painting Arnaud had brought in at her request.

Meera wasn't related in any way, but she was Clare's companion and a buffer against excessive virility. Lavender sat next to her, but she was seventeen, and her enthusiasm was not always useful.

Having her sensible, slightly older cousin at her side was almost like having her late sister, Bea. Of course, Bea would have taken command, asserted her authority, and left everyone to carry out her orders. Clare lacked that temerity. Apparently, so did Elspeth.

At their entrance, the men politely stood. Knowing Hunt's knee often ached, Clare hastily made the presentation. "I believe you've all met, but let me properly introduce you. Lady Elspeth Villiers is the granddaughter of the earl's third child. She prefers to be called Mrs. Evans, if we can all remember that, please. I believe that is her grandmother's portrait Arnaud has just finished cleaning."

Hunt generally demanded documentation of any person claiming a family relationship. Lady Elsa demanded nothing, but Clare meant to establish her credentials anyway.

She took a chair at the table and Elspeth sat beside her while studying the painting.

"Your grandmother looks very much like you, Miss Villiers," Arnaud said as they all found chairs.

Oliver settled in a corner with a book.

"Blond hair and blue eyes perhaps," Elspeth acknowledged, studying the portrait. "But I was born in the wrong century. The corsetry, billowing robes, and panniers of my grandmother's era added to her grandeur." She glanced down at her bosom, concealed by her high bodice. "Broadcloth isn't as bad as muslin, but today's thin gowns do not hide or ameliorate a less-than-perfect figure."

Clare hid a chuckle. Her cousin was not shy.

"You would look wonderful in the new French bodices I saw in the. . ." At Clare's raised eyebrow, Lavender bit back her eagerness to discuss fashion. "Sorry. The painting was to discuss jewels, wasn't it?"

Lavender had been sent to boarding school to hide the disgrace of her birth from society, but like most Reids, she had a mind that did not fit any proper mold. The manor's inhabitants had been left to steer her along what passed for proper paths.

"One of many topics," Hunt acknowledged. He turned to their newest family member. "You are familiar with the Wycliffe jewels?"

Elspeth shrugged. "I recognize the ruby pendant in the painting. My mother wore it on a heavy gold chain. She had it redesigned in gold filigree for my presentation. Our family regularly makes their presence known by wearing jewels when they should not."

Clare widened her eyes. "I hadn't thought of that! Unmarried maidens only wear pearls. I was never presented, but Bea complained about the restraint until my mother conceded to let her wear the Wycliffe sapphire."

Elspeth nodded. "The biddies clucked at the ostentation, but it's a family tradition."

"So you have the necklace in the portrait, *oui*?" Henri asked.

With his faint French accent, Hunt's darkly handsome cousin exuded smiling charm. About the same age as Elspeth, Henri spoke with such interest that he almost turned Clare's head.

Instead of responding to the handsome Frenchman's flirtation, Elspeth examined the portrait. "I've only seen the pendant, not all those diamonds and pearls. That's amazingly ostentatious. I daresay my stepfather sold everything else, if we ever had it. I think the only reason he didn't sell the ruby was that the jeweler was working on the filigree when he died."

"Bluntness runs in the family, I see." Clare toyed with Oliver's dragon eggs. "It could also mean the earl only gave the pendants to his children and kept the rest of the gems. My mother only had the sapphire. Hunt's mother only had a ruby. If yours only had a ruby too, that sets a pattern. We have some reason to believe the rest may be hidden."

~

"MAY WE CALL YOU ELSPETH?" HUNT INTERRUPTED CLARE'S conclusion. "Working together as we must, we tend to be casual."

Elsa thought the captain's raw-boned, piratical counte-nance ought to be frightening. He was a big man, with shoul-ders as wide as the painting they perused. But she was still unbalanced by being treated as *family* by strangers. They knew things about her that even she did not.

"Call me Elsa, please. No one has called me Elspeth since my grandmother died." And Jack left. He'd always been quite rude about treating her as a child.

She studied the portrait of her grandmother as a very young woman—serious, with a slight frown already marring the space between her eyes. The future Lady Hardwick had inherited a fortune. Her marriage had been planned since birth. She'd grown immensely fat with indolence—and possibly to keep her elderly husband away. Grandmother had never spoken of her married years.

The captain continued. "The portraits in the gallery display a fortune in gems that were not included in the earl's inventory. So far, no current family member recalls seeing anything other than the pendants. There is mention of the necklaces in the early diaries of the late viscountess, but not after she was widowed, when presumably the jewels returned to Wycliffe's vaults. The earl lived years after his son's death."

"I've been reading inheritance laws." The African steward —Walker?—looked up from a ledger he'd been perusing. "The jewels would have been entailed to the earl's estate and passed down to his son. Once his only heir died, the earl broke the entail and could have sold them. If he didn't, he should have left instructions in his will for their distribution. As far as we can determine, he did neither."

Elspeth finally pulled her attention from her grandmother to the company. Having family around her, having a real conversation over matters presumably of importance, was a rarity. So rare, she could not remember the last time it had happened—unless one counted countless scolding.

And now, she not only had family, but Frenchmen and an African and a brown-skinned Jewish lady. She had never met the like before, even in her brief sojourn in London. She was appalled at her rural ignorance. Having the world under one rather large roof should be an educational experience.

"I'm sorry I cannot be of any help." Jewels didn't hold her interest. One couldn't eat a diamond. The bread in the oven, now, was important, no matter who one was. "I have never seen my mother wear anything except pearls and the pendant. She had a few rings and brooches that her husbands gave her, but the gems were mere chips in comparison to these."

Lavender sighed. "Old people keep too many secrets. Just think of the fabric only one of those diamonds could buy."

Gossip below stairs said Miss Marlowe was illegitimate, but she seemed to participate in family discussions as an equal. Elsa's mother would faint should she ever visit—which Elsa prayed she never did.

Clare chuckled. "We need a treasure trove to restore the estate and you would house us in silk?"

Ah, so that explained this jewel discussion. The manor needed funds. Elsa squirmed uncomfortably as she always did at any discussion of money. Trustees handled hers. She had little say in the disbursal of anything except her allowance.

The captain led the discussion to the next topic. "Henri, do you know any magistrate who might take interest in Mr. Culpepper's untimely demise?" He gestured at the box containing the dead man's belongings. The tops of a pair of boots stood out.

The dark-eyed Frenchman grimaced. "Unless we have a highwayman robbing merchants traveling to the city, I doubt any magistrate has an interest. If we knew the family, they might exert pressure for action."

"De Sackville might. We've been waiting for him to come around. Otherwise, no, we have no idea how to notify Culpepper's family." Hunt looked disgruntled.

Elsa swallowed. This was why she wanted to be Mrs. Evans, the invisible cook who knew nothing and nobody. She wanted to forget her old life and start anew. She didn't want to deceive these nice people, but she didn't know them well enough to confide her darkest secrets.

But Culpepper's poor parents needed to be told of their son's demise. She could wait for Jack to recover or do the right thing now. Not knowing how long he might remain fevered, she swallowed hard and clasped her hands in her lap. "I believe Mr. Culpepper's family normally reside in London this time of year, but they have a small estate near Bath. Their staff should know how to reach them."

Whether or not his noble parents cared to pursue their depraved younger son's killer was another matter entirely.

Ignoring excited questions, Elsa stood. "The bread will be burning. Thank you for including me in your meeting, but I must go."

If feet could fly, she would have flown back to the kitchen.

Once safe in her cellar hideaway, she set it to order again. With the bread cooling, she hummed contentedly and stupidly stirred dough for the biscuits Jack favored.

Clare could play lady of the manor all she liked. Elsa was tired of beating her head against stone walls. Now that the kitchen staff had been informed she was family, they didn't seem quite so wary of her, so that was all right. If she never ventured above, they might forget all about it, eventually. Happiness was a productive kitchen and good food.

She had attended Culpepper's burial yesterday to verify it was him. A funeral was a perfectly acceptable reason to mix with her betters. She supposed it had been impulsively idiotic to run upstairs when she'd learned Jack was the fevered patient Meera was nursing. She wouldn't repeat that foolishness.

Jack had looked so handsome, even with his lively eyes closed and his bronzed complexion pale as his sheets. It had hurt to see him in pain.

She gathered from the meeting that he was out of danger. She hoped he would take her advice and return to visit his old dad. The baron was well respected in Newchurch, but he loved his studies more than the land, and his pockets suffered for it. Jack's older brother wasn't any better. He'd taken off to Edinburgh to become a physician.

Bright young men didn't stay in a backwater village that was dying as surely as Gravesyde Priory. The captain and Clare were fighting a losing battle trying to restore this rural outpost. With Birmingham so close, industrialization and money lured families away.

Elsa was fine with that. All she'd ever wanted to do was cook. Yes, once she'd thought she could love the village vicar. Certainly, she'd loved the safe haven the vicarage had offered. She'd grown up since then.

Wycliffe Manor couldn't replace the tidy estate she'd called home, until her father's death. But she didn't need tidy so much as she needed a welcoming haven where she was needed.

She worried about her horses, but her estate steward was a good man. He'd take care of them. They were hers. Frederick couldn't touch them, she hoped. She suffered no guilt in refusing to be a target for abuse any longer. She knew she was no slender sylph and that men would only court her for her money, as they had her poor grandmother. She'd proudly donned her cap and called herself off the shelf.

Oliver clattered into the kitchen from the outside stairs holding a book and a pail. The meeting must be over. Elsa smiled at the dirty little boy and gestured at the plate of warm biscuits on the table.

Always wary, he eyed her for a moment to be certain it wasn't a trick, then grabbed a treat, and made a polite bow. "Thank you, miss. May I have some milk for my dragon?"

"How could I say no to such a charming young knight?" She took the terra cotta pitcher from the slate board in the pantry where she kept it cool and poured a tin mugful. "Will this be all right?"

He considered it solemnly. "He may swallow the mug. I brought my pail. They won't let me milk the cow." He poured the liquid into the empty tin bucket. "Thank you. If the eggs hatch, I will let you have one of the babies."

He was off before she could expound upon mothers not willingly giving up babies. Even at an early age, men had odd fantasies.

"You do know that his dragon eggs are rare gems?" A male voice asked from the landing.

Jack! *Botheration.* And after just vowing to never mix with the gentry again. Wiping her hands on her apron, she returned to stirring dough, keeping her back to the stairs.

"Iz dat so, sir," she said, mimicking the locals as best as she was able.

"I am looking for the angel who sent up my favorite cake. Would that be you?" His voice came closer. The damned man knew no rules or respect. He was entering *her* domain, without invitation.

This was Jack. She might want to swat him for his arrogance, but she would not fear him as she did some others. Yes, he'd been a soldier and had probably committed brutal acts in the heat of battle, but she would swear he'd not raise a hand to a woman.

Only—he knew everyone she knew, and eventually, word would travel, and there were people she didn't want knowing her hiding place for very good reasons.

"Betsy, wilt thee and Ned escort the gen'lmen above stairs, wheres't he belongs?" She hid her regret in giving the order.

SIX

STILL WEAK ENOUGH NOT TO FIGHT WITH THE BURLY MAID AND the muscled stable hand escorting him from the kitchen, Jack pulled himself back up the stairs where he apparently belonged.

He'd only wanted to thank the baker. He'd hoped to hear the welcome accents of home again. The cook's dialect had been crude and not the least warm, so maybe he'd dreamed the angel.

That didn't make him any less disgruntled. The angel had told him to go home, and he needed to. But as weak as he was, he'd fall off a horse. And the rain would probably return his fever. If he wanted to join Wellington, he needed to be in fighting shape, damn it all.

Presumably, whatever Culpepper had planned was postponed with his death, but he still needed to warn Elspeth that danger lurked. He hadn't seen her since buying his colors, but she was the only heiress in that part of the county—unless the rat had been seducing merchants' daughters now.

Even then, Elspeth would know who to warn, in case Culpepper had hired thugs. His father had kept him informed of the lady's habits, and he knew how she loved Newchurch. She'd not be gadding about London.

If he couldn't ride. . . He went in search of writing material. The young footman—there only seemed to be the one tall lad—directed him to the library. Before Jack passed the marble stairs, the little apothecary entered from the front foyer, shaking water drops from her hooded pelisse.

"Mr. de Sackville, you should be resting," she scolded. "You risk the fever returning. Are you drinking the broth I ordered?"

"There is only so much broth and tea one can drink, my dear lady. And it's too early to start on brandy."

The massive butler—whose mushed nose and scars gave away his boxing origins—arrived to take her pelisse. Once divested of her outer garments, the colorful Mrs. Abrams revealed a handful of mail.

He was too late to send his letter this morning.

"Very humorous, I'm sure," she said, flipping through the letters. "I'll ask the kitchen if they can make apple juice. If they can't, I suppose watered cider wouldn't hurt. Beef broth and tea would be better. Sit and read a book and recover." She bustled off.

Grimacing at the thought of more broth, Jack changed course to the windowed gallery that always seemed filled with people. He had time before the afternoon mail. He'd write later. He'd find out what the captain had done about Culpepper first.

The enormous ballroom was a hive of activity on this gray day. The young blond flirt, Lavender, was busily cutting up fabric and giving orders to several women sitting on fading sofas. They had threads and pincushions scattered around them as they sewed.

Another table was littered with bits of metal and paint-boxes and ceramic buttons. A couple of young people and an older woman had formed a production line that appeared to be painting or wrapping round bits, adding backs to them, and fixing the finished buttons to cards.

Under the low murmur of voices, an erratic tattoo of raps emerged from the floor. Jack grimaced at the din and aimed for the big man painting at an easel by the windows. Hunt's cousin could probably answer questions.

"Do I address you as comte, monsieur, or Mister Lavigne?" he asked, strolling up to admire the artwork.

"Arnaud, please. My titles are meaningless." Taller and broader than Jack, the artist would have made a good soldier, if he had more meat on his bones. "How may I help you?"

"I'm concerned about Culpepper's family and whatever mischief he was up to, as well as the thieves who attacked him. I feel I ought to be doing something, but I don't know what has already been done."

Arnaud nodded and cleaned his brush. "We have sent word to his family estate in Bath and consulted a magistrate in Birmingham. My brother claims that it is unlikely to find common thieves bearing pistols this far off the highway. None of us are familiar enough with the locals to guess as to who may have stolen the horse and robbed him."

Jack rubbed the back of his head. "I'd like to believe he rode with someone who decided to put an end to his black heart, but that seems far-fetched. I should probably ride back along that route to ask if anyone saw him and if he was with anyone.'"

Arnaud picked up another brush and dipped it in a different color. "Henri is doing that now. He travels the roads frequently and people will talk to a peddler. I imagine Meera has told you to rest."

"If I'm of no use here, I need to ride on. I can't continue to impose on your hospitality." Jack would much rather linger and eat cake and be visited by angels, but he would go mad doing nothing.

Arnaud pointed at a row of portraits. "Do you know aught of code?"

Jack glanced at the newly cleaned but ancient oils. "I know a few, played with a few more. Why?"

"Because we found what appears to be code etched into each of those paintings. Henri and I are French. Hunt and Walker are American. None of us recognize the combination. I assume the code was printed by an Englishman, possibly the earl or viscount. . ."

Jack caught on. "So maybe it's a particularly English code? Do you have it written down or do I need to study those bewigged nobles and gaudy ladies?"

"We've written them out, but we thought the placement might also be relevant. It's hidden in different places on each work." Arnaud completed a few strokes, dropped the brush in cleaning fluid, and rummaged in a stack of papers on the windowsill.

Producing one, the artist gestured at the first painting in line, a bewigged young man wearing an enormous jeweled tie pin. "That's the oldest painting, the late earl as a youth, we believe. The code is scratched into the shadows of the lapel. The same paint was used on each portrait, so it's possible to detect where they daubed it."

Jack crouched down to examine the portrait. "Did they cover the code with paint and you uncovered it?"

"No, they daubed a small thick glob that was easier to scratch than the original. Time and exposure darkened all the colors so the daub blended in until I cleaned them."

Jack located the shinier dark spot. Closer inspection revealed the scratches. It took more study to make out letters and numbers. "It's not striking me as anything mean-ingful. Too few figures to say much. Could it represent a location—like left at the second door—in a shortened code?"

"My thought too, but I can't find a pattern." Arnaud

handed over his list. "I've noted which painting and the section the code comes from."

"A puzzle." Intrigued, Jack scanned the jumble of numbers and letters, but nothing leaped out at him. "I'll copy this and work on it a bit. I can't stay long, but it will keep me occupied for now."

Arnaud saluted and returned to his painting.

Jack wasn't much at sitting still, but a puzzle now. . . that could occupy a gray day.

First, he needed to write Elsa. It wasn't proper to write a woman to whom he wasn't related or engaged, but she was no longer an adolescent, and her parents weren't available. He hoped the lady didn't tear up anything from him without opening.

He'd write his father as well, just in case. And perhaps a word of condolence to Culpepper's family.

He despised paperwork and would much rather ride and see them in person, but he'd learned expedience and caution in his grand old age.

HAVING BATHED OFF THE DAY'S DIRT AND DRESSED FOR DINNER, Hunt settled in front of the fire in his study to work his way through the papers that had accumulated on his desk while he'd been banging away in the dungeon. The coal retort was coming along well. Piping the gas into the house. . . that would take a great deal of work that would drive the household to distraction. It had to be done. This huge fortress might have sufficed for knights and knaves, but the lack of windows in the corridors and stairs did not suit modern use. Light was required.

He propped a foot on a stool to warm his throbbing knee. Meera's unguent eased the ache, but heat also soothed.

A brisk, light knock on the door had him looking up

again. There had been a time when the lady wouldn't go anywhere near him without a guard. It made him ridiculously happy that Clare now dared to enter his lair alone. "Come in. Just don't expect me to stand now that I'm comfortable."

Also dressed for dinner, Clare wore a gown of pale yellow silk with a blue bodice to set off the eyes she currently hid behind spectacles. She carried in more mail. "Mary just brought up the afternoon post. These looked official."

She flipped through an assortment and kept two to herself. Hunt gave her his knife to pry open the seals, then went to work opening his own. Letters from solicitors and bankers seldom carried good news.

Clare made a soft little noise and dropped into a straight-legged chair.

In concern, Hunt looked up. Her complexion had gained a hint of rose, and he wished he dared kiss her again. But they weren't children. Clare was a lady and kisses led ladies to marriage. He still had a bad taste in his mouth from his last failure to keep a fiancée. Distance was the only solution until they'd resolved the issues of the manor and whether or not they stayed. That didn't prevent his half-state of arousal now.

"Bad news?" he asked when she said nothing but read and re-read her letter.

She shook her blond ringlets. "No, unexpectedly excellent news. I now have the funds to pay whatever is needed to hire Oliver's tutor for a full year, if only I could find a good one willing to work for me."

He considered that. "I had not realized the problem was you. Tutors do not work for women?"

"An all-female household and a male tutor. . . I'd need someone quite old. And the only replies I receive are from ones who believe students must be constrained to desks and books, which will never work with Oliver. He needs to explore."

"Or he needs a tutor who understands that books are a type of exploration. But it is not tomes on Latin and Greek that Oliver favors, is it?" Hunt considered that problem rather than the ones in his hand.

"Not *any* language," she said dryly. "Math, the sciences, any of those. He's just not very verbal. I'd hoped a tutor might draw him out, but not if they spend all day rapping his knuckles for not replying to questions."

"What if I did the hiring? Once someone is hired, you can determine if he is what Oliver needs, and then decide what to do about the all-female household if you return to London. You have a few more months here." He hoped she'd stay for the winter, but she was a city girl, and the winters here were no doubt grim.

And they might lose the manor anyway, if the letters in his hand meant anything.

She took off her spectacles and her eyes were shining. "Do you think that might work? I feared a respectable tutor might not wish to work so far from a city, but Birmingham is large, isn't it?"

"He won't be able to walk to a library or theater from here, and we have no fancy carriage. You might have to give him more than one day off if he needs intellectual pursuits," Hunt said dryly.

She nodded absently. "That's a good thought. If I draft a letter as if it came from you, will you have Walker copy it out so you can sign it?"

"Or just tell Walker to do it. Give him a list of agencies, and he'll handle everything. That's what a good steward does." Hunt loved the way she beamed at him as if he'd handed her diamonds.

"I wish I could handle *your* problems with such ease." She nodded at his letters. "Did Bosworth decide to sue us over those poorly written deeds?"

Hunt turned back to his desk, where he'd set up a lamp

59

and a magnifier to read with his one good eye. "The estate solicitors are looking into our requests to have illegitimate heirs claim their share of the manor under the terms of the will. We cannot offer Bosworth—or Lavender—a share until the courts approve it."

"That might only take to the next century. Have you asked the marquess if he can forward the case? I'm sure your aunt will encourage him to take the task if you ask." She leaned over the desk to read the letter upside down.

The Marquess of Spalding was his aunt's stepson and looked after her affairs. The marquess had no real reason to care about an estate that wouldn't come to him.

Hunt turned the solicitor's letter so Clare could peruse it at will, then picked up the one from the bank. "I've had Walker write Spalding to ask if there is any possibility the case might proceed. He is aware."

"But I assume the bank still insists that they be repaid, even if the deed they hold isn't exactly legal? I do feel bad that the viscount cheated them." She wrinkled up her nose in distaste.

After scanning the bank's letter and seeing nothing new, he pushed it toward her. "They are willing to extend the terms another year if we make up the payments. I assume that's Bosworth's doing. He wants the place, but he's waited this long, he's willing to see how badly we fail, especially if we hold out the temptation of allowing him to be a legitimate claimant, and we do all the work of improving the place."

"I am trying to like the poor man, but he doesn't make it easy. Still, he's the only son of the earl's blood, however illegitimate. He really shouldn't be left out. But we have no means of making any payments." She shoved the letters back. "It would be lovely if he worked with us instead of against us. To change the subject, did Walker send letters to Mr. Culpepper's family?"

"And to our solicitors asking them to locate his family, in

case that one goes astray. I wish I knew more people so we could learn more about him." Hunt sat back in his chair. He hadn't fully understood how valuable it was to know people until he'd arrived here not knowing a soul.

He recognized Clare's uneasiness when she twisted her hands in her lap. He waited for her to find the words. She often had a creative perspective that escaped him.

"It occurs to me. . ." She grimaced and gestured help-lessly. "That it is very odd for two gentlemen to be on this barely traveled lane within days of each other. If Mr. Culpepper came from London and was going to Birming-ham, there are more direct routes. I might think he'd followed Mr. de Sackville, except he had to have been ahead of him by at least a day to be found in the hedgerows like that."

"We only have de Sackville's word about how he found him." Hunt rubbed his hand over his scarred temple. "I hate your imagination. I much prefer events to be straightforward. We should inquire more into de Sackville's whereabouts as well?"

Clare nodded sadly. "I like him. Maybe Mr. Culpepper did something he shouldn't and Mr. de Sackville had to defend himself. I can make up many stories. But we only have his word for it that Mr. Culpepper was not a nice man."

"Our lady cook knew how to find his family." Hunt didn't know what to make of an earl's daughter who preferred to live in a cellar and work like a servant or if she could be believed. But they should at least ask questions.

Clare snickered at the appellation. "Lady Cook—that would simplify what we call her. I shall try again to speak with her, but she bolts like a rabbit any time a conversation becomes too personal."

"Do we dare ask the solicitors to locate her family and find out her story? Maybe she's killed a husband. If she hadn't been working so hard in the kitchen, I'd wonder if *she* bashed

Culpepper over the head. And now I'm making up stories just like you."

"Elspeth arrived weeks ago. I'm fairly certain there would be no body left to find if she killed him before arriving. But an earl's daughter hiding in a kitchen. . . does lead one to ask questions, doesn't it?" She rose and drifted out on a scent of lilies and roses.

Leaving Hunt adjusting his trousers and wishing he was still young and whole and confident enough to believe he might support a wife and family without the decrepit manor.

With only one eye, he no longer had the future he'd planned.

SEVEN

CRUSHING THE LETTER FROM HER PUBLISHER IN HER EXCITEMENT, Clare wanted to wave it in front of the world.

Her book had sold enough copies to earn twenty-five pounds. Twenty-five pounds! And the publisher actually offered to *pay her* for the one she'd just sent in!

She'd had to pay to publish the first one.

Her head spun and her heart pounded, and she thought she understood why women had the vapors. There was only so much excitement a body could take. She'd like to dance down the hall. *People were buying her book and—reading it!*

Her pragmatic side eventually raised its sensible head. Much of the twenty-five pounds would go to pay the debt she'd incurred in printing the first novel. But if she accepted the publisher's offer. . . It wasn't a fortune, but with the rent she received from the townhouse she might afford the fifty or sixty pounds a year the best tutors cost. It would mean staying here. . .

Unless she wrote faster. . . Only there was no guarantee that the publisher would want her novels faster. Her first task was to find a tutor.

Excited, she hastened into the family parlor where they

gathered before dinner. Meera was already there, talking with Walker, as usual. Walker was a good man, but like Hunt, he most likely would return to America if they could not make the manor financially viable. She hoped her friend wouldn't have her heart broken again. Meera's last love had been a scoundrel who had wanted her only for her father's apothecary and pharmacopeia.

She didn't want to intrude on their conversation. To protect her family from scandal, Clare wrote under a male pseudonym. No one else besides Meera knew of her novels, so she had to impatiently accept a glass of sherry from the maid and listen to Lavender prattle about the design of the staff's new uniforms.

Hunt finally arrived, and the dinner bell rang, just as the front door knocker rapped. Desperate to speak with her friend, Clare was inclined to leave it to the butler and go on to dinner. But everyone else waited. Spring evenings might not be dark at this early hour, but it was still not a time to be making a casual visit.

Quincy returned without a calling card. Proper butler that he was, he approached Hunt first. Clare wanted to stamp her foot in frustration. Instead, she crossed the room to Meera, freeing Walker to go with Hunt, as was his habit.

"You are practically bouncing," Meera whispered as the men left the room. "What is happening?"

"I sold *another book*! And the publisher has sent money for royalties earned on the first. I earned as much as rent on the house!" She'd thought renting the house had been a coup, but to earn it on her own. . . Clare tried to be pragmatic.

Meera hugged her in excitement. "Can we tell everyone now that you are a published author? You will be famous!"

Clare shook her head vehemently. "No, no, it will never do. Aunt Martha would have hysterics and insist Oliver be taken away. Besides, if the book is to sell, the world must think the author is male. And can you imagine trying to hire a tutor if he knew I wrote gothic novels?"

Meera sighed. "Men are so foolish. We need to buy an island and leave them off."

Clare laughed. "And adopt orphaned girls so the population does not die away?"

Meera nodded emphatically. "Exactly."

Hunt returned with a weary rider in an aging greatcoat a size too large. The gentleman doffed his old-fashioned round hat and bowed to the room at large.

Quincy announced in a doleful bass, "Mr. Geoffrey Garrett, vicar of Newchurch."

Mr. de Sackville swung around in such surprise that the brandy in his glass sloshed. "Geoff? You're still around?" He crossed the room to shake the visitor's hand.

The vicar seemed visibly startled that anyone knew him, but Clare couldn't hear the words exchanged.

Since it was obvious that neither Hunt nor Quincy had invited the guest to stay, and her curiosity was aroused, she approached as well. "Quincy, if you would take our guest's overcoat, please?"

"I really cannot impose on you," the vicar said nervously, reclaiming his hand to hold his hat.

"There's room at the table for one more, isn't there?" de Sackville asked eagerly. "I'm anxious to catch up on news from home."

That's when the name of the village struck her. *Newchurch* —where the late Mr. Culpepper meant to go? *Both* Culpepper and Jack knew the village? As well as the vicar? Was a conspiracy to use Wycliffe Manor as a meeting place afoot? It had been abandoned for years, after all.

Clare concealed her surprise. "Of course, there is always room for one more. And the roads are treacherous these days. You must stay the night, Mr. Garrett. I assure you, it is no difficulty."

The vicar reluctantly gave up his outer garments and bowed, apparently not knowing what to do with his hands. He wasn't an imposing figure, just a man in his early thirties with a receding hairline and a slight paunch. A vicar from a rural parish couldn't be expected to dress in the height of fashion. His outdated coat and boots were well-tended and only slightly disarranged from his long ride.

"That is very generous of you, Lady. . ." He hesitated, as no one had introduced her.

"Just Miss Knightley. I trust Captain Huntley has introduced himself. Quincy, why don't you have Adam show our guest to a chamber and take up some hot water so he can refresh himself? We can hold dinner a while longer."

"This is unexpected. Really, I'll find an inn. . ."

De Sackville shoved him by the shoulder toward the door. "Fustian. There are no inns, and I truly wish to catch up on the news. I'll go up with you, see you—"

Hunt intruded. "We need you to settle a matter down here, de Sackville. Adam and Quincy can take care of our guest."

Clare tightened her grip on her glass. Hunt wanted to keep the visitors separate—because they both came from the town where Culpepper might have been headed?

Surely, he did not think a *vicar* could be a killer?

～

"HOLD DINNER FOR HALF AN HOUR, WHY?" ELSA ASKED IN dismay, checking the delicate souffle in the horrible oven. After it fell, she supposed she could call it an *omelette*. . .

"A vicar, ma'am," Marie, the upstairs maid, said excitedly. "Do you think they might be thinking of having church again? My nan would love that."

"Keep that sauce stirred," Elsa ordered Anne, the new hire, a girl barely past adolescence. Wiping her hands, she considered all the simmering pots and pans. "A vicar, at this hour. Has someone died?"

"No, ma'am, he didn't say nuffin. He's from a long ways off. Maybe it's about the. . ." She nodded at the back door, indicating the new grave.

Having mentally considered all she had to do to delay dinner, Elsa finally gave the idle gossip a thought—and a chill of fear settled over her heart. Culpepper and Jack and now, a *vicar*? Could it be. . .? It didn't seem plausible.

"Did you hear where he was from? I heard there was a vicar in Newchurch who might need a position. . ." That was an utter lie. Geoffrey was entrenched there since her estate supported the vicarage. But she needed to test her suspicion.

Marie bobbed her head enthusiastically. "That's it. I heard Quincy say it. But our chapel is collapsing! He'll leave."

Elsa had to stay busy to prevent her frozen heart from sinking to her feet. "He may just be visiting. Take up these stuffed mushrooms and pass them around to keep everyone from starving. Add some cheese and those crackers that the captain likes."

Ever obedient, Marie bobbed a curtsy. Elsa gave her a tray and helped her dish the small offerings onto plates. The men would eat anything with their fingers. She wasn't too worried about the ladies disdaining food meant to keep the gentlemen from griping.

She couldn't *think* properly. Her dinner had to be paramount, but Geoffrey. . . Mr. Garrett was upstairs! Why? He couldn't know she was here. No one did, not even Jack. She was simply scaring herself for naught, surely.

True, it had been foolish of her to see Jack when he was fevered. She had hoped that once he recovered, he wouldn't remember and would ride on. But he hadn't.

Sometimes, she was so *stupid*. That's why she belonged in the kitchen, where she knew what she was doing. She basted the lamb on the spit and raked the coals to the side to keep it from drying out. The meat pies. . ."Warming dishes, Anne, over the pies. I'll watch the sauce and peas."

The men in her life had always left her alone when she was in the kitchen. As long as they were being fed, they didn't care if she existed. Uneasily, she realized that wasn't the same here. But she had work to do and no one else to do it.

She simply wished she could be a mouse under the table to hear why Mr. Garrett was so far from home—at the same time as Jack was returning.

~

JACK TASTED THE MUSHROOMS AND WAITED IMPATIENTLY FOR THE vicar to return. He could think of no good reason for Garrett to be visiting the manor where Culpepper had been buried. Jack's letters couldn't have reached Newchurch yet, and Culpepper had no connection with that rural area. From missives he'd received while overseas, he knew of Elsa's disastrous encounter with Culpepper during her presentation, but that had been in London.

"Do you know the vicar well?" Hunt asked, helping himself to a handful of crackers and topping them with cheese. "You should try these. I asked our cook to make them, and she's created perfection."

Absently, Jack picked up a *cracker* and imitated his host by adding cheese. "Garrett's father was vicar before him. We attended different schools, but we're much of an age, and it's a small town. We more or less grew up together." He bit into the cheese thing.

"But he has no reason to know Culpepper?"

Jack looked at the dry cracker he'd bitten into. "They make these things where you come from? Interesting."

"They keep well and are tastier than hardtack on the road.

Crumble though. Culpepper?" Hunt brushed off his lapel and watched the women gossiping across the room.

Jack shrugged. "I've been gone ten years. I never knew Culpepper to leave London unless someone invited him to the country where he could eat for free. For all I know, he married some wealthy woman and was traveling for fun. I can't think of a reason the vicar would know him. Should we have him say a few words over the grave?"

"I'm more interested in finding who killed our victim than having him blessed. A stranger showing up at the door arouses curiosity given our isolation." Hunt sipped his brandy.

"Did he not give a reason for his appearance?" Jack watched in disappointment as the maid left with an empty tray. A diet of broth and tea had left him starved.

"He said he was looking for someone and unfamiliar with the roads. Night fell before he found an inn. The gossips in the village told him we had guests, so he came to make inquiries. If I mentioned that to Clare, she would be creating a romantic fantasy about a lover run off and a villain on the trail." Hunt turned back to the doorway as their guest returned.

The captain might be half blind, but Jack thought he must have the ears of a canine to hear Garrett creep in. He led his host to the drab vicar dawdling uncomfortably at the entrance.

"Come along, old boy, let me introduce you around. How have you been keeping?" Jack gestured at Hunt. "You've met Captain Huntley, I assume. His feminine counterpart is Miss Clarissa Knightley, the lady watching us expectantly."

Garrett nodded. "I truly do not wish to bother the ladies. I'm amazed and relieved to find you here, Jack. Have you heard aught from Lady Elspeth? She seems to have vanished." The vicar reluctantly crossed the drawing room with them.

Jack halted abruptly, fighting off panic. Culpepper's note. . . had he been too late? "She has gone missing?"

"Lady Elspeth?" the captain asked at the same time.

At their questions, Garrett stopped out of hearing of the ladies. Alarmed, Jack tried not to shake the man into speaking faster. *Elspeth*? Missing? Impossible. Culpepper couldn't have reached her. An heiress was surrounded by servants. . .

"Lady Elspeth Villiers, a spinster," the vicar explained to Hunt. "She and her mother share a life estate in one of Lord Villiers' smaller properties. Her younger stepbrother has been overseeing the estate, but he recently married and moved away. She has a most excellent steward but. . ."

Jack bunched his fists in fury and frustration. "What do you mean, *vanished*? It's not as if she can go anywhere without a carriage, a maid, a driver, and a caravan of trunks!"

The vicar raised his palms helplessly. "The carriage has gone nowhere. Her lady's maid said she was to stay with friends in town to do some shopping and didn't require her services. She never returned. When we made inquiries, the friend knew little. She had sent her carriage to pick up the lady. They had shopped. And then Lady Elspeth insisted on hiring a carriage to take her home. That's the last anyone has seen of her."

With no outlet for his fury, Jack tossed back the rest of his brandy and refrained from strangling everyone in Elsa's life. She'd never had anyone looking after her. She'd always more or less run wild. And this was the result. "There's more, isn't there, Garrett? What do you know?"

The vicar shuffled and glanced at the ladies across the room, watching. "It is gossip, sir. I am sure I cannot say. . ."

"Out with it, Garrett! The world spins on gossip." Jack didn't even wait for Hunt to speak. The captain seemed content to listen.

"It's only. . . Mr. Aloysius Smythe, the owner of several factories in town. . ." The vicar seemed unable to explain.

"Henri!" The captain shouted at his younger cousin, who stood with the other gentlemen, surreptitiously observing. "Do you know anything of Aloysius Smythe?"

The Frenchman sauntered over to join them. "Inherited a lot of factories, filthy rich, haven't met him personally. Why?"

Jack growled at the vicar until he hurriedly answered.

"He has bought an estate in Newchurch, my parish. He is very generous to the church, very generous. He is courting Lady Elspeth. Their estates run together, I believe. Only. . ."

"Elsa ran away, didn't she?" Jack demanded. "You let this rich Cit hound her now that she has no one to protect her, and she picked up her skirts and fled."

Garrett nodded miserably.

EIGHT

Dinner at the manor was usually an informal affair. With more men than women, the company simply paired off with whomever they were conversing, with no concern for etiquette. Clare arranged it so Mr. de Sackville and Mr. Garrett sat near Hunt and herself. She'd already missed something that had the captain's jaw muscles twitching angrily.

But the men didn't reveal what their conversation had been about, and she was left to stew in curiosity. What could a village vicar have told them?

Since they weren't talking, dinner was an uncomfortable affair. Their guests complimented the cook, the wine, and the company and pretended naught was wrong. The vicar had appeared startled at seeing Walker and Meera seated at the table, but he was too visibly rattled by his own concerns to take offense, if he were inclined that way.

They were generally in the habit of going their way after dinner, although Clare, Meera, Lavender, and her puppy usually withdrew to the cozy blue salon upstairs to discuss work that might need doing before following their pursuits. The men lingered over whiskey to do the same.

To her surprise, the captain abandoned the whiskey to

steer her into the large downstairs parlor once the pudding was cleared. Her heart sang that he actually sought her out— even though it meant he had a knotty problem he couldn't solve. She apparently liked being seen as a problem-solver.

"Our cook is a runaway," he stated bluntly.

Clare nearly laughed at his shock. She teasingly tapped his lapel. "And you have just worked this out? Do they not have runaways where you come from?"

"Not heiresses." He glared at her glumly. "You knew? And said nothing?"

"I surmised. One does not often find the granddaughter of earls in kitchens, using an alias. Is she in danger? Do we have a need for concern?" Clare tried very hard to curb her wild imagination, but it was running in circles and becoming overexcited, rather like Lavender's puppy.

"She is an *heiress*, with a large dowry and a life estate in a lucrative property. Her father's son by a first marriage is the heir, but he leaves an elderly steward in charge. Her mother remarried after the earl's death, to a ne'er-do-well, it seems. They produced a son. The stepfather apparently drank himself into an early grave, and her stepbrother is recently married and moved away. In their absence, the predators are circling." Hunt looked uncomfortable.

There was a time when Hunt would have reached for more whiskey and flung books at the fireplace in his frustration. He was coming to terms with his limitations, Clare hoped. There would be no heroic riding to the rescue, even if his leg allowed. The American soldier knew nothing of England except what was on this estate.

Which was why he relied on her. Clare appreciated that he didn't ignore her knowledge because she was female. "And I suppose our Mr. Culpepper was one of the predators?"

"We don't know. The scrap of paper he carried indicated he knew about what we assume was an illegal mission. One cannot question a dead man. The vicar fears a wealthy landowner has set his sights on Elsa, and she objected. How do we persuade her to tell us the story?" He leaned against the mantel and rubbed his temple. "I did not think running an estate involved so much melodrama."

"We live for melodrama. What else is there?" she asked dryly. "I will have Elsa come to my sitting room again. Perhaps she will wish to see the vicar? And you say *Jack* knows her?" That was a bit of news their cook had not imparted.

He nodded. "He's not seen her since he left home, doesn't know she's here, but their home village is not large and they're close enough in age."

"I am afraid she will only run away again. Did either of them mention how Mr. Culpepper is involved? Surely it's too much coincidence that he was nearby?" She was quite certain Elsa had been inspecting the deceased before he was buried. She must have recognized his name.

"Apparently there was a scandal the year the lady was presented? I don't know these things. Culpepper was involved, her reputation was ruined in some way, and she retreated to her estate. Jack wasn't too happy with the vicar about something, but they did not let me in on what is old news."

"Elspeth is a few years older than I, closer to my sister's age. Bea might have known about the scandal, but my father died, and I was never presented. I have little more knowledge than you. We will have to step carefully to earn her trust." Clare bit her bottom lip and studied the problem. "I assume we can do that by abiding by her wishes if she prefers to stay hidden."

Hunt groaned. "It would be much simpler if everyone simply talked!"

She daringly tapped his lapel again. "We are not all engineers. We muddle about as we can."

This time, he grabbed her hand and kissed it. But he let her go and returned to the table and the brandy.

Clare held his regard close to her heart and tried to make nothing of a pounding pulse. She glanced at the clock. The staff would be sitting down to their dinner. She hated to intrude, but it had to be done.

Lady Elspeth was on her feet as soon as Clare arrived on the landing. So, she'd heard about the guest and recognized his name. The heiress wiped her hands on her apron and removed it, then followed Clare without speaking until they reached the small upstairs sitting room Clare had usurped as her writing study.

"Mr. Garrett is here. Has he said why?" Even wearing servant's garb, the lady spoke with the authority of her station.

Clare gestured for her to take a seat. "The gentlemen are not communicating with anyone but Captain Huntley. He has asked me to inform you that the vicar says you have vanished and fears the worst. Mr. de Sackville is upbraiding him severely and is ready to ride out in the morning to look for you, even though he is not fully recovered."

The cook buried her face in her hands. "Why can Garrett not leave well enough alone? I imagine Smythe put him up to this. The church always comes first, and Smythe contributes generously."

She looked up, and her eyes flashed with fury. "They had to have gone through my desk for Garrett to find the name of the manor!"

"The matter of the manor's inheritance is well known in the family. Your mother, your aunts, any of them may have mentioned it. He seems genuinely concerned," Clare said, choosing her words with care. "Not many men would ride these lanes at this hour in hopes of finding you."

"Smythe didn't," the lady said with a bitter laugh. "He sent the vicar as his minion."

Clare clasped her fingers on the desk and puzzled through what little she knew. "Was Mr. Culpepper a minion? Could the note in his boot have been instructions related to you?"

The runaway looked startled. "What note?"

"He had a scrap of paper indicating he was to meet someone in Newchurch and to find horses for some inn on the way to Liverpool. Unless you were planning an elopement, we do not have any idea what it means."

"Another minion," she agreed bitterly. "Although how Smythe would know Culpepper is beyond my knowledge. I cannot think a factory owner like Mr. Smythe would be accepted in Culpepper's noble circles."

"Someone killed Mr. Culpepper for a reason. Unless you wish to suspect Jack or Mr. Garrett, then I suppose the captain will need to talk to this Mr. Smythe. Henri has not yet found anyone who saw Mr. Culpepper on the road, so we have no suspects. We don't even know what his horse looks like."

The cook shook her mob-capped head. "I cannot help with any of that. I ran to the manor because I wanted to cook, and I saw an opportunity. If there was aught nefarious happening behind my back, I did not know of it. But you can see why I prefer my privacy. I hate deceiving Jack and the vicar, but they know everyone at home. They could not resist reassuring people that I am safe. One thing would lead to another. . ."

"So I should let them worry, or reassure them that you are safe and let them hunt for you? If word has spread that you are one of the manor's heirs, then you are already exposed." Clare shook her head. "We need to solve the problem, not avoid it. You are a lady. You have family who will not allow you to come to harm. If you trust Mr. Garrett and Mr. de Sackville, talk to them. You may stay here and cook all you like. But don't make others suffer."

The lady's lips set stubbornly. "I will think on it." She rose and left without being dismissed—as she had every right to do. It wasn't as if Clare had any rank at all.

~

ELSA CRIED HERSELF TO SLEEP FOR THE FIRST TIME IN YEARS. SHE didn't want Jack riding out to look for her, but he was a soldier. He'd performed far more dangerous feats. And Mr. Garrett—he was a fine one to worry about her now. Had he not backed out of courting her after the scandal, they could be happily married with half a dozen children. But his position was more important to him than she was.

She supposed she should be grateful that the vicar wasn't after her wealth, but he probably didn't know anything about her dowry. She had never informed him that it was her husband's upon marriage and had nothing to do with obtaining anyone's approval.

And Culpepper! Could he really have been planning something that involved her? Why, after all these years?

She had so hoped. . . What? That she could spend a lonely life in an ancient kitchen with an old brick stove when she could have her own modern cast iron one? Did she think she would marry a stable hand and take him home? What future did she have like this? And if word of the manor had already spread. . .

She wanted to cook. She could no longer live at home with her neighbor conspiring against her and Freddy lurking every time he needed funds.

She dried her tears and tried to muddle through it, but she fell asleep. And when she woke late the next morning, she hadn't decided anything except she wished to see Jack. He was a troublemaker, beyond a doubt. The military had been the perfect choice for a boy who rode horses as if he were a centaur and who couldn't sit still long enough to hear a sermon.

His father wasn't rich, but Jack hadn't tried to woo her for her money. Admittedly, a man as handsome as he could have any woman he liked, and except monetarily, she was no prize. But he hadn't married. After a year or so of carousing through London, he'd ultimately made his own way in the world instead of marrying wealth. She thought that meant he had integrity.

She dressed and summoned Ned, the deaf mute who helped wherever he could. Ned was good with horses, but he had difficulty communicating with the stable hands. He could read though. She gave him a note.

In her absence, the kitchen staff was worriedly attempting their breakfast routines while the stove sat empty. She was late. Elsa hurriedly threw rashers in a pan, seasoned the beans she'd left soaking and set them on to boil, and broke eggs into a bowl. "Betsy, prepare the toast, please. Anne, you'll need to stir the eggs in the pan if I'm not back by seven. You can read the clock, can't you?"

Wide-eyed, her young assistant nodded.

Scattering orders, Elsa donned a cloak she'd borrowed from her maid, pulled up the hood, and hurried out the back door with the meager bucket of scraps she usually left for evening.

The day was dawning clear for a change, but it was cool enough to justify hiding under a cloak. She'd never been svelte, but she'd rather Jack remember her as a much younger, slimmer woman.

He came hurrying toward her garden from the carriage side of the house. Ned had done a fine job of dragging a gentleman from his slumbers. Or the fool soldier had already been dressed and prepared to ride out. From the looks of his neatly tied neckcloth and flapping capes of his greatcoat, she assumed the latter.

He looked wonderful, more than wonderful. Ten years had added muscle to fill out his tailored attire and chiseled his square jaw and cheekbones to refinement. As he approached, she could see weary lines on his face that hadn't been there as a youth, but they only added to the character shining in his eyes as he saw her.

"Elsa? Is that really you?" With his usual carelessness, he flung off her hood, kissed her cheek, then hugged, lifted her, and spun her around. "Elsa, my old girl! You are a sight for these weary eyes. And now I am going to scold you."

She thought she might melt against his strong chest and weep. It had been so long since anyone had held her. . .

Elsa straightened and pushed away. "Don't you dare, Jack. You went off a-soldiering without asking my permission, leaving me to worry about you for years. You aren't allowed an opinion on what I choose to do. I simply wanted to let you know I'm fine, so you won't be riding needlessly about when you should be resting."

He beamed down on her and brushed a straying hair from her cheek. "You were my angel of the biscuits, weren't you? You told me to go home. Is my father doing well? He never tells me otherwise."

Her cheeks heated, but Jack always had a way of making her blush. "He is older but still healthy and sharp. I cannot even say for certain if he is lonely since he keeps so much to himself. We all try to stop by when we can, but I always feel as if I'm interrupting his studies."

Jack nodded. "Or his articles. He has a vast correspondence with those of more intelligence than I. So let us talk about you. A cook, Elsa? Did you grow bored cooking for your own staff?"

This was where the conversation became difficult. She gestured at the aging manor. "My great-grandfather left me a share in this. I thought it might be exciting to know more of my family and share in their effort to restore it."

He crossed his arms and glared at her. "You were never good at fibbing, Elsa. Your eyes crinkle and you don't look at me. Did you know your eyes are almost the color of turquoise? I've seen turquoise, so I know this now. And your mouth is prettier than rubies. Rubies are plain ugly when they're unpolished."

She smacked his broad chest. "Stop flirting. We're too old for that. I am happy here. What will you do next?"

"Stay here until I find out why you ran away. If you had simply wished to know family, you could have arrived in a carriage with all your trunks instead of disguising yourself as a mere cook. I understand the manor needs a good carriage, although the stable might not be up to the standards of your horses." He bent his head down to hers. "You can trust me, Elsa. Whom do you fear?"

"No one. I am fine. Go home, Jack. Where will you go after that? I know you don't wish to be a farmer." She turned the conversation on him.

It didn't work. He took her arm and her empty bucket and led her through the kitchen garden. "Culpepper didn't end up dead on your doorstep for no reason, my dumpling. Unless you wish to say you bashed him over the head with a skillet and hired a thug to put a bullet through his skull, then I have to assume his killer is still loose. He was carrying a note that immediately reminded me that you are an heiress with little or no protection. And I hear a bullying Cit has been courting you. I may be incompetent at managing a farm, but I am not *stupid*."

She wished he'd hold her in his arms again. She'd felt safe like that. She hadn't felt safe in a very long time. Unfortunately or not, she was learning to resist impulse. "Tell me what you intend to do after you visit your father."

He halted and stared down at her. "Join Wellington, of course. Napoleon can't be allowed to return."

She studied his face. "You look half starved, and your eyes have dark circles. You were just confined to bed with a raging fever. If you go a-soldiering again, you'll likely die before you reach the battlefield."

"I've nearly died any number of times. What I just suffered was nothing compared to the original bout of illness. Soldiering is what I do. I know naught else. You cannot divert the subject. You are a female. You can't expect to defend yourself against villains like Culpepper and Smythe."

Foolish longing made her answer as she had as a child. "You love horses, Jack. You helped me pick a stable that men would weep to own. You could easily earn a living helping others as you have me."

"I want to *own* horses," he told her gently. "I want my own stable. I have saved nearly enough to buy land if I can find the right property. I will never be wealthy, but I will be happy, like my father in his little world. That is why I soldier, to earn enough for horses. What's your excuse?"

"I want to cook." And because this was Jack, she bared her soul. "I want a family I can trust not to sell me to the highest bidder. Go home, Jack. You cannot help me."

He glared at her relentlessly. "A dragon's gold requires a dragon to guard it. These good people are not dragons." He gestured at the manor. "Until you find your dragon and marry him, I will have to slay the thieves who would steal you away."

She didn't know whether to laugh or cry at his foolishness. Instead, she picked up her skirt and fled back to the kitchen where he could not go.

NINE

After the frustrating encounter with Elsa, Jack stormed into the manor, heading for the breakfast room where he assumed everyone would gather at this ungodly hour. He found only the boy—the owner of a fortune in gems that he carried in his pocket as if they were jackstones. Well, Jack had thrown them in a trunk and forgotten about them, so he was not one to criticize.

But the boy was another innocent who needed a dragon guardian, not a slip of a female who couldn't even manage a seven-year-old.

"Did you find a cave for the dragon eggs?" Jack asked, filling his plate with burned bacon and cold toast—because Elsa had not been overseeing the kitchen.

The boy nodded and smushed his toast into his milk.

"I trust you know they're very rare and valuable, and your aunt could probably use the money one would earn if you were to sell it to another dragon lover?" Not that it would be a wise idea for Miss Knightley to walk into a jeweler with one. The men in that business would cheat her blind, as they did each other when they could. Jack had learned the cut-throat competition in India.

How much did little boys understand of money? Not much, he'd surmise. This one frowned and sucked on his mushy toast. Jack could do no more.

He couldn't do anything about any damned thing, not even the frustrating, annoying, irritating, damnable Lady Elspeth. He could slay an army, sail the seas, and earn a modest fortune, but he could not force one little female to listen to sense. It had always been that way. He'd tell her what she should do, and she'd do the opposite.

To be fair, it worked the other way around. She'd told him to stay and help her with the horses instead of riding off to be a soldier. But he hadn't wanted a woman to be his employer. And he'd hated watching her being neglected when he could do nothing about it. He'd been a stripling then. He'd hoped to come home a hero and save the princess. Instead, he'd run off to India when she'd turned twenty-one and came into some of her fortune. Fine hero he made.

The boy ran off as the others trickled in. Jack wasn't certain who knew what about whom, so he figured he'd have to wait until Huntley was done breaking his fast before he could corner him. He didn't know what he wanted to say, so he ate his food in silence and pondered.

The captain wasn't so circumspect. He crunched on the burned bacon and glared at Jack. "Did you succeed in seducing our cook?"

"If the lady could be seduced, she wouldn't be in your kitchen now." Disgruntled, Jack spooned up half-cooked beans.

"I'd hate to lose her. You haven't frightened her into flee-ing? I spent too many years eating army mess. I'm just learning to appreciate good food." Hunt stood as Miss Knightley and Mrs. Abrams joined them.

Jack pulled out a chair for the apothecary while Hunt seated Miss Knightley.

"Has the vicar departed already? Or is he not down yet?" Miss Knightley asked, reaching for the teapot on the table and frowning at the plate she'd filled from the buffet. "And has Mrs. Evans run away? Perhaps with the vicar?"

Jack processed this while chewing his toast, took a sip of tea, and did his best to translate without giving anyone away to eavesdropping servants. "The vicar's nag is still in the stable. If Mrs. Evans is your cook, then she was feeding the chickens instead of cooking, so fleeing is a possibility. I have suggested that she needs a dragon to protect her. She disagrees."

Miss Knightley sent him what appeared to be a grateful smile, so presumably she understood the nonsense. The captain grunted and made inroads into his food.

Arnaud entered, filled his plate with everything on the buffet, then added another plate for toast and a hot sweetbread the maid had just delivered. "Any luck deciphering that code?" he asked, sitting next to Jack.

He recognized Elsa's decadent shortbread. She was back in the kitchen. He helped himself to a large slice before replying. "I attempted to discern a pattern. Each cipher so far contains from five to seven alphanumeric characters. The numbers run from one to thirty-three, or one to nine if we look at the 33 as two single numbers. There are only ten different letters used. I am attempting to calculate all the directional words those letters might represent if they do indicate location."

The African steward entered as Jack was explaining. Helping himself to the stewed beans and bacon, Walker settled at the far end of the small breakfast table, near Mrs. Abrams, and joined the discussion. "I have been counting rooms in a futile attempt to match numbers. But if we count the new wings, the manor has nearly thirty suites on the family floor alone. If we count the ground floor and the attic. . . That doesn't work."

The massive butler scratched a warning at the paneled door, and when he had their attention, announced, "There is a young man at the carriage entrance. He says he has found a horse."

Jack was on his feet instantly. Hunt took a moment longer to engage his injured knee. Walker and Arnaud placidly continued eating.

"You spoke with Lady Elspeth?" Hunt inquired as they traversed the corridor to the side entrance.

"*She* spoke with *me*," Jack corrected dryly. "She's happy here, claims everything is fine, and refuses to tell me anything that might cause concern. But she'll run at the first sign of a threat. I assume she does not consider Garrett to be a threat."

Hunt nodded. "If she is afraid of someone, I'll add another bolt to the kitchen door. Lavender's ball of fluff doesn't make much of a guard dog. I'll see if I can find a hound."

"An entire pack of dogs roaming the grounds at night might give warning, I suppose. I'd feel better if the lady were above stairs, but she'll want to go to the market and feed the chickens and harvest the garden. . . There is no imprisoning her."

"You think there is a danger?" Hunt halted before opening the door and watched Jack carefully.

Jack nodded. "Definitely. Always has been. She's an heiress with no family to watch over her. Seduction hasn't worked since Culpepper. With her last male family gone, she's ripe for abduction, and she knows it."

"My assessment too." Hunt yanked open the door to find a young man sitting on the step.

He held the reins of a massive gray hunter Jack recognized from his last sojourn in town, before he bought his colors, before Elsa had been presented. In that more innocent time, he'd helped Culpepper buy the sturdy mare.

∼

Hunt ordered the horse's gear carried into the gallery and spread out on the tiles. He'd left Jack tending to the weary, hungry animal. There was little in the way of fodder in winter fields.

He was amazed no one had claimed the mare. Clare had sent the honest lad to the kitchen for feeding. Hunt would question him later and provide a reward.

Walker silently pointed to dark drops on the saddle blanket spread across the floor. *Blood*. Hunt pointed at cuts on the leather of the reins and the girth dents where it would normally be fastened. The buckle had been in different notches when he'd taken it off the horse. Stupid bastard hadn't checked his leathers before riding out.

Arnaud and Henri joined them, crouching down to examine what Hunt didn't want to have to kneel and inspect. "Loosened the girth," Arnaud agreed.

"Reins would have broken had he let the horse have its head." Henri folded up on the floor to better examine the saddle stitching. "Seam is loose here."

Arnaud started emptying the saddlebags.

"So the killer hoped to spook the horse into a gallop, let the saddle slip or the reins break, and send the rider flying into the hedgerow. Although if the thief meant to rifle his bags, he wasn't as smart as he thought. Horses run when frightened." Hunt half-sat on one of Lavender's sewing tables. "Not exactly a recipe for murder but close enough."

"If murder was the intent, the killer most likely doctored the tack when Culpepper made a stop, then followed behind, pistol ready. A servant?" Walker handed a knife to Henri so he could slit the saddle seams.

"Could be anyone. Someone he met on the road who thought he looked a likely mark. Someone who detested him, and I gather that may be more than a few." Hunt studied the contents of the saddlebag without interest. The man liked clothes but packed no purse or weapon. "What are the chances that he carried a pistol and someone turned it on him?" Who traveled alone without weapons?

"A pistol would ruin the cut of his clothes," Arnaud said dryly. "And one needs to know how to use a sword. There is no scabbard."

Henri searched the pockets of the clothes without luck. Arnaud had more success with the saddle seam. With a whoop, he slid out a collection of banknotes and spread them across the floor. "Promissory notes, with assigned receivers. We'll need Mr. de Sackville to recognize the names."

"Jack, call me Jack." The gentleman in question entered the gallery still wearing his boots and smelling of horse. "The mare is in reasonably good condition for having roamed the fields on her own. Ned is picking out the burrs and will have her in shape in no time. What do you need me for?"

Hunt gestured at the banknotes. "I gather they contain names. Do you recognize any of them?"

Jack picked them up, flipped through them, and whistled. He handed one to Hunt. "Lady Elsa's stepbrother, the one who just married and abandoned her and the estate."

Hunt could make out the scrawl with his one eye but handed it to Walker to read aloud. "Frederick Turner."

The vicar walked in, wearing his overcoat and carrying his hat. He halted as Walker read the name. "Lady Elspeth's stepbrother. Does he know where she has gone?"

"Why would Culpepper be carrying banknotes made out to others?" Walker asked, ignoring a question no one could answer. "Can he cash them?"

"If they signed them over. . . after he completed a task, perhaps?" Henri began reading off names. "Any of those mean anything?"

Frowning, Jack shook his head and handed them to the

vicar. "I've been gone too long. I don't know Culpepper's cronies these days."

The vicar looked them over, and his Adam's apple bobbed up and down as he handed them back. "Reginald Hill. I believe he is employed by Aloysius Smythe."

"Huh. Looks like I have more reason to speak with Mr. Aloysius Smythe." Hunt slid off the table. "Henri, you want to go with me? We can see if he needs any workers or supplies or whatever his factories might need, strike up a conversation."

Jack carried one of the notes over to a window and shook his head. "Better let me see the rest of these."

Hunt took one before they could all be gathered. With his one eye, he likely couldn't see whatever Jack had, but he needed to learn about his new home—if he meant to stay. The note bore the name of Liverpool Bank and was signed by their cashier, as far as he could determine. What had made Jack suspicious?

"The paper is flimsy," Jack said, holding it up to the meager morning sun. "The name of the bank is printed in poor ink, and the word *cashier* is misspelled." He fanned the notes like an expert card player. "These are counterfeit."

Henri crossed the gallery to examine them. "I don't handle sums of this amount, but it's good to know what to look for. I might have been fooled."

"Unless you knew what to look for. Did Culpepper?" Jack returned to hand the paper around so others could look. "Or was it his intent to defraud these people? Since the banks are now restricted from paying out gold, counterfeiting has soared, but I didn't think anyone forged hundred-pound notes. Most merchants and all banks would notice. It's usually small notes that go to the illiterate that are counterfeited and certainly not assigned ones."

"Printing isn't cheap," Walker argued. "More profitable to write them for large amounts."

"But whoever handed them out would be in certain trouble once the receiver attempted to cash the note. Tradesmen would hunt him down. And men of respectability would ruin him." Arnaud frowned at the one he held.

"Maybe that's what happened." Hunt headed for the door, although he was torn between destinations. "Culpepper handed out one of these notes, the victim couldn't cash it, and he came after him. We need to take that horse to his family in Bath."

"I need to continue to look for Lady Elspeth, or I would take on the task of speaking with the grieving family." The vicar crushed his hat brim.

Hunt glanced at Jack, who shook his head. The lady hadn't given permission to reveal her whereabouts. He frowned and borrowed Clare's imaginative thinking. "Might the lady have gone to friends or family in Bath? I understand it is a congenial place for society to gather?"

"Not in Apr—" Jack winced when Hunt kicked him.

The vicar didn't notice. "Mr. Turner, her stepbrother, lives near Bath. Perhaps he might know where Lady Elspeth is. I can visit Mr. Culpepper's family estate while I am there. Does anyone have the direction?"

Within the hour, they had bundled the vicar off with the horse, Culpepper's effects, and what limited directions they possessed. Jack glared at Hunt throughout the process.

"The family will be in London at this time of year. What do you mean by sending the bumbling nodcock on a fool's errand?" he demanded after the vicar rode off, leading the weary mare. "And that poor horse needs a week's rest, at least."

Hunt headed for his study. "Do you want him returning to Newchurch and telling everyone that Culpepper died on the way to Gravesyde Priory and was carrying fraudulent bank notes? If Mr. Smythe is searching for the lady and using

Culpepper as his lackey, how long would it be before he sent one of his men poking around the manor?"

Jack muttered imprecations under his breath.

Hunt ignored them. "How do you know about counter-feiting if you've been in India?"

"Happens everywhere." Jack shrugged as they entered Hunt's lair. "I started as an officer in the East India army, guarding tax collections. I had to learn to count the collections so I knew they made it to their destination intact. Some taxes were paid in jewels and some in notes. I learned as I went."

"Not useful knowledge unless you're a jeweler or banker, I suppose, but a boon to us. Can I ask you to delay visiting your father until Henri and I call on Mr. Smythe? I dislike leaving the ladies alone. Arnaud and Walker are good men, but not trained soldiers." Hunt limped to his desk chair. He needed to draw out coins for his journey. Did he trust an officer in the Company's army with his purse?

Jack paced. "I dislike sitting still. I can work on the code a bit, but I need more. I'm sorry to see Culpepper's mare leave. You need a stable."

"I need a land agent who knows farming," Hunt said dryly. "Then I'll worry about a stable. The code Arnaud gave you might be a clue to the location of the gems in those paint-ings. Perhaps you could hunt for jewels. The bank is demanding we repay funds that the late viscount borrowed. We could use your expertise in determining the value of the jewels should any be found."

Jack shoved his hands in his pockets, rocked back on his boot heels, and nodded. "Perhaps I can persuade Elsa that she needn't hide in a cellar."

Hunt snorted. "Good luck with persuading any woman to do anything sensible."

"I'll make her help me hunt jewels." He wandered off, apparently not distressed that he wouldn't be rejoining the army soon.

Hunt pocketed a few coins and the banknote made out to Reginald Hill. He'd let the others go to Culpepper's parents but kept this one as evidence.

He might make a bad magistrate, but perhaps he could learn to investigate criminals.

TEN

Hunt and Henri left for Birmingham in the peddler's cart after breakfast. Since their last housekeeper had drowned in a fit of madness and not been replaced, Clare spent the morning overseeing the maids and the cleaning. After lunch, she settled Oliver in the library with some mathematical problems. She was finally sitting down to work on her new novel when Betsy pounded down the narrow back hall from the kitchen stairs, shrieking, "Fire, fire!"

Fire? My Lord in Heaven, she had no plans for dealing with fire. Terrified, Clare dropped her pen and ran out of her study to catch the hysterical maid before she sent everyone straight into the flames. "Where?"

"The chimney, the chimney's on fire! We'll all die." Still shrieking in alarm, Betsy pushed past her to race out the garden door.

A kitchen chimney fire? Clare desperately wished Hunt were here. Should she run down to see how serious it was? Had the staff evacuated yet?

Oliver popped out of the library. Clare pointed him toward the front door, away from the kitchen. Ever vigilant, Quincy and his son materialized in the corridor. At Clare's gesture, they began ushering people from the gallery work-shop. Emerging with fabric in their arms, Lavender and her workers glanced about in confusion.

"Outside," Clare shouted. "Everyone outside. See if the stable has buckets."

Arnaud carried armloads of paintings from the workshop. He shoved them at everyone in the hall, returning to collect more as soon as his arms were empty.

Too rattled to think clearly, Clare checked the back hall. Smoke seeped under the door of the kitchen stairs at the far end.

Pulse pounding, she dashed back for her manuscript box and returned to the back hall just as Meera emerged from the infirmary carrying a box with her jars and tins. They were nearest to the rear door. How dangerous was the smoke?

Worried about the kitchen staff, she chose the closer garden exit. Carrying her box of pages and following Meera, Clare held her breath through the smoke and gasped for air once they were outside.

With all her dreams literally going up in smoke, she hurried through the parterre gardens of the courtyard with her box. Smoke poured up the outside cellar stairs. She counted heads of the staff milling uncertainly in the garden. Where was Elsa?

In a panic, she almost ran into Jack. "Why isn't everyone carrying buckets from the well?" She shoved the box at him, prepared to find buckets. Was Elsa still in the cellar? Had someone already stolen her?

Jack caught her before she ran off. "Elsa has it under control."

To prove his words, the lady cook stumbled up the outside kitchen stairs, flapping her apron at the smoke and cursing like a trooper.

With relief, Clare clung to Jack's arm to steady herself—and to listen in awe to Elsa's voluble opinion of. . . the *stove*?

"Where did she learn those words?" she asked. She'd thought Meera had an immense vocabulary of epithets. The chilly wind almost whipped her question away as they hastened across the garden.

"Servants, her brothers, stepfather, the stable. . ." Jack followed on her heels. "She did not lead a protected life."

As Clare had, up until Egypt, leastways. Even then, until the riot anyway, her escorts had been mostly civilized in her company.

She didn't dare hug her coughing cousin but offered Elsa a handkerchief for the soot. "What happened?"

"Mrs. Evans threw dirt on the fire, she did," the young assistant cook said excitedly, responding when Elsa could not. "And the kitchen scraps and the water bucket and put a cauldron over the last of it! I'd never have thought to do such a thing."

"Blasted bloody old rotten pile of mule dung." Elsa finally muttered, scrubbing at her face. "Stove is done for. Blew a hole through the mortar, cracked the top. No telling what it did to the chimney. We'll be eating cheese until we fix the firebox."

That stunned everyone into silence.

Coming around the corner from the front, Walker and Arnaud raced toward the stable where presumably buckets were stored. They halted at seeing the crowd idly milling in the garden.

Clare could almost feel Jack's indecision as he glanced from Lady Elspeth to Walker and Arnaud. Unable to acknowledge the heiress in public, he reluctantly trotted over to explain the dilemma.

Clare had no notion of how one cleared smoke from a cellar. So she took Elsa by her soot-covered shoulders and led her back inside the upper hall, where reality hit. "No hot water for a bath?"

She thought Elsa chuckled. She was no doubt hysterical.

"Giant fireplaces everywhere. How good are the rest of your chimneys?" Tears streaked down her filthy cheeks.

"What a wretched time for Hunt to be away." Clare led a subdued Elsa up the stairs, to her bedchamber. She knew the coal grate worked, and she had a tea kettle. They could start there. "How does one buy stoves?"

"Ones like that are built with bricks and mortar and cast iron. Even the cast iron cracked. I have a new Rumford on my estate, but it's immense and took an army to install," Elsa replied with a watery laugh. "All that work, and it's sitting there going to waste."

It sounded to Clare as if a great deal more than a stove was going to waste, but that wasn't for her to say. "Thank you for saving the manor. I know nothing of kitchens and would have been helpless."

She removed a robe from the armoire. "I had no notion that stoves could be so dangerous."

Elsa unbuttoned her ruined servant's garb. The water in the kettle was still barely tepid by the time her cousin had discarded the filthy rag. "I've never had a stove catch fire, admittedly, although I've set fire to pans. It's all my fault, I suppose. I had a boiling soup on the fire and needed to fry the fish. So I fired up the box to boil the soup, fry the fish, and bake bread at the same time. I don't think it's been tested like that in years."

"Certainly not by the caretaker who lived here. Have you burned yourself?" Seeing the reddened skin emerging from the soot as Elsa washed, Clare panicked again. "I'll call Meera with her unguents. She needs to look at those burns."

Else glanced at them and shrugged. "I've done worse. It's a hazard of cooking."

"Meera will come anyway. She's had trouble with the child she's carrying, and I don't want her climbing stairs. I'll be right back." Clare rushed out, meeting Meera before she was halfway up.

"Has the staff gone back to clean up? What are the men doing?" Clare asked her apothecary friend, taking the tray of jars and bandages.

"I've told the staff to sit in the fresh air awhile, clear the smoke from their lungs. I believe Quincy and Adam have gone down to open doors in hopes it will dissipate and to pour water on embers. The men are holding a discussion in the captain's study. I expect shouting shortly." Meera reluctantly gave up possession of the tray. "She is all right?"

"Coughing a bit, some burns on her hands. I'm not sure she'll even allow us to treat them. Tell the men her estate has a brand new fancy stove and let the shouting begin." Clare sailed back up the stairs, knowing she'd just flung grease on the. . . metaphorical. . . fire.

If they couldn't feed family and the staff, all the effort they'd made these last months would be for naught.

~

DRESSED IN ONE OF THE *ENCEINTE* MRS. ABRAMS' LESS outlandishly hued gowns—Clare's were too long and small in the bodice—Elsa inspected the mirror and sighed. "I look like a circus tent. Could I hide in the attic until Lavender sews a uniform for me?"

Her prim and proper cousin snipped at a few more of Elsa's burnt hair ends and began pinning it up in ribbons. "Has no one ever told you how lovely that shade of blue is on you? I couldn't wear it, but it almost exactly matches your eyes."

Jack had said her eyes were turquoise. Elsa just thought them weird. And *turquoise* was much too bright. It drew attention, unlike her favored blacks and browns.

Elsa sighed and wrapped an equally colorful peacock-adorned shawl around the flesh spilling from the top of her gown. "I am a fubsy squab. No one looks at anything but my bosom. I despise fashionable gowns and haven't worn them in years."

"You are not a *squab*!" Clare sounded horrified. "Men look at every woman's bosom. I think they're taught that in school. That's why we wear shawls, to tease and taunt. When you wear a uniform, you become part of the furniture. It's foolish to be a table when you can be the lady sitting at the table." She added a few pins to the neat twist in Elsa's hair. "Now, we must go to whatever remains of dinner and make your wishes known."

Elsa attempted to draw on a pair of Mrs. Abrams' gloves to disguise the bandaging. "Mr. Garrett is gone? It is only just us and Jack now?"

"Yes. And the staff already knows you're an eccentric lady, even if they don't know your name. So you're as safe as it is possible under the circumstances." Clare stepped back to admire her handiwork. "You really should be one of the leading ladies of London society. You just need a ridiculous hat with a plume for the full effect."

Elsa had to giggle at that. "Would ladies follow me to the kitchen so I can teach them to bake? I can't do much of anything else."

"Well, they can't do more than gossip from all I can tell. Let us go down to see if your assistant figured out how to finish the soup over an open fire. We'd better not let the gentlemen have too much brandy. They won't have enough food to soak it up."

"I haven't eaten a proper meal in a dining room in ages." Elsa glanced at her hands. "I suppose if we must eat cheese and crackers, that doesn't exactly qualify as a proper meal, especially while wearing gloves."

"We shall be very informal. You will come to know us a little better. Jack will quit glowering at everyone and perhaps smile a bit. It will be fun."

Thinking of Jack sitting at the table with her caused

unnecessary fluttering in the vicinity of her vast bosom. Jack was a flirt, she reminded herself. A safe one, perhaps, one she might test her few social skills on, but not someone who should cause fluttering.

The company, such as it was, had gathered in the family parlor. As she entered, Elsa admired the oak coffered ceiling and strained to see the decorations carved into the squares. They might once have had gilding, but the light in here was too poor to examine them closely. The mirror over the mantel allowed for suffused light from the candelabra, and table lamps illuminated dark corners, but even the gold-framed oil paintings vanished into shadows. Her ancestors were evidently into ostentation without practicality.

The captain and the peddler had not returned. Elsa wasn't exactly shy, but she remained behind Clare while studying the occupants of the dusky chamber.

The men she knew as Arnaud and Walker performed cursory bows at their entrance and returned to their conversation. Uninhibited Lavender hurried over to examine Elsa's peacock shawl, exclaiming over its beauty, and adjusting it to her satisfaction. Mrs. Abrams—Meera—nodded approval of the gloves.

Jack—Jack stood there in stupefaction. She swallowed. Did she look that dreadful? She'd gained weight in the ten years since she'd seen him, but she'd never been slender.

He finally approached to gently take her gloved hand and bow. "You have only grown more beautiful, my lady. I do not understand why you hide. It is akin to growing a rose in darkness." He bent over to whisper in her ear. "But roses don't cook as well as you do."

She felt the heat in her cheeks again and giggled at his silliness. The man was very bad for her. "You are hungry and the emptiness has gone to your skull, sir." She removed her fingers and gazed in the direction of the dining room. She was

98

starving. Had Anne at least the sense to bake potatoes in the coals?

"Has anyone decided on a course of action?" Clare asked, sensible as always. "Walker, do the accounts allow for building a new stove?"

The African gentleman straightened. "If we delay buying the captain's fittings for the gas lighting, possibly. I don't know the cost involved."

"Unlike most homes, the manor has a kitchen large enough for the new Rumford, but you don't need anything that large for the few people living here." Elsa brightened to the subject. "I can give you the name of the firm who rebuilt our chimney, though. The new flue design allows more heat to stay in the stove and sends more of the smoke up the chimney. And then perhaps the captain might rebuild along the lines of the old stove, except it will heat better."

"Speak of the devil." Arnaud headed for the door. "I hear the cart on the drive. I hope they thought to stop for provisions while they were in town."

Jack poured glasses of sherry. "I suppose that means we must delay dinner again. Should I send Adam down to see if the cheese and crackers are ready?"

Clare laughed and agreed. Elsa frowned. "I think I'd better go. Anne has no experience. And unless they scrubbed the utensils, we could be eating ashes with our cheese."

"If you go, I go," Jack warned. "It is a pleasure to see you in a lovely gown. I don't want you using your poor burned hands or finding a reason to linger below. You may order me about."

Cousin Clare frowned at this apparent breach of protocol, then gestured at the tall young footman. "Adam, will you go to the kitchen and bring back a report of how the staff is faring? Tell them we need to set dinner back half an hour, please."

Elsa sighed. She was running away. Again. But she had

good reason. "You think I'll learn to be comfortable fussed up like this? My mother insisted that I dress to the nines. It didn't work then. I doubt it will now."

"We are not your mother. And do you not wish to hear what the captain has to say about his visit with Aloysius Smythe?" Like a know-it-all younger sister, Clare sipped her sherry and nodded toward the door.

Allowing Quincy to divest them of their coats but unconcerned about travel dust, Hunt and Henri strode in and headed for the decanter. The family parlor possessed a collection of fine furniture, a bit worn from use. But the silver drink tray gleamed, and the crystal glassware sparkled in the candlelight. It had been quite a while since Elsa had indulged in such niceties. Despite the extravagant furnishings, informality did seem to be the order of the day, though.

Elsa clung to her glass as the men approached, not certain she wished to know what Smythe might have said. Men didn't see him as she did.

Before the new arrivals could speak, Lavender raced over from the window to join them, deluging them in excited questions. Elsa wanted to know where the child fit into the family tree, but she'd been too busy to ask. She was starting to see Clare's point. This was family. She should learn more.

"There are crates from the mill in the cart," Lavender cried. "What did you buy?"

The captain looked over the adolescent's head to Clare, then noticing Elsa, raised his eyebrows and nodded acknowledgment of her presence. "Don't you think we should save the news for the dinner table where we may all converse properly?"

Lavender almost stamped her foot in frustration. "We are having naught but cheese and crackers. We could eat that in here without dirtying dishes."

"That sounds as if you might have more to share than we do." Henri sipped his drink and waited for explanation.

Elsa sighed. Here was where she admitted her complete idiocy. "I blew up the stove. To be fair, it was a medieval waste of mortar, but I knew better."

She'd been trying to impress Jack and work off frustration, but that didn't need to be said.

Hunt set his drink aside and started for the door. "I'd better take a look. That chimney might fall in—"

Clare protested. Jack stepped in. "I've already looked. I'm no engineer, but the damage is mostly to the stove box. A good chimney sweep might tell us if there is more damage. Do you have any notion when it was last cleaned?"

"The caretakers had all the chimneys regularly cleaned," Walker said, crossing the room to join the discussion. "It was last done only a year or so ago. We should probably ask him to return to inspect this one as a precaution."

"I know one in Birmingham I trust." Elsa spoke up. Kitchen business, she understood. "I will pay for the damage and repairs. I would order a new stove built, as well, but an amount that large would need to go through my trustees, and. . ." She gestured helplessly.

"You don't want them to know where you are. Rightfully so." Hunt nodded approval. "The manor's maintenance fund will cover replacement. I advise you not to access your funds for now. It seems your Mr. Smythe has your bank in his pocket. It may be necessary for you to find new solicitors and a new bank once you've decided where you wish to live."

Elsa threw back the rest of her sherry and let it burn to her gullet. The news did not entirely surprise her. The realization that she could never go home finally sank in.

ELEVEN

April 30, Sunday

The next morning, while the staff listened to Clare read the Sunday scripture in the gallery, Jack explored the ruined oven with his host. He had stewed all night over the realization that Elsa really did have reason to run and hide. A man with the power to control bankers. . . The implications were vaster than his weak brain could conceive.

So he stayed busy with things he could do. While Hunt sketched dimensions, Jack measured.

"Elsa's right. This was pretty primitive. They have stoves now that allow the pots to be lowered closer to the heat inside the box while keeping the fire in the chimney, where it belongs." Jack stuck his head up the massive medieval fireplace designed for roasting a wild boar or two. "This must smoke badly."

His host ducked down to take a look. "I build bridges and dams, not chimneys, but I can see the design is defective for stoves. There's a fellow back in Philadelphia, Orr, I believe is his name. He's selling cast iron stoves for heating and cook-ing. Wonder if we could do anything similar?"

"I'd think that would use less wood and hold heat better. But can they make anything large enough for Elsa? Will the manor hold more people in the future?" Jack sat back on his heels and grimaced at the filth in which he was coated.

"If Clare has her way, it would hold every dangling leaf on the family tree and a village full of servants. We have the space. Whether it's practical remains to be seen." Hunt crawled back to the hearth and lurched into a chair. "Of course, if we don't settle the suit with the bank, we may all be out on our ears."

Jack pumped water into a basin and scrubbed his hands. "With a poisonous spider like Smythe weaving his web, I can't leave Elsa unprotected. If you'll have me, I'll be staying a while longer. If Culpepper carried a bank note to Smythe's assistant, then it's likely Smythe knew him as well."

"I disliked the smarmy gent, but a banknote doesn't mean much. Smythe seemed perfectly respectable, but he handed us over to Hill. Your knowledge of English society and rank might fare better. Apparently, I am not important enough to rate his company." Hunt took his turn washing at the basin. "But Henri learned enough from other merchants to know Smythe is not to be trusted."

"A wolf in sheep's clothes, the perfect villain. How would a London fellow like Culpepper know a Birmingham merchant? And Smythe does not sound like the type who might shoot pistols in hedgerows, even if he thought Culpepper was competition for Elsa's hand. If you will be about for a while, perhaps I should ride into Newchurch, visit my father, make more inquiries? I can make it there and back in two days." Jack thought he felt well enough to manage that.

His rank as the younger son of a minor baron did not

amount to much, but Jack could see where it might be above that of an American ex-soldier and a French peddler.

"I wish you would fetch my stove while you're at it," Elsa said wistfully from the landing. Having just arrived, she studied the remains of her ruined kitchen.

"Difficult stealing a stove without alerting the household," Jack said dryly, bowing.

"It is not stealing since I bought it, but it would be rather easy to follow a stove down the road," she replied in the same tone.

"Are services over? Do you need to return to work?" Hunt asked.

"We need to go over every surface with a scrub brush. I have potatoes baking on all the grates upstairs, and a stew in the fireplace in the great hall. Thank you for setting up the spit and hooks, captain." Wearing a dark skirt and white bodice, she clasped her arms to gaze in dismay at the disaster. "It didn't look quite so bad at dawn."

"A good scrubbing will do wonders. I believe I can mend the cracked stove top," their engineering host offered. "Rebuilding the brick stove box will require materials, so that might take a day or two. Stealing a stove shouldn't be necessary."

Jack could read her disappointment but didn't dare offer what he couldn't give. "Tell me who built your fancy stove. I will talk with him, if I can. Or I can take you with me back to Newchurch, if you're tired of playing here." He had to offer that much, although every bone in his body rebelled at the thought of putting her in reach of Smythe.

She shook her head until her cap nearly flew off. "I am staying here. At least the manor is a small part mine. The Newchurch estate belongs to the earl and is merely a roof over my head."

"A rather impressive roof." Jack turned to his host. "Give me a list of what is needed in town, since I'll have to traverse it to reach my father. If there's more I can do, let me know before I leave."

Elsa hurried down the steps to take his arm. In surprise at this intimacy, he studied her expression, but he couldn't read it. Just having her turn to him spun his empty head around.

"The horses in the stable are mine, Jack, bought with my own money. Two of them are due to foal. Is there any way. . .?"

Jack didn't know how to respond. "You want to move your stable? Here? Why?"

"Because Freddy will steal and sell them if he's desperate enough. I need them safe, Jack. Please? I've been so worried. . ."

He glanced at the captain. "The stable here? I have not done more than make certain my mount is comfortable."

Hunt grunted and gestured to encompass the crumbling kitchen. "Much like the manor. The earl kept it up, I suppose, but the viscountess did not. Roof needs replacing, at best. Good stone walls though."

"I will give you a bill of sale, Jack," Elsa insisted. "You may show it to my steward, tell him you're taking them to Tattersalls. He will recognize my signature. I will give you a letter to him to say I am fine and do not wish to be found. He's a good man. I trust him. We were talking of selling a gelding. It should bring enough funds to buy a roof for the stable."

"Wouldn't it be better to buy your stove with those funds?" Despite his question, Jack was already considering all the ramifications of transporting horses without being followed, replacing a roof, feeding her expensive stable. . .

This time, one of Elsa's blond curls fell loose as she shook her head. "I can buy the stove by selling the mares after they give birth, if need be. I've learned patience, Jack."

He snorted. "No, you haven't. If anyone follows me, they'll know I'm not taking the horses to London. This is just

the sort of impulsiveness that always got you into trouble."
Moving her stable meant the pampered heiress intended to
continue living under these conditions. . . He couldn't
fathom it.

But in his heart of hearts, he admired her for not aban-
doning her animals, especially if they were endangered by
fools.

"How many horses?" Hunt asked, ending the argument
with pragmatism. "How many men are needed to transport
them? Will your grooms be willing to accompany them? We
have no one qualified."

Elsa went wide-eyed. Jack could almost see her thoughts
spinning behind those glorious eyes. She hadn't given the
practicalities a whit of consideration.

Jack knuckled her noggin and brushed her nose as he used
to do when she ran wild with ideas. "I'll speak with the lads.
The older ones will still know me, won't they?"

She offered a weak smile. "Hank is still there. He's head
groom now. He'll sort what's mine and know which of the
men might wish to stay in my employ. Rely on his advice,
please. He's all I've had these past years. I'm sure you can
convince everyone you've bought my stable."

When Jack had left Newchurch, she'd been an adolescent
in the care of an older half-brother who'd inherited the title, a
stepfather who had ruled the roost, and a stepbrother who
ought to be old enough to be useful by now. And she only
had an elderly steward and a half-pint groom to protect her
from the likes of Smythe? Jack gritted his teeth and reined in
his anger. He had no right to question.

"I'll have a look at the manor's stable, see what it needs,"
was all he managed to say. "You and Hunt have a good talk
about what is best for all. Just let me know." He stalked up
the outside exit stairs.

If Elsa was upset with him, he didn't care. This wasn't his
home. If she wanted to make it hers, she would be in safe

hands, and he could move on. He didn't have the where-withal to keep an heiress in the luxury to which she should be accustomed.

~

SUNDAY EVENING AFTER THEIR MEAGER DINNER, HAVING SENT Jack on his mission with their two stable lads, Hunt remained in the blue upstairs salon rather than withdraw to his study. Little by little, family and guests drifted off to their own pursuits, no doubt gnawing on their fingers in hunger. Elsa had prepared a hearty beef stew and adorned the baked pota-toes with cheese and green onions, but lacking bread and puddings, dinner had not been up to the standards they'd enjoyed since her arrival.

The reason for his lingering sat beside him on the sofa, scribbling notes on one of her never-ending scraps of paper. Walker had told him the only thing Clare had saved from potential fire was that wooden box she kept in her study. Hunt was tempted to peek, but he'd prefer she trusted him with her secrets.

"What do you think of your cousin's plan to move her stable here?" he asked, propping his leg on a stool. Reading a book with one weak eye gave him headaches, so he whittled at a model latch for the cellar door that he meant to show to a blacksmith.

Huh, if they had a stable, maybe they could entice a black-smith to the village. A working forge would make repairing— or even building—the stove top easier.

Clare set her pen across her pad and sighed. "I know nothing of stables or much of anything. And here Elsa has been running a kitchen and a stable and no doubt the entire business of an estate. I suspect if I return to London in the autumn, she will run the manor far more capably than I."

Alarmed at this direction to her thoughts, Hunt stared at

her in incredulity. "Surely, you jest! Does the lady strike you as the domestic sort who might direct the servants and guests at the same time as she runs the kitchen?"

He'd much rather say, *Don't abandon me here!* But he had no right to say that.

A smile teased the corner of her lips. "I should hire a housekeeper before I leave? And I'm fairly certain, should we ever have guests, that they would be better behaved than we are. You simply don't want to deal with any of it, do you?"

He didn't. But more than that, he couldn't imagine sitting here of an evening with anyone else but Clare. He knew he looked the part of beast with his eyepatch and scars and bearish size, but she didn't seem to notice. She didn't demand that he dance at balls or visit tailors and dress like a dandy. Although he probably ought to look into a new coat or two now that the trust executors had agreed to pay him for his engineering skills.

He didn't know how to express any of this. Unlike Jack of the smooth tongue, he could only stutter over practicalities. "You make this place a home instead of a shelter for wayward strays. You are the glue that keeps us from wandering off again."

Her smile flickered away, and she studied her hands. "I grew up in that house in London. It's all I really know. I can return there easily, slip into my prior life, go to my favorite seamstress, stop at the market and the lending library. . . Staying here for the summer was a frightening notion driven by desperation in hopes I could save money for Oliver's education. But now. . ."

"He has dragon eggs," Hunt said ruefully. "And you have somehow come into sufficient funds to pay a tutor. And this will be a cold and lonely place come winter. I understand."

No, he didn't, not really. But he wanted her to be happy. He thought *he* could be happy here. He'd been a miserable bastard a few months ago, believing his career was over, and that he'd never so much as own the roof over his head. But she'd given him hope that the manor wasn't a pile of crumbling stone.

"I am a trifle overwhelmed at having choices," she admitted. "Well, and overwhelmed by the size of the manor and amount of work it requires, but you and Walker have much of that in hand. I'd like to meet more of my family. It was fun coming to know the marchioness and the baroness, even if they are haughty curmudgeons. I'd never have met them had I stayed at home. So, for now, I shall try to be your domestic goddess on the very few funds we have for feathering our giant nest."

"While hoping someone breaks the code and finds the jewels?" he asked with a laugh, disguising his fear that she would leave.

She laughed too. "I am already making up stories of princesses in towers saved by the jewels they find in unlikely places. It's an exciting thought but probably not realistic. The manor is good for dreaming and is giving me some good—" She cut herself off with a shrug. "I dream too much. I need to see that Oliver is tucked up in bed. Do you think we might hear from the agencies soon about a tutor?"

He stood to assist her to her feet. "I have no idea, but we will keep writing until we do." He bowed over her hand. "I am eternally grateful that you accepted our invitation to stay. I cannot imagine what we would have done without you."

Her smile was so brilliant that he could not resist bending over to kiss her cheek. He meant it only to be a kiss on the cheek.

But her lips were right there, and he wasn't made of stone.

TWELVE

May 1, Monday

CLARE SPENT A RESTLESS NIGHT TOSSING AND TURNING AFTER Hunt's kisses had heated and their passion become ardent. Her breasts ached with need, and she'd had to pull the pillow over her head in hopes of burying her revolving recollections of every delicious moment.

By morning, she was so muddled that she was considering fleeing back to London, while wondering what it would be like sharing a bed, and fearing Hunt had kissed her just to make her stay. This daft looby was not who she was, was it?

While Hunt worked on mending the stove, and the other men examined the stable to determine what repairs it needed, Clare resolutely turned her dizzy mind to the practical. First, she checked on Lavender and her sewing ladies. They extolled the virtues of the linen and notions Henri had brought and excitedly discussed which of the buttons and trim would be proper for undergarments. Clare fingered a beautiful satin and wondered if it could be made into a night-dress and robe.

Realizing where her thoughts had traveled—again—she hastily left them deciding what to make next and checked on Oliver in the library. Walker had set him to doing sums, and Clare had asked him to report on any book he read. He had dutifully done both and was now poring over the paper on which Jack had been attempting to decipher codes. She kissed his head, making him squirm.

"I have had two letters this morning from prospective tutors," she told him. "They sound rather more promising than the others we've received. Will you like having real lessons?"

He shrugged and continued working.

With a sigh, Clare drifted away. She wondered if her nephew might be more normal if he had friends to play with. But families had yet to return to the village. Given its state of disrepair, that was understandable.

She had just settled at her desk to write when Adam came in bearing the visitor tray. "Mr. Benedict Bosworth Jr., miss." He presented the card.

"Oh, fustian," she muttered. "He cannot lower himself to speak with men working in a stable?"

"He wishes to speak with you, miss. Shall I say you are not at home?"

She was tempted, but then he'd only ask to wait. The ride from Stratford was quite long. He must have set out early to have arrived before noon. "No, show him to the great hall and ask Meera if she would join us, please."

Not that she expected a middle-aged man like the banker to importune her in any way, but she preferred relying on propriety when dealing with the toady. She had wanted to meet family. She had not expected one of them to be a greedy, baseborn banker. She supposed upbringing had much to do with how a person turned out.

Meera wore one of her rainbow-colored shawls, and her thick black hair had been hastily pinned and held with what appeared to be a knitting needle. "I was trying to mix a creamier unguent for our lady cook so she would use it more often. Those burns will peel raw if she's not careful."

"You will need to set up an apothecary shop in Birmingham if you don't mean to return to London. Your talents shouldn't be limited to us." Clare reluctantly strode toward the great hall.

"I need a shop somewhere," Meera replied ambiguously. "We will have to see what the future holds."

The banker rose when they entered. He'd kept his greatcoat and hat, understandable given the chilly day and the even chillier two-story hall. Clare hadn't ordered the fires lit.

"Miss Knightley, Mrs. Abrams." He bowed punctiliously.

They took seats in chairs across from the sofa he'd chosen. "How good to see you, Mr. Bosworth. How might I help you?"

He nervously worked the brim of his top hat. "W-would it be possible to see the journals that may or may not refer to my birth?"

He'd seen them once, but under pressing circumstances that had not allowed him to study the details.

"Our translation of the passage is surmise, of course," Clare reminded him. "Have you not spoken with your father?"

"I h-have. He's unwilling to d-discuss it. He is nearly ninety and s-set in his ways. He says he's—he is leaving me the b-bank shares and the house, and I should be grateful for what I have." Red-faced at the effort to speak his thoughts, he waited.

Clare wished Hunt were here. He was certain the banker meant to claim the manor as his own as soon as the debt was called, and they couldn't pay. But she was very bad at playing the kind of games that men excelled in. The man deserved to know his heritage.

"The journal only describes the circumstances as the

viscountess chose to write them. The more telling features are your looks." She turned to Meera. "Do you know where that particular volume is stored?"

"Walker installed shelves in the cabinet. We ordered them by date after we received the volumes from Arnaud's family." She rose to open the doors of a chinoiserie armoire.

Meera and Walker were much of a kind, organized, highly intelligent, and thoughtful. One was mathematical and the other scientific, but those factors worked well together. Clare's romantic heart wanted them to make a match, but their precarious circumstances activated their cautious natures.

Bosworth touched his fading blond hair. "I-I fail to see the family resemblance," he admitted. "Many p-people have yellow hair."

"And blue eyes, dimples, widow's peaks, and the Reid backward thumb," she acknowledged. "Altogether, along with the viscountess's tale, we can still only surmise. Even if it is possible to prove to a court that you are the viscount's direct descendant, what do you think can be done about it? The law does not acknowledge children outside the bonds of matrimony."

In prior encounters, the banker had been much more lofty and arrogant. Today, he seemed somewhat subdued, running his hand nervously over his receding hair. "I-I never under-stood that I had been adopted. But I have made inquiries. . ."

"Your parents never told you?" Shocked, Clare took the volume Meera handed her. The spiky handwriting was all in French, but she'd been practicing her knowledge of that language lately. "I am so sorry if we have disturbed your father by telling tales that were never meant to be spoken."

"Everyone knew I was a b-bastard except me," he said with bitterness. "Even my old nanny. N-no one t-told me."

"It may have been a promise to the viscountess. She does not go into any detail about the circumstances of your adoption, only that the viscount's natural child was sent to Strat-ford to a gentleman able to support him in comfort. Her ire was saved for your natural father." Sympathizing with his predicament, even if she did not like the man, she handed him the journal open to the appropriate pages.

He read silently, mouthing the words as he translated, running his finger underneath the lines. Once he read the brief passage, he returned to the beginning and read again, shaking his head in what appeared to be dismay.

Closing the half-century-old book, he held onto it. "My mother was no more than a *scullery maid*?"

"She became the manor's extremely efficient housekeeper and caretaker," Clare reminded him. "She was never given an education. The manor is all she knew."

"But she carried on with her employer! She was no more than a. . ." He bit back a word that most likely shouldn't be said in respectable company. "No wonder my p-parents did not tell me."

"And what does that make the viscount?" Clare asked sharply, losing sympathy with his plight. She had no patience with society's condemnation of the woman and not the man. "He was older, experienced, and even if he was a drunkard, he knew perfectly well what he was doing. What are the chances that a foolish sixteen-year-old had any idea? He no doubt gave her pretty presents and flattery she'd never known before. And ultimately, what he did drove her mad. If you wish to look at your birth through eyes of shame, then know both your parents behaved badly. Where does that leave you?"

"He wanted to have me *killed*." He stared at the book with what looked like horror. "I-I think I-I'd rather claim my adopted p-parents than admit to my true birth. My father is a respected gentleman in the community."

Clare had a notion this affected how he viewed the manor's debt, and her insides clenched. "You are perfectly entitled to do so. As I said, I am sorry to have informed you of something you were not supposed to know."

He finally handed back the diary as if it were repugnant. "The man who built this manor was a kn-night, a true hero who served his king and was rewarded with an earldom. He would be appalled to know how his d-descendants failed their heritage."

"Actually," Meera finally spoke. "Our research shows that your ancestor destroyed the priory, slaughtered many of the inhabitants when they objected, and was rewarded the remains of his carnage by the king. Wycliffe Manor was built on blood and bones."

Clare winced. "I did not know you were researching."

Meera shrugged. "Walker and I were curious. So were previous earls. They gathered quite a collection of histories. Gravesyde Priory was once a flourishing destination."

Bosworth rose precipitously. "All the more reason to r-remove the *remains* to more Christian hands. I thank you for your time, ladies, and g-give you good day."

Christian hands? Like his own? And what did that make her and Hunt? Pagans?

Clare let him storm off, not bothering to ask him for luncheon. It was likely to be wizened apples and the last of the crackers anyway.

"He must be riding to Birmingham," Meera said, watching out the window. "Should I have not spoken out of turn?"

Clare held the condemning volume and tried to think, but she was not a greedy, jealous man nor a banker. "I must wonder if he's not a trifle disturbed, like his mother. I felt sorry for him until he turned vindictive. One cannot know what to expect."

Bankers knew men of wealth and power—like Aloysius Smythe. Money could buy almost anything, including the courts.

THIRTEEN

On Monday morning, Elsa picked through the baskets at the village market. In early May, the pickings were still slim. Clare had said there had been only one old woman selling potatoes when they'd first arrived. At least now, a few more people were bringing in greens. The men wouldn't appreciate a green salad for dinner, though.

Fortunately, the woman who sold bread had sent her son in with extra loaves. Elsa had been attempting to bake dough in a covered iron pot, but she hadn't found the right temperature. Baking in a fireplace required skills she did not possess. Yet.

"Thee will make the sauce and butter when the apples come on?" a wizened, red-cheeked woman asked as Elsa picked through her onions.

Elsa had been told the estate had apples. She'd need to be here in the autumn to cook them. Thinking of all the wonderful recipes she could make with apples, she absently nodded. "I mean to."

She tried not to speak too much. The villagers didn't know her origins.

Still, the woman looked a little startled before hiding her surprise. "Along back, when I's a girl, the house had great cauldrons of apples and ever'un gathered to stir. We'uns took home enough for our families. Not there's much in the way of families nowabouts."

Elsa had no idea there were that many apple trees. Rather than speak, she nodded and moved on. She had experimented with boiling jellies and jams in jars and sealing them with wax according to scientific papers she'd read from France. Sugary fruit had worked reasonably well, but anything else had spoiled. Could apple butter be sealed in jars?

With her basket full, she had just crossed the road to the walking path to the manor when a man galloped into town on a fine steed she recognized at once—*Frederick's*. Her stepbrother had found her.

"Bootless dog-hearted lout," she muttered, hurrying into the pines where he could not see anything but the back of her cloak. "Hedge-born moldwarp." She'd spent years poring over the classics in search of words to describe the codswallop. Cursing hid her fear.

Frederick had found her. No one came this way unless they were headed for the manor. The vicar must have told him she had vanished from Newchurch and about the invitation she'd received as one of the heirs. *Bloodydamnhell.*

He had a horse and could travel faster than she could walk, but he'd already missed the drive. Once he turned around, the carriage drive was a much longer, circular distance than the walking path straight up the hill. She reached the manor before he was in sight. She raced in the front door rather than stay exposed running around to the kitchen.

Adam looked startled and hastened to take her basket and cloak.

"I am not here to the man coming up the drive. I have never been here. No one like me is here. You have no cook except for Anne. Forget I exist. Tell Quincy and anyone else to say the same. Please send Miss Knightley upstairs to the blue salon." She lifted her old skirt and raced up instead of down. Frederick was a mean bastard, but he wasn't stupid. He'd search the kitchen if he could.

She repeated those instructions to the startled maid cleaning the rooms. By the time she reached the blue salon where the family gathered at the end of the day, Clare was already running after her.

"What is it? What has happened?" She dragged Elsa into the room, checked the corridor, and closed the door. Cool light from the open draperies didn't warm the feminine room with its silk upholstery and delicate furniture.

"My stepbrother has come in search of me. Mr. Garrett must have let him know I've left the estate. He or my mother may have told Freddy about the manor. I assume she received an invitation?"

Clare's eyes widened. "Of course. Your mother is one of the heirs. She never responded, but. . ."

Elsa gritted her teeth. "She may have considered it unimportant, but if Freddy told her I am missing, she'd remember the invitation. I have nowhere else to hide. What do I do now?" Rather than reveal her anguish, she bent to the task of lighting a fire.

"Tell your brother to go back where he belongs?" Clare suggested. "Why do you not want him to find you?"

"He's a bully. He has no claim to my father's estate and resents it that I do. He was only a toddler when his father married my mother, so it is the only home he knows. Mother allowed him to continue living there, but his new bride wanted a house of her own." She laughed bitterly. "But I control the purse strings. He likes to bully in comfort."

"He hurts you?" Clare asked in alarm.

"From the moment he stumbles out of bed to the moment he falls back in, death by a thousand cuts. He is fortunate I am not violently inclined, or I could have carved out his gizzard at any time over the years. I hoped the Wastrel would go the way of the Sot and soak his liver and die of pneumonia or worse, but Frederick is too lazy to even do that." She ignored Clare's shock.

Elsa peered out the window, but it overlooked the court-yard. "May we go across the hall to see if he is riding up the drive?" Elsa opened the door to peer out and listen. No one at the door yet. Without waiting for permission, she crossed over to Clare's chamber. Claret-colored velvet draperies adorned the windows and heavy, old tester bed. Wine-and-pink cushions and upholstery added feminine touches, along with the striped wallpaper—which curled a little in the corners from age.

"He insults you?" Clare asked, peering around the draperies.

"Insults me, hits me, pushes me around, and tries to sell me to men like Smythe, bringing them home for drunken revels and taking them down to the kitchen when I refuse to go up. I will not speak with him ever again." Peering through the opening, Elsa cringed at sight of the beast riding to the rear of the house. She hoped Quincy had barred the door to the kitchen.

"Your brother's name was on one of those bank notes," Clare said, finally understanding. "He knows Culpepper?"

Elsa shrugged. "Possibly. They are the same sort of useless fop, although Frederick is younger."

A few minutes later, horse and rider reappeared and followed the drive to the front. Thank all the heavens, he'd been prevented from harming anyone in the kitchen.

They couldn't hear the door knocker from here. Frustrated, Elsa cracked open the chamber door to listen. Clare held a finger to her lips and gestured, slipping into the hall.

Out of curiosity, Elsa followed. She still couldn't hear anyone. The entrance vestibule was well-built.

They crept down the long upper corridor, past the suites the men occupied, to the marble stairs and narrow visitors' hall at the end. From the upper gallery loft, they could see Arnaud in the ballroom below, working on his paintings. Lavender and her workers stitched and chattered as usual. The paneled wall at this side of the loft would overlook the two-story entrance vestibule, had there been a window.

The manor was the perfect hiding place, Elsa realized. The old building sprawled over so much acreage, that it would be possible to always be five steps ahead of anyone looking for her.

Clare slid a small panel in the woodwork—a spy window!

"I found this when I was searching for jewels," Clare whispered. "We can observe anyone visiting."

Frederick stood below, blocked from entering the main house by the massive butler at the interior door. He paced the entrance, the capes of his greatcoat flapping in his agitation. "If she is not here, I must speak with your master. It is a matter of life and death."

"Fustian," Elsa muttered. "His life, mayhap. Not mine."

"Captain Huntley is unavailable, sir. Perhaps another time?" Quincy remained immovable.

"Your mistress then. Surely, she is about?" Frederick did not use his polite voice with servants.

"The captain is unmarried, sir. We are not prepared for visitors." Stoically, Quincy began to close the door between the vestibule and the main corridor.

Frederick slammed his fist against the panel, attempting to stop it from closing. He failed. The click of a bolt falling into place defeated any violence. Smacking his hat against his thigh, he spun around, glared at the waist-high lion statue, then strode out.

Every nerve in her body on edge at that performance, Elsa didn't breathe a sigh of relief. "He will go to the stable and find the captain. How do we warn him?" She ran through a host of scenarios.

Jack had left to fetch her horses. Jack didn't know what a bastard Frederick was. No one did. Her mother would just say that little Freddy was looking out for her and wasn't he a fine lad? Even the damned vicar said she should listen to her little brother, that he had her best interests at heart. Her best interest apparently was marrying the first toad who bribed him enough and removed her from the estate. She was certain the marriage contracts would include a nice slice of her considerable dowry for Frederick.

Clare hurried along the upper corridor where no one could see them from below. "Adam was sending staff hither and yon to warn them. Word will have reached Hunt. Let us return to the blue salon where we can sit in comfort and wait to hear all reports."

Elsa had always thought the ancient manor cumbersome compared to her light-filled home, but she could see a fortress had its uses. No spacious central hall with windowed domes lit the middle as in more modern manors. Only the medieval chapel windows in the gallery and great hall provided light. The rest was a solid block with rooms on either side of a dismal corridor lit only by flickering sconces. She suspected many of the chambers had adjoining doors that she could run through and never touch the hall, if necessary.

"Do the rooms in the east wing overlook the stable?" she asked, out of curiosity.

"No doubt, although our explorations were mostly in search of hiding places for the journals and the jewels. Since we found the books on the ground floor, I haven't explored the upper ones yet. The previous caretakers closed off the wings. We lack the staff to open them."

"If I didn't have to hide, I'd send for my lady's maid. She could keep my room clean. The cook's chambers below need complete refurbishment, especially after the fire. The stench of smoke is dreadful." *If she didn't have to hide. . .* Would such a day ever come?

It had to. She needed to move her personal funds out of reach of the greedy Smythe. She couldn't do that while hiding.

"I do not fully understand the threat," Clare acknowledged, closing the door of the salon behind them, and turning the key. "You are of age. You possess a fortune. Why can you not do as you like?"

"A single kiss and I am a ruined woman and free game." Elsa flounced down on a blue silk sofa and picked up a book from the table next to it. "Frederick had my tea laced with laudanum once. One of his friends with pockets to let had a carriage waiting. My groom and my maid saved me that time. It wasn't the only time. I had to quit going into the village on my own." She lit the lamp and read the book's title—apparently one of the late viscountess's journals.

"My word." Clare sank into another chair. "This is worse than a novel. You need to marry simply so you may live!"

Elsa sank into the cushions and tried not to sound pathetic. She'd had years to study her difficulty and accept her fate. "Culpepper saw to it that I could not be respectably courted, even by aristocratic fortune hunters. And to anyone else, I am not only fat, but I'm a managing sort with no desire to play demure and obedient wife. I suppose I might disguise myself as a poor spinster, find an elderly gentleman looking for a caretaker, and persuade him to marry me. But I'd have the same problem once he popped off. I cannot control my dowry or write my marriage documents. The earl's solicitors handle all that. My older half-brother is reasonable, but he is a busy lord with his own family, estate, and politics. He does not have time for my plight."

"I see why you prefer to be a cook. But marrying a butler just so you might have your freedom. . ."

Elsa giggled. "I would terrify Quincy."

Clare laughed. "Quite so. Still, I don't know why you underrate your looks. Pleasantly plump is the fashion. I'm considered a skinny scarecrow. My sister said there is no pleasing people and to look for someone who likes you for who you are. She never listened when she was called stout. She married quite happily. A meeting of the minds is more important than our appearances."

Which might explain why pretty Clare looked on the grim, one-eyed captain with starry eyes. Elsa filed that notion away for a time when she wasn't terrified of losing her new home.

A light knock on the door followed by a key in the lock warned of company. Hunt strode in, covered in soot and smelling of the stable.

Clare's expression lit with welcome, and Elsa bit back a nervous laugh.

The captain walked up to the fire to warm his hands and regarded them warily. "At least you're not armed. I expected swords and muskets."

Elsa raised her eyebrows, but Clare just laughed. "We watched through the peephole. Did our visitor berate you as he did poor Quincy?"

Hunt shrugged. "A rather rude young man. Had he been one of my soldiers, he would have landed in the trough. I told him we didn't have visitors, except for the late Mr. Culpepper. Your young man then went off in a bit of a tirade believing the *rattling cove meant to bilk him of his game*. Took a bit to translate. I had to inform him that his competition was six feet under."

"He thought *Culpepper* had stolen me? Fool." Elsa tried to relax, but the captain's words only made her more restless.

"It does show your brother knew Culpepper but did not kill him, and that they think you are still fair game," Clare pointed out. "Did you learn anything else?"

"Gave me his direction, assured me I'd be rewarded if we found his poor, addled sister, and then asked if he might stop by the kitchen for a spot of tea. I told him the stove blew up, and he'd have to fix his tea over a campfire. He was not pleased. I have a nasty suspicion that any newcomer from here on should be regarded as a spy." Huntley turned his back on the fire to warm his other side.

Elsa squirmed under his regard. "I should leave," she acknowledged. "I just don't know where else to go."

"You're better off here, surrounded by friends and family, than on your own," the captain admonished. "We simply need to make it clear that you are under our protection. I've talked to a few people about buying hounds, but I need a trainer. I will teach young Ned and Adam how to use weapons. They're already handy with fists. If Jack returns with servants you trust, then I will train them as well. Security is always a good idea when isolated as we are."

Elsa felt tears forming. She swallowed hard and clenched her hands. "I am too much trouble for someone you scarcely know."

Clare cried out in protest. "Good heavens, were you raised by *wolves*? Even a complete stranger would take you in out of the cold. We are family and friends and you are beyond value to us!"

"Well, to our stomachs, anyway," Hunt added in his pragmatic tone that passed for humor.

Elsa choked on a giggle. "That's all right then. I'll blow up a few more stoves for you, if you keep everyone I know away from me."

"I'll growl at them." The one-eyed captain stalked out, apparently content that he could personally prevent anyone from stealing his cook.

Elsa was fairly certain the unsophisticated American soldier had utterly no idea how scary society could be. After all, Culpepper had been on his way here with *counterfeit banknotes,* and one of his aristocratic friends most likely shot him. Even if the villain was caught—which was unlikely—they would not be sent to gaol. Men of influence got away with murder all the time.

FOURTEEN

MAY 3, WEDNESDAY

JACK RODE IN WEDNESDAY NIGHT, PAINFULLY AWARE THAT HIS strength still wasn't what it should be. Leading Elsa's stable of horses and grooms up the drive, he nearly slipped from his saddle in weariness. It was damned humiliating not to be able to manage a few days in the saddle when he'd once lived in one.

The sight of Elsa running out the side door, beaming with excitement, erased the low moment. She flung herself at him as if he were her brother, hugging him and talking so fast, he could scarcely sort the words. He simply understood that she appreciated his efforts.

Blackguard that he was, he hugged her back, relishing the soft scent and touch of woman for the first time in what felt like decades. He brushed his scruffy cheek against her silken hair—her cap had fallen askew, as usual—and allowed himself this moment of ease before releasing her. He righted her cap, brushed loose strands of gold behind her ears, and let her run to her favorite mare, where she repeated her hug and

126

cries of joy.

Elsa was meant to be a joyful woman. He didn't know how life had battered her down so that she hid in a sooty kitchen. But if he did nothing else with his worthless time on earth, he'd know he brought her this moment of happiness.

Hunt and his cousins examined the thoroughbreds for injuries and showed the grooms to the stalls that had been prepared. Jack wandered inside the barn to take a good look at what they'd done since he'd left.

Elsa took his arm. "It's all right. I watched over every improvement and made certain they did as you liked. It's old, but the stone walls are sound and well-mortared. I think the stalls are actually larger than mine."

"You remember how I had our stable constructed?" he asked in amazement. "That was eons ago."

"But you were so proud and excited when your father agreed to improve his old one, I had to pay attention. I hope you stopped to see him while you were there?"

Jack nodded. "He even stopped writing to have tea with me," he said wryly. "He looks older but seems healthy. He was concerned about you."

"I hope you reassured him that I am well."

"I did. Smythe has been at his new estate this past week or more, paying calls on his neighbors. Father says he asked about you, which worried him. He's taken a dislike to the man, called him an encroaching mushroom."

"Smythe gives mushrooms a bad name then. Did he say if Freddy has been about?"

"He didn't mention him. I asked around to be certain I could talk to your groom without interference, and no one has seen him recently. I hope you don't plan on hiding any more. Your staff was all over me." Word had spread quickly through her household that he'd seen her. He'd had difficulty persuading them that he only needed a few grooms.

Servants were better off staying in their comfortable quarters with the wages an earl could afford. He still didn't think Elsa's impulsive escape would last long. Women liked their creature comforts. There was a world of difference between this grim, gothic rambling horror and Elsa's elegantly furnished, multi-windowed Georgian manor.

Elsa happily pointed out the new wood in the stalls as she showed him around. "You once instructed my trainer on the proper feed and bins, so I told the captain what to use. The roof has been repaired so the upper story is fine for the grooms. I'm so glad you persuaded Hank to come. He'll handle everything."

"I don't think he would have allowed the horses to leave if he didn't go with them," Jack admitted. "Your entire staff is worried about you. I had to assure them you're with family and happy. I didn't know what else to do."

She huffed. "It's all right. Freddy has already been here. The captain scared him off, but he'll be back. And now the horses are here, he'll know I am. I simply have to be smart and not let myself be alone with anyone I don't trust."

Jack wondered why her young idiot of a stepbrother should be scared off, but now was not the time to question. They were surrounded by eavesdropping servants. "I want to take a good look at the broodmares. I think they traveled well, but it won't hurt to keep an eye on them."

Instead of leaving him there, Elsa followed right on his heels, holding the mares' heads, whispering nonsense, and feeding them apples while he inspected other parts. She even had carrots for the high-strung stallion they installed on the opposite end of the barn. Jack wanted to warn her away, but Lady Elspeth had grown up with animals and knew her way around them as well as he did.

The last rays of sun had fallen before he persuaded her to leave her horses and go inside. He desperately needed a bath, but he assumed hot water would be at a minimum. "How has Hunt progressed on your stove?"

"He's hired a bricklayer who knows how to rebuild the chimney and firebox to his specifications. And now he's trying to restore the forge at the old blacksmith shop in town so he can mend the cracked top. And I am learning to bake over an open fire." Elsa cheerfully entered the main house through the carriage door rather than escape to the kitchen stairs as she usually did.

"I might have help with the forge. I should go back and find Hunt. . ." Distracted by Elsa, he'd forgotten to speak with the captain.

"No, you will not, not now. I'll have Adam carry up hot water, and one of the maids will follow shortly with what passes for a meal. I've learned to make an excellent skillet bread if naught else." She bustled off.

He watched her curvaceous hips sway as she departed and smiled at what she called her *managing* ways. Why would any man object to being fussed over, especially by a beautiful woman?

He was scrubbed and had consumed hearty soup and bread before the captain knocked on his chamber door. Too weary to dress again, Jack wore trousers and banyan to greet his host. He'd collected a few more civilian clothes while he was home.

Hunt had divested himself of his outerwear but not his filthy boots. He hadn't shaved for dinner either. He looked the part of rough soldier, not polished officer. But Jack did not allow his host's coarse demeanor to fool him into believing he was anything less than in command.

"Lady Elspeth tells me you wish to speak with me?" Hunt flung coal on the fire. "You look like hell, if you don't mind my saying so. Should I ask Meera for restoratives?"

Lowering himself to a chair, Jack shook his head. "No, I just need rest. We've pretty much been riding day and night. Since I brought all the lady's grooms with me, there was none

PATRICIA RICE

to complain of my robbing the stable. I trust you can house everyone?"

"With a few roof repairs, the whole upper story of the stable will be in solid shape. Didn't know how many beds to set up, but I gave the head groom permission to sort it out. Plenty of wood and coal and the chimney functions. If nothing else, the caretakers were scrupulous in spending the trust funds to maintain this fortress. I suspect our lady cook is sending the entire contents of the pantry out to feed the lads."

Jack snorted. "Most likely. Next to her kitchen, she prized her stable most. That's why I exceeded my authority, I'll warn you now. By tomorrow, the village will have a new black-smith. I promised him that he'd have his own shop and cottage. Newchurch already has a blacksmith, so Elsa couldn't set his assistant up in his place. He's still a bit young but skilled."

Hunt merely raised his scarred eyebrow and nodded. "That will help in repairing the stove. If he's good, perhaps he could follow my specifications for a new one. Don't know if our stable will be sufficient business to support him. And the smithy and cottage is a disgrace. Does he have a family?"

"He hopes to marry, which is why he needed this place. You don't mind?" Jack leaned back in the chair and tried not to let his eyes close.

"I assume the lady wouldn't have used him if he couldn't do the job. Why would I mind? Get some sleep. We'll go down and look at the forge in the morning." Hunt let himself out.

Jack thought maybe he didn't need to buy colors to become a soldier again. The captain was forming his own army.

❧

WITH NO FORMAL DINNER TO FORCE HIM INTO SHAVING AND dressing properly, Hunt fell back on bad habits. He foraged for food when he wanted it, stayed in his filth-coated clothes, and enjoyed the hell out of being useful again. He preferred tinkering with the stove and the coal retort, but he was trained in making men jump at his command.

By mid-morning on the day after Jack returned, he had taken the measure of Hank, the new groom, had him learning to communicate with deaf Ned, and discussed positions for the new stable lads. He had a groom saddling his horse to ride into the village when Jack emerged from the house. He hadn't expected the gentleman to rise so early. Riding herd on a stable of high-strung thoroughbreds for that distance was exhausting for a healthy man. And Jack didn't strike him as fully returned to health.

"Thought you'd take a day of respite." Hunt held his restive gelding's head.

"Old habits die hard," Jack acknowledged. "Are you going into the blacksmith's shop? I can meet you there."

"I expect I'm exceeding the bounds of the manor's trust fund by repairing the smithy or any other part of the Priory village while the ownership is disputed. I thought I'd just make a list of what's needed and see if Walker can fiddle the expenses." Hunt mounted with less difficulty than when he'd first arrived. The knee was improving.

"I'll be down shortly. First, I want to warn the head groom to notify us should any strangers arrive while we're about. Elsa is in a bit of a pother, and I promised she'd be safe here." Their guest glanced at the massive manor. "As long as she stays inside, there shouldn't be a problem, but she never stays in one place."

"I have a lead on some hounds. We can visit them after the smithy. If the unpleasant young fellow who visited yesterday is any example, I don't think we have much to worry about."

Physical confrontation, Hunt was prepared to handle. Financial and legal battles were far more worrisome.

Jack saluted and Hunt let his horse have its head down the drive. He wished horses and ovens would excite Clare as they did Lady Elspeth. He didn't know what would entice the bookish lady to remain at the manor. She loved the library but gave no indication that she wanted to give up her comfortable home for it. She enjoyed the puzzle of the missing jewels but was too sensible to set any hopes on them. A tutor would only hold her here for a short while.

Her kisses sizzled, but he didn't dare seek them too often without an arrangement. What else could he offer?

There were probably entire books written on what ladies wanted, Hunt thought in disgruntlement as he rode up to the abandoned smithy. The door hung loose on its hinges, but it was a sturdy door, not rotten. He'd already cleaned and repaired the forge in order to work on the stovetop.

Studying the rotten timber beneath a leaking roof and debating the need for a lumber mill to turn the manor's wilderness into planks, he heard horses passing by on the lane to the village. He stepped out, wondering if Jack had forgotten the location.

A closed carriage accompanied by four sturdy outriders rolled past. The riders wore swords and had muskets attached to their saddles. This wasn't the London highway. Did they expect to be robbed by farmers?

Unless they were lost, they were almost certainly headed toward the manor. They'd already passed the drive, but it was overgrown, shabby, not exactly welcoming, and the manor was invisible. They'd inquire at the village and turn around shortly.

Hunt's instinct for danger had him returning to the saddle and dangerously galloping up the footpath.

He met Jack on the upper drive. "Visitors," was all he said. Jack turned his mount without questioning.

For all they knew, the carriage could carry Lady Spalding or Lady Lavinia, the late earl's daughter and granddaughter. Or perhaps more of the heirs had decided to take advantage of the warming weather to venture out and explore their new home.

Most people would not arrive with armed outriders. Polite visitors sent messages ahead of time.

They left their mounts with a stable lad and ran for the manor before the carriage rattled up the long drive.

"I'll warn Elsa and the kitchen staff." Jack dashed toward the back of the house.

Hunt took the side entrance. He could hear Clare instructing Oliver in his lessons in the library. He warned the butler and footman to keep visitors out until instructed otherwise and ducked in to disturb the lessons.

"Carriage and four with armed outriders arriving," he said curtly. "Suggestions?"

"If there are ladies, you must let them in. They'll need the retiring room. The one adjoining the great hall should suit." She rose and shook out her drab skirt. "If we are to become a public inn, I really should learn to dress accordingly."

He snorted. "As an innkeeper? Perhaps we should charge for the facilities. Wait until I join you before allowing Quincy to bring in anyone. The outriders will go to the stable where Jack will deal with them. I want all the doors locked."

He strode to his study where he loaded his pistols and his American sharpshooter rifle. Clare hated weapons, but these guests did not come unarmed. From the earl's armory, he handed a pistol and musket to Walker when he joined him.

"If it's Bosworth, may I shoot him?" Walker asked, checking the ammunition, then hiding the pistol on a shelf. Powder-loaded weapons were too unwieldy to be carried in company, and Walker didn't do swords.

"In self-defense, certainly, although I'll have taken off his

133

head before you fire a shot." Hunt donned a rapier. "I'm beginning to feel ridiculous."

"Defending a cook and a house you don't even want? Perhaps. Defending people who can't defend themselves? Not ridiculous."

"I'd like to keep the cook." Hunt strode out, leaving Walker chuckling.

Henri and Arnaud were running down the main stairs, buckling on swords.

"I love dressing for company," Henri called down, stashing a knife in a belt under his coat. His younger cousin was grinning, apparently enjoying the excitement.

Henri had never fought as a soldier and had little understanding of the horrors of battle. Arnaud was an artist pressed into service defending their home. He understood too well. He looked grim.

"One of you at the carriage door, the other at the garden exit. Jack has the stable. Consider this good practice. I don't think thieves arrive in a coach and four." Hunt nodded at Quincy, who apparently kept fireplace pokers in his coat stand. The butler's size alone should terrify any fops.

Lavender popped out of the gallery carrying her fuzzy puppy, took one look at the weaponry, and hied herself into the great hall with Clare. Meera hurried from her infirmary in the rear, her expression defiant. What the devil had she been told? Hunt rolled his eyes at a front line of an adolescent seamstress, pregnant pharmacist, and bookish spinster. Civilian life took some adjustment.

Hunt joined Oliver in the library and waited for the drama to unfold.

"Boiling oil from the ramparts," the boy said, looking up from his book.

"Drawbridge and portcullis," Hunt countered. "But your aunt objects to treating visitors as enemies."

They listened as Quincy answered the knock. Hunt was

fairly certain that was Bosworth's voice. Had the banker brought armed lawyers with him this time?

He eased open the connecting door between the library and the great hall in time to hear Quincy announce, "Sir George and Lady Culpepper, Mr. Benedict Bosworth, and Mr. Reginald Hill to see you, miss."

Clare's response was clipped. "I am quite certain the gentlemen wish to see Captain Hunt, but please bring in the Culpeppers. I assume they're poor Mr. Culpepper's parents?"

Hunt bit back a curse. The dead man's parents? Accompanied by the usurious banker and the minion of Lady Elspeth's unwanted suitor. They damned well were under siege.

FIFTEEN

THE PARLOR MAID EXCITEDLY RUSHED INTO THE KITCHEN TO recite the name of the visitors.

Elsa nearly cast up her breakfast at hearing Hill was on her doorstep. Why was Smythe's smarmy clerk in the company of the poor Culpeppers?

Because Smythe was spying on her. She had known once Jack took her horses, it was only a matter of time. Short time, apparently.

With malice aforethought, she armed herself with a meat cleaver. Catching her alarm, deaf-mute but sturdy Ned grabbed an iron poker. Not entirely certain what the trouble might be, her staff set iron skillets and rolling pins at hand. She ought to be safe enough from kitchen intruders. For now.

In time, one or two of the servants might learn to line their pockets by giving away her activities and whereabouts, as they had in Newchurch, but for now, this group was loyal to the captain, and perhaps, to her.

Feeling brave, she whacked onions with her cleaver. The

household would tire of stew and soup eventually. She knew how to cook on a spit and had chickens over the fire. But bread and side dishes. . . Took more thought than she could spare these days.

Down the hall, past the laundry rooms, the lock on the outside door rattled. Ned stayed on alert. The captain had installed good bolts, so she had nothing to fear.

Until she heard Jack shouting. Her heart raced, and she gripped the cleaver tighter.

Adam raced down the interior stairs. "There's fighting in the yard, miss, my lady. And the captain and Miss Knightly are busy with guests. Do I go out or stay?"

The question that haunted her life—run or fight? She needed more information. Jack was a soldier and could defend himself, but she had a stable of horses and unarmed grooms. . . Surely they wouldn't be attacked by Smythe's bullies?

She wasn't a general. She didn't know how to position troops.

She might not be a general, but she was a *lady*. For the first time in a long time, she recognized she had powerful friends and family willing to defend her.

At this realization, Elsa felt a surge of unwarranted courage and mule-headed obstinacy. She threw off her mobcap and apron, grabbed her cleaver and a skillet for good measure, and stalked up the interior stairs to the ground floor. She was curbing her impulse to race directly outside. She'd see if she could gather an army first.

Here in the narrow service hall by the courtyard, noise from the stable yard could barely be discerned. The manor's walls were thick and the windows, few. She couldn't see Quincy at the front. She simply assumed he was there.

"The captain's cousins? His steward?" she asked the footman who had followed her up, looking anxious. The butler's son was taller than his prizefighter father, but not as bulky or experienced.

"Mr. Walker is in the library. Mr. Arnaud and Mr. Henri have gone into the yard." The staff had taken to calling Hunt's cousins by their first name rather than attempt distinguishing one Monsieur Lavigne from the other. Or pronouncing *monsieur*.

Adam followed her to the courtyard exit. She didn't even know that the commotion was about her, although every instinct said it had to be if Smythe's toady was here. But with Hunt's cousins and Jack and an entire stable of grooms in the yard, it shouldn't matter, unless Smythe had hired an army. She could go out and tell them all to go to hell, and there wasn't a thing they could do about it. Even Smythe would resist outright abduction in front of witnesses.

She was a lady, daughter of an earl. Unless she wished to live her life in terror, the time had come to behave like one.

"Very well, Adam, continue guarding the door." His station was here at the garden exit, protecting the manor and its occupants. "I will put an end to this nonsense. Step aside, please."

"But the captain, he said—" Adam grimaced when she held up her cleaver. He hastily opened the door.

She stepped into the courtyard, neatly edged by low brick walls, the spring greens just starting to fill the brown earth. From the other side of the wing forming the east wall of the garden, she could hear shouts and metal clanging, with Jack's voice overriding the clamor of panicked horses.

Her feeble insides froze in terror. She wanted to turn and run, as she always had. She'd always been smaller and weaker than the men in her life. Dodging their curses, drunken fists, and sticks and whips had become a wearisome game.

She should have poisoned them. Too late now. Jack was

out there, endangering himself for a useless coward. If nothing else, she had to help Jack.

Swinging her skillet and cleaver, she marched through the garden gate, past the safety of the wall to the muddy stable yard.

"There she is—grab her!" Freddy's voice shouted over a clash of steel.

~

CLARE POURED ANOTHER CUP OF TEA FOR THE SOBBING LADY Culpepper, who had arrived draped in black crepe and netting from head to foot. The lady still managed to find her mouth well enough.

The Culpeppers had been extolling the virtues of their younger, restless son through the course of two pots of tea and a plate of scones. Apparently, Elsa had learned to bake scones over an open fire.

Clare had offered to take the couple to their son's grave, but they had dithered and wept, while their companions had kept Hunt occupied in an argument about business on the other end of the enormous chamber. Meera had offered smelling salts to the weeping mother. Lavender had offered to let them cuddle her puppy. Nothing consoled the Culpeppers.

Over by the windows, the banker, Bosworth, and Mr. Reginald Hill ignored the grieving parents. Mr. Smythe's factotum was a rather gangling, middle-aged man who wore spectacles and a jacket that didn't fit him properly. He had *clerk* written all over him.

Clare thought she might as well attempt to learn something while suffering through this. "Do you think your brilliant, brave son might have been on the way to alerting banks of the forgeries?"

"By Jove, I believe you have hit on it," the florid baronet declared, pounding his cane for emphasis.

139

Clare was happy to have finally said something worthwhile.

The baronet shouted to the men by the window. "Bosworth, did my boy consult with you about the forged notes?"

Distracted from the financial argument, the banker turned his attention to the baronet. "What forged notes?"

Clare sipped her tea and awaited enlightenment. The recently deceased had been riding toward the manor for a reason. Now that she realized Culpepper had known Bosworth, she wondered if the banker had sent him. Why?

"The notes my boy was carrying when some scoundrel killed him, of course," Lord Culpepper shouted, turning a dangerous shade of red. "Could he have been working for the bank and someone wanted to prevent him from warning you? We showed you the damned notes."

Lady Culpepper murmured a remonstration about language.

"I told your son they were counterfeit," Boswell said coolly. "I warned the Liverpool Bank they might have forged notes circulating. As I told you, I have no notion what Basil meant to do with the notes or where he obtained them."

The use of Mr. Culpepper's name said Bosworth knew the dead man and his activities more intimately than he'd admitted. Bankers were seldom on casual terms with the gentry.

"You overstep yourself, Bosworth," the baronet warned, apparently irritated by the familiarity.

Hunt abandoned the businessmen to join Clare on the sofa, helping himself to the last scone. "Bosworth may be kin to the earl," he warned their angry visitor. "We can probably all trace our lineage to royalty. I'd rather think it's what we accomplish, not who our ancestors are, that matters." He covered his mild reprimand with the usual courtesy. "I am sorry for your loss, sir, my lady. Will you accompany us to the cemetery and express your wishes for his grave?"

Clare thought Hunt might be impatient to see what was happening elsewhere.

Smythe's toady turned his attention away from Bosworth. "I'd like to see the button factory your cousin spoke of. Is it in the village?"

Clare smothered a laugh at Hill's expression when Lavender popped up and said, "I'll show you, sir. We have buttons and toys, and Arnaud has painted the most exquisite. . ." She nattered happily on the way to the door.

When the Culpeppers dithered, eyeing the empty teapot, Clare refused to call for another round. She rose, brushed down her old gray skirt, and gestured for the hovering maid to bring her wrap. "Meera, would you mind accompanying Lavender? She forgets the need for chaperones."

And Meera's more sensible head would keep the businessmen in line. Her friend hid a smile and solemnly agreed, as if she and Lavender were proper ladies. Society was all in how one behaved, after all—until one's antecedents were known, at least. So silly.

Appropriating Hunt's arm, Clare abandoned the chilly great hall, giving the Culpeppers little choice but to follow. Quincy looked worried as he handed out coats and hats. Clare glimpsed enough of the far end of the corridor to see Adam glancing anxiously from the company to the door. Her insides knotted.

Hunt pressed her hand on his arm reassuringly, but he seemed a tad grim.

"Really, you needn't do this," Lady Culpepper insisted as the butler all but pushed her after Clare and Hunt. "It is too sad. We didn't bring flowers."

Clare ignored her. Something was happening in the yard. Violence terrified her. Experience had shown her she could not stop it. What she couldn't control, she feared.

Quincy and Adam would block armed intruders to the interior. She had chosen the two large men to guard the

141

ground floor for good reason—they had fists and didn't need weapons. But who was outside?

Hiding her terror, she sought Arnaud and Henri. Were they still in the gallery?

"We've only begun restoring the estate," she nattered mindlessly, ignoring her guest's complaint as they strolled down the dark hall. "The gallery occupies the original priory chapel. The cemetery is in back. Do you think you might wish to place a gravestone? We don't have a stone carver and couldn't do more than leave a wooden marker."

Hunt remained silent and let her chatter pave the way to the side exit. He opened the door and gestured for her to proceed him, followed by the Culpeppers.

The screams and shouts immediately reached their ears. Panicking, Clare froze. Hunt caught her arm and pushed her behind his broad back. From this perspective, the stable yard appeared to have become a battleground of swords and horses.

RIDING BEANSTALK, JACK TORE THE WHIP FROM THE CARRIAGE groom's hand. Spinning the gelding to lash at the man on the ground attacking him, he caught sight of an outrider grabbing Elsa's arm. He nearly had an apoplexy. What the devil was she doing out here? With a boot kick to the interfering groom's jaw, he swung Beans toward Elsa.

She wielded a wicked-looking cleaver, but her large attacker easily dodged the blow. She fought when he grabbed her wrist, but she wasn't strong enough to fight his crushing hold. Forced to drop the cleaver, she swung with her pan.

Jack kicked his horse into a dangerous spring past Arnaud and Henri, on foot, battling two more of the mounted carriage guards. A third deliberately blocked Jack, angling his horse to prevent him from galloping across the rutted drive.

To hell with that. Jack reared Beanstalk, ripped his sword from his scabbard, and smacked the rider with the flat of his blade. Rapiers were for gentlemen. Jack had a soldier's weapon. Caught by surprise, the other man tried to dodge the blow, lost his grip, and his horse skittered from under him. He hit the ground with a curse. Jack jumped his gelding over the bastard and galloped across the rutted ground.

Another outrider followed, but Jack lifted his pistol, turned, and fired over his shoulder, knocking the fool's hat off, and grazing his empty skull sufficiently to cause him to fall into the hands of Arnaud.

Elsa screamed and kicked as her attacker attempted to wrench the weapon from her other hand. Her bloody war cries mixed with male curses, and she was still slamming her assailant with the iron skillet by the time Jack arrived. Years of wielding heavy pots had given her a wicked strength. The outrider staggered but didn't release her.

Jack couldn't risk firing the second shot in his pistol, not when they grappled so close. Even his sword might maim her if he didn't swing accurately enough. That left brute force. He wasn't in the best of shape, and the other man wasn't small, but Jack had rage on his side. Beanstalk was well trained and didn't object when Jack flung his leg over the saddle and shoved off, leaping onto the miscreant's back.

Clutching the man with an arm around his throat, Jack applied pressure until his opponent gagged and had to release Elsa to defend himself. Elsa swung her skillet and belted her attacker in the breadbasket, causing him to weaken, giving Jack the momentum to floor the brute. Standing over his prone opponent, he held his boot on his Adam's apple, while Elsa screamed and kicked him where it had to hurt. Their prisoner writhed in agony.

"Don't do anything I wouldn't do," Jack warned, biting back a laugh that concealed his abject terror at what might have happened had they not been forewarned. "We need him to talk."

"Then kick him in the head. He doesn't use it." Elsa picked up her cleaver and crossed her arms over her ample chest, looking like a disheveled warrior goddess. "That's Frederick."

Jack glanced down in astonishment at the choking, weeping scoundrel beneath his boot. "This sniveling snot is little Freddy? The boy never was much of a fighter. What's got into him?"

"His father died and my mother quit funding his excesses. He had to marry or starve." Elsa kicked him again.

Shouts from the manor turned their attention back to the fight. Clare and a pair of black-clad guests huddled near the side door, while Hunt roared toward the action, firing a pistol at the hooves of an outrider's horse to prevent him from hitting Henri with his rapier.

The captain's commands loosed a veritable army of hired hands. They poured from the stable, grabbing reins, wielding pitchforks and whatever weapons came to hand. Hunt's stalwart cousins joined in with their punishing fists.

Frederick wouldn't be receiving help from those quarters.

"I don't suppose we can kill him?" Elsa asked wistfully, kicking at her stepbrother's ribs. "Could I pay the captain to build a prison? Isn't there a dungeon?"

With the outriders and coachman at the point of pitchforks and knives, Hunt limped across the barren ground in their direction. After one quick glance of concern at Elsa, he focused on their captive.

"Rude fellow from yesterday, right?" Hunt leaned over, caught Frederick's collar, and with a withering glance at Jack to move aside, yanked him to his heels.

"She's my sister. You've no right to. . ."

With impatience, the captain swung a punishing fist into Freddy's jaw, rendering him unconscious.

"Not supposed to mistreat prisoners," Jack said laconically, grabbing Freddy before he fell. "I volunteer to take him to a magistrate and have him locked up for assizes."

"Legally, you'd have to take him all the way to Shrewsbury. One of these days, I ought to look into having Gravesyde Priory returned to Worcestershire, but today isn't that day."

Hunt nodded at the older gentlemen joining the black-clad couple on the drive. "You'll have difficulty persuading anyone but the grooms to testify against him. Whom do you think the judge will believe, a distinguished banker, businessman, and baronet, or two penniless Frenchmen and an American who looks like a pirate?"

"I'll testify," Elsa said defiantly.

"They won't let women into the courtroom," Jack said in defeat. "I could go, but they'll all accuse me of assault. With my luck, I'd be the one in gaol."

Their prisoner stirred, and Hunt frog-marched him across the drive, in the direction of Arnaud and Henri, one grim, the other grinning.

Elsa fell into Jack's arms the instant Frederick was gone. She shivered, and he wrapped his greatcoat around her, hating that her stepbrother had caused her fear. "Let's take you back inside," he murmured into her hair. "Even warrior goddesses need to wear more than a skimpy gown in this wind."

"Not a warrior or goddess," she muttered. "I wanted to kill him and couldn't. If it weren't for you, he'd be riding off with me right now."

She didn't argue more but allowed him to lead her to the kitchen stairs.

Marveling that a sheltered lady could survive such horrific intimidation for so long, Jack hated himself for not having known. "You would have escaped. You're smarter than he is," he said reassuringly.

"He brought reinforcements. And Mr. Hill is not dumb." She shook her head and continued trembling as he led her downstairs. "Can Culpepper's *parents* be involved in kidnapping? Does that make sense?"

"Hunt will find out what he can. I think they may have been a Trojan horse to slip the others past our guard. Not sure how the banker is involved." Jack tried to puzzle that out while he had his arms full of warm, round woman who smelled of vanilla and violets. But his thinking apparatus was rapidly sinking to lower parts.

"I am so very glad you're here, Jack," she whispered as they entered the warmth of the kitchen under the concerned watch of her staff. "You're my hero."

She hugged him hard, her soft bosom pushing against him, and what remained of his wits went south. With no idea of what she did to him, she detached herself and transformed into efficient cook to order everyone back to work.

Jack let her praise whistle through his empty head. He'd never been a hero, never aspired to be one. All he'd ever wanted to do was own a little land, raise a few good horses, have a good time. Maybe he should have more purpose than just sliding by?

If he wanted a valiant woman like Elsa, he probably ought to consider a world outside himself, one he'd mostly ignored all his life.

A woman *like* Elsa? No such creature existed. Watching her dive into a bowl of dough after thrashing a kidnapper, he didn't think he could ever want anyone else. The child who had followed him around like a puppy was now a woman he could only watch in distant admiration. She was an heiress. He was not a termite to live on anyone's support.

Maybe he should ask the captain if there was a reward if he found the manor's jewels.

146

SIXTEEN

"You can't hold Mr. Turner," Bosworth argued. "You may be magistrate, but he's entitled to a trial."

Hunt nursed a whiskey and a pounding head. He'd had people nattering at him for an hour now, while he left young Frederick cooling his heels in the crypt. If Fate were kind, the ghosts of the monks buried beneath the cellar floor would rise and scare the excrement out of the cur.

Hunt needed to see to Clare. Gunfire and violence reduced his brave co-general to quivering hysterics. This bunch of selfish clods would be enough to reduce *anyone* to quivering hysterics, although he'd rather punch nattering jaws.

He'd been hoping for a calm discussion, but tempers were rising.

"Mr. Turner attempted to *kidnap* the daughter of an earl," he said through gritted teeth. "I'm fairly certain, even in England, that is not acceptable behavior. Why don't you take the Culpeppers back to whatever rock they crawled from under? We have no stove and a cook who'd rather poison than feed them, so staying here is not wise." Hunt closed his eyes and pretended to be a vegetable. Maybe the banker would catch a clue.

"Mr. Turner is the head of his household. He had every right to return his wayward sister to the man to whom she is affianced," the unctuous Reginald Hill protested.

"Turner is *not* head of the household. Lord Villiers is. Turner is merely a worm who crawled into the earl's woodwork and wants to stay. Given that Lady Elspeth is of age and sound mind, she cannot be affianced against her will. Give it up, both of you. I draw the line at kidnapping." Hunt returned his chair to all four legs and stood, effectively dismissing the late viscount's bastard son and the factotum of a wealthy Cit.

Bosworth's soft jaw worked as if grinding molars. "You don't know the power of wealth as I do. Aloysius Smythe claims Lady Elspeth is his fiancée. Mr. Hill verifies it. It is not our place to call them liars. The lady's *brother* supports the claim. She is merely a hysterical, spoiled female who wants her own way. Imagine, a lady hiding in a cellar as a cook! Does that sound as if she is in her right mind? Do us all a favor and give her up."

Hunt snorted and pointed at the door. "Line drawn, remember? Go away before I have Quincy fling you out."

He knew that English law treated women as property and not human beings with wits and wills of their own. Anyone with half a brain observing the women running this decrepit manor knew better. His rage simmered at the overt bigotry. Much more of this, and he couldn't be responsible for his actions.

The two men stalked out. Too furious to sit still, Hunt slammed the door after them, then took the library exit in search of Clare. How had she fared through this tarradiddle?

Oliver sat at the library table studying his dinosaur eggs and a drawing book of rocks. The boy was only seven but his reading skills improved hourly. He glanced up at Hunt with a troubled look. "Mr. Jack says my eggs might help Aunt Clare. Will they pay to make the bad men go away?"

Hunt bit back a few blasphemous phrases. Oliver seldom spoke. That he'd been forced to do so by the likes of Freddy Turner. . . Realizing the boy had come to trust him enough to express his concern, Hunt gathered his composure. "The bad men won't hurt you or your Aunt Clare. No amount of dinosaur eggs will turn greedy men into nice ones. When you are old enough to understand the ways of the world better, you might use your eggs to help others, if you can. But for now, they are a treasure from your father, and your only task is to keep them safe."

Oliver nodded solemnly, although the frown didn't leave his brow. "Yes, sir." He gathered the rough gems into a handkerchief and held them up to Hunt. "Would you keep them safe, sir? I do not want to lose them like the earl lost his jewels. I think dragon hoards may not be very smart."

Hunt carefully put the bundle into his pocket, then lifted the boy and hugged him. "Your aunt has raised an intelligent young man. Your father would be proud of you. I will show you the safe I put them in when I'm done talking with your aunt. You should always know where your hoard is kept."

The boy beamed shyly when Hunt set him down. "Thank you, sir."

Clare should not worry about the boy. She'd done a fine job of raising him.

Hunt tousled his hair, then eased the great hall door open to peer through the crack.

Clare wasn't there. He hoped that didn't mean she'd taken to her bed.

She'd left Lavender showing Lady Culpepper a fashion design book, while Meera and Walker played chess by the cold fire, providing a chaperone and no more. Sir George, Culpepper's father, sipped Hunt's brandy, looking ill-tempered.

Reginald Hill kept some exalted company for a clerk. A baronet, a banker, Elsa's brother. . . Who was he? Hunt would

149

have to investigate when he had a few days to himself—as if that would happen anytime soon.

Bosworth stormed into the formal chamber, accompanied by a cold-faced Hill. Quincy followed them in with coats and hats.

Ah. . . Brilliant tactician that she was, Clare had deliberately abandoned their guests, instructing Quincy to give them no choice but to leave. Society was little more than a war zone, it seemed. The best tactician won.

Stoic Walker rose to bow out their unwanted guests. Lavender's ribbons wafted in the breeze of her cheerful farewell. The manor possessed the world's most eccentric army, but they'd succeeded in routing the wealthy enemy and protecting their cook.

The cook, Lady Elspeth. . . That's where Clare would be.

Hunt would like to join her, but he supposed he needed to do something about the young hellion moldering in the cellar.

His cousins waited in Walker's office near the back door where they could keep an eye on staff running up and down the kitchen stairs. Someone had provided sandwiches, and they'd worked their way through the stack, leaving Hunt the dregs. He grabbed the remainder.

"Not enjoying foraging for food again," he said grumpily, taking Walker's desk chair. "Who do you have guarding the dungeon door?"

"Lady Elspeth's grooms. They're a bloodthirsty lot and don't like Master Freddy much. Armed themselves with whips and pitchforks. They're hiding in the shrubbery, eager for battle. Even if our visitors figure out where the door is, which is unlikely, they won't sneak past the guards." Looking smug, Henri finished off his mug of ale.

"They haven't had enough fighting?" Disgruntled, Hunt debated ripping out walls so he could have windows. But the infirmary and service hall stood between Walker's office and the outside, and they overlooked the courtyard, not the drive.

"Now what do we do? Truss the fellow and throw him on a magistrate's doorstep with a note?"

"The foolish Brits only allow landowners to be magistrates," Arnaud said, filling one of the chairs by the fire and studying a ledger, his boots propped on the andirons. "That would be you, since their law does not recognize women."

"Charming." Hunt finished his sandwich. "Since I'm not the law, I guess I'll ask the women."

"That's fair. If Lady Elspeth says hang him, may we?" Leaning his hip against the desk, Henri waited with interest.

"Shouldn't you be out peddling trinkets?" Irritably, Hunt stood up. "Are the women in the kitchen?"

"Upstairs. Now that her whereabouts are known far and wide, the lady is choosing a decent chamber. And I'm heading to town in the morning with a wagonload of goods to sell to manufacturers other than Smythe, if any dare buy from me any longer. I can put your prisoner in my cart and dump him anywhere you like." Henri didn't appear too upset about potentially losing all his customers.

Hunt snarled. "Dump him on a Navy ship, maybe. Anywhere else is useless."

Deciding not to disturb the women while they were playing house, Hunt returned to Oliver. He needed to clear his head before making decisions in anger. He took the boy to his study and showed him the locked iron cash box he'd installed behind a painting. Together, they placed the dinosaur eggs inside. If the earl had only used one of these. . .

Hunt shook his head. A fortune in jewels belonged in a bank vault.

Would *Bosworth* be hiding the existence of the jewels? Another question for the solicitors.

He returned the box to its hiding place and swung the painting over it. "Do not tell anyone but your Aunt Clare where you've hidden your treasure. If you wish to see it at any time, just ask me."

"Will the bad man try to steal them?" Oliver asked in concern.

"We'll put him in chains," Hunt said to reassure the boy, then liked the notion so well, he played with it as he went in search of the women.

After all, a blacksmith was supposed to be arriving today. . .

For the first time since entering Wycliffe Manor, Hunt had confidence that even if a maimed engineer couldn't lead an army troop, he might still suit the role of protecting an eccentric household. It wasn't quite the same as battling for home and country, but it was better than the life he'd expected after his injuries.

~

CLARE LAUGHED AT HUNT'S SUGGESTION THAT THEY LOCK Frederick in chains, but Elsa lit up like a lantern. Clare hadn't thought him serious, but she had given little consideration to protecting an earl's daughter. She must now.

They adjourned the matter until dinner, where they could all sit down and discuss the prisoner rationally, she hoped. Apparently, no one cared that a newly married man was left rotting all afternoon in a muddy crypt beneath a medieval hall.

After choosing a bedchamber near the service stairs, Elsa abandoned Clare and hurried down to the kitchen to oversee the dinner preparation. With time to spare, Hunt and Jack rode into the village to work on the smithy and meet with the new smith.

Clare retired to her small sitting room and writing. At times like this, she wondered what her brave sister might have done, but even Bea was unlikely to keep a prisoner.

She had no experience at running a manor this enormous, much less dealing with all the family accumulating. What would happen if she returned to London in the autumn? Would Elsa stay? It seemed unlikely when she had an estate of her own.

It might be a moot point if the bank won the suit over the mortgage. She was learning so much about the world, forged bank notes, fraudulent deeds. . . Perhaps she should be writing contemporary novels instead of medieval. If she found out, her aunt would dissolve into rampant hysterics. Fun to watch, if it did not jeopardize Oliver's future, which it would.

At dinner time, she had to extract Elsa from the kitchen. "You are a rather necessary part of tonight's dinner discussion, my lady. You will have to let your assistant take over from here."

"I'm not dressed for dinner." Elsa finished gutting a fish. "Anne doesn't have the experience to plate everything appropriately and have it delivered in order."

"The men would dump their food into a bowl and eat with their fingers if given a choice. Hot water being at a premium, none of us are dressing for dinner. Come along, the family board meeting awaits." She took off Elsa's cap and helped her remove the apron.

"You are more despotic than I am," Elsa complained, hastily washing her hands. She rearranged the pins in her hair as she followed Clare upstairs. "Have you always been this way?"

Clare thought about it. "I've not had an estate to manage, but someone had to tell the servants what to do after my sister died and my mother fell ill. That's the extent of my experience. How about you?"

As they climbed the stairs, Elsa explained, "After the death of my father and stepfather, my mother ran the household by simply telling the housekeeper what was needed. I stepped in after she left for London, but we have an enormous staff. Consulting a steward or housekeeper was merely

153

a formality. I suppose I took over the kitchen on my own because it was a good hiding place. I've never tried to manage family or my equals. You do it without any semblance of effort."

Clare had not given what Hunt called her co-general duties much thought. She was older and more experienced than Lavender, knew more about English society than Hunt, and she'd simply assumed whatever task needed doing. Hm. Maybe she was needed, at least a little bit.

If it only paid as well as novel writing, she might consider the manor a safer future than risking her family discovering her scandalous career. Or even the family of Oliver's father. But the manor might be gone by year's end, and she *liked* writing.

"Give yourself time, Elsa. The manor requires constant attention, and we all have to do our share. If you simply take charge of the kitchen, we'll all be eternally grateful. But for now, you eat with us." She ushered the earl's daughter to the table, where everyone had already taken a seat and waited impatiently.

Or not at all, since the soup was almost gone.

"Rude, the lot of you," Clare admonished. "Lady Elspeth should have been seated first."

"We're half-starved, and the food was on the table, going cold." Henri reached for the tureen to ladle out the last of the broth before catching himself and passing it down to the empty seats so Clare and Elsa could have what was left.

"Shall I send for more of my servants?" their lady cook asked, attempting to manage the unwieldy bowl. "We really should have a footman to serve."

"I'd rather spend our trust allowance on improving the estate, unless you're offering to pay them from your own funds." Hunt took a piece of skillet bread from a basket and passed it on.

"My estate is paying them to do nothing as it is. Some of

154

them have family in Newchurch and won't want to come. It will take a bit of sorting. I'd like to bring my assistant cook, only my staff needs feeding too." Elsa took bread and passed it to Clare.

"You would prefer to stay in this ramshackle edifice than your own comfortable home?" Jack asked in surprise.

Their cook thought about it for perhaps half a second. "This is the most fun I've had in forever."

Clare tried not to blink her surprise. Fire, combat, and kidnapping constituted fun?

Elsa glanced around the table. "I prefer to be with people who like me and appreciate my efforts. As I mightily appreciate your efforts, thank you."

Clare had led a protected life indeed if an earl's daughter appreciated this disparate, inelegant company. She tried to imagine what it must be like to only be wanted for one's money and to live in fear of abduction by people one knew. She could use that in her novel.

Adam arrived with the roasted chickens. Betsy followed with a bowl of mashed turnips. Clare kept an eye on Oliver to be certain he took a little of everything. At least he was sitting at the table now, instead of under it. Coming here had been good for him.

Hunt waited until everyone had eaten their fill of the main course, and awaited the fruit and cheese, before opening the subject that preyed on Clare's mind. She wasn't certain the men had given their prisoner a second thought since he'd been locked up.

"As much as I would like to keep young Mr. Turner imprisoned for the rest of his days, guarding the door and sending servants out to feed him three times a day is a damn. . . a blood. . ." Hunt growled and finally managed to finish without a curse, "A nuisance. I am open to suggestion as to his fate."

"Execution," Elsa muttered.

"No guillotine," Hunt retorted. "I don't know English law, but I'll assume transportation is more likely for the offense of attempted kidnapping, at least for the gentry."

"Can't transport him," Jack objected. "He's newly married, and it's not his bride's fault that she married a dolt."

"I suspect they've been married long enough for her to be grateful if we dumped Freddy on a ship and sent him out." Elsa remained mulishly adamant.

"Perhaps we should ask," Clare murmured in amusement. "Dear Mrs. Turner, would you prefer your husband returned in chains or simply shipped to the antipodes?"

"If he has given her any hope of moving into Elsa's estate, she'll not be cooperative," Jack argued. "Unless you wish to ship him to Shrewsbury and trial, we are judge and jury."

"I think we all agree he's guilty." Hunt looked up and apparently saw no objection. "It's just a matter of determining how to keep him from harming Lady Elspeth."

"Elsa. Call me Elsa as you call everyone else by name. And there is no way of stopping him as long as we're both alive."

"Unless you marry," Clare corrected. "Once you're married, there is naught else he can do, unless he's inclined toward murder."

"It's only one step from kidnapping to murder. She needs a husband who can snap Freddy's neck if needed." Jack's expression was bleak as he drained his ale.

The men had poured themselves *ale* for dinner. Clare refrained from rolling her eyes. The manor would become a tavern or worse if the men were left to themselves.

Had she forced them into domesticity? Now was not the time to ponder.

"Are there any potential suitors you would like us to invite?" she asked.

Elsa laughed bitterly. "Even the vicar has rejected me. The only ones interested are men who want my dowry, not me."

"That's ridiculous." Jack appeared to be in an argumentative mood. "Anyone with wits in their brainpan would want you. Even I want you, and I know what a bull-headed termagant you can be, and I'd have you without your bloody land and money. You simply haven't given yourself a chance."

Clare noticed Elsa's cheeks pinken as she ducked her head to apply a bit of cheese to her old apple. She would correct Jack's language, but the conversation had taken an interesting turn.

Even more interesting, the heavy scent of jasmine perfume drifted around them. She'd start believing the ghost of the viscountess lingered. Judging by the sachets they'd found, jasmine had been her favorite scent.

"There you go, then." Henri poured more ale. "If neither of you has any other plans, marry. Make little Freddy witness. The end."

The independent heiress's eyes went wide. The penniless soldier choked on his ale. Clare bit back laughter and offered a less dramatic solution. "Or we can have Mr. Turner watch a fake ceremony. We'd need a counterfeit special license and a fake vicar, but that's all manageable, isn't it?"

"Counterfeit bank notes, fraudulent deeds, why not a fake marriage?" Hunt muttered. "Instead of Wycliffe Manor, we should call ourselves a House of Cards."

"May I make your wedding dress?" Lavender asked eagerly, finally contributing to the conversation.

Clare did giggle then. As the absurdity asserted itself, Elsa joined her. Jack's expression of relief was so obvious that the other men roared and pounded him on the back.

Undeterred by hysterics, Hunt poured wine all around and held up his glass, "To false nuptials, may they end Freddy's reign of terror."

Even Elsa and Jack raised glasses to the toast.

SEVENTEEN

AFTER A NIGHT OF TOSSING ABOUT IN SHEER TERROR AT THE insane plans her ramshackle family merrily fashioned, Elsa woke up on Friday morning determined to make her fake nuptials work if they would drive off Freddy forever.

By afternoon, as plans proceeded resolutely toward reality, she was back to terror.

Elsa bottled up her fear and senseless excitement while Lavender pinned her hem. Her young seamstress cousin had located an ancient cream-colored satin gown in one of the manor's moldering wardrobes. She was now fitting it to Elsa's lack of height and the absence of panniers.

With no desire to be married for her money, Elsa had never expected to wear a wedding gown, even a fake one. She had to find the logic again that had made this seem feasible. "This would never work if the manor wasn't so isolated."

"Or if your stepbrother wasn't such a dolt." Clare removed pins from her mouth and sat back to admire their handiwork. "Jack will want to call a real vicar after he sees you in this. You look like an angel."

Elsa rolled her eyes and lifted her haystack of hair. "A mad angel. I'd fare better waving a meat pie under his nose to induce eagerness." She would never be desirable as a *woman*, just a cook and moneybags.

"We'll set one on the fake altar." Meera glued a bit of stiff paper to a scrap of linen for the fake vicar's collar. "No one will believe the ceremony is real if you're both petrified."

"Freddy is too stupid and selfish to notice. A vicar, a wedding party, witnessing a document. . . he'll believe it even if I'm in chains. Walker could misspell everything on the license, and he'd not know the difference."

"I daresay he will believe anything to prevent Hunt from keeping him in chains. He'll be so happy to be out of that awful cellar that he'll grovel at your feet." Clare took a brush to Elsa's long blond hair. "This has a lovely curl to it! You shouldn't hide it beneath those ugly caps."

"It's an uncontrollable haystack. Just tack a piece of lace on top and don't trouble yourself." Elsa squirmed under the unfamiliar attention. She should probably send for her maid, but she was enjoying the lack of carping. "My maid hates my hair."

"Who hired her?" Meera asked, pressing the fake collar with her fingers.

Elsa wrinkled her nose. "My mother, when I first went to London. I don't have much use for her, but it seemed a shame to turn her off for no fault of her own. She's quite good at her duties. Why?"

"Because your hair is beautiful, and your maid is either a lazy liar or knows nothing about fixing hair. Why surround yourself with people who disparage you? Send her back to your mother." Clare tugged her around to face a mirror. "You are beautiful. Look at yourself through our eyes."

Elsa studied the small oval mirror on the washstand. Clare

had used a curling iron, then tied the curls with cream and gold ribbons and pinned up the length with sparkly pins. With pale strands dangling by her cheeks, she almost looked demure, instead of like a savage Viking battleax. The old-fashioned gown was designed for a woman of ample bosom, so she actually had a waist below the brief bodice and above the billows of creamy fabric. The hairstyle accentuated the wide oval of her weird turquoise eyes, so they looked large. Or maybe just scared.

"I don't look like me." Elsa wrinkled her nose and stuck out her tongue, but she couldn't deny that the gown suited her. "Lavender, you are a fashion genius."

The girl sat back on her heels and beamed. "I know."

They all laughed, and Clare swatted the youngster with a fan. "What do we need to do with that black abomination to make it look like a clergyman's robe?"

Lavender shrugged. "I've tacked a sort of sleeve he can put his arms through. The stitches can be removed later. I hate to waste good bombazine on something that will never be used again. I hope Mr. Oswald won't mind standing still until the robe comes off. I don't want to have to hem it."

They had been shocked when one of the kitchen maids had offered her grandfather, Mr. Oswald, the village postmaster, to play the charade of vicar. The postmaster had once been a schoolteacher and enjoyed parlor games. Elsa thought it was a good thing she'd never dreamed of cathedral weddings and bishops.

She still couldn't believe Jack had agreed to this. Or that he meant what he'd said last night at dinner. He *wanted* her? What precisely did that mean? He'd called her a bull-headed termagant, then said he'd take her without land or money. She wished men were a little more clear in expressing themselves. Freddy had tried to *take* her. Smythe *wanted* her land and money. Jack had seemed to mean something different. Perhaps she represented home to a lonely soldier.

Admittedly, handsome Jack had always turned her foolish head, probably because he spoke to her as if she weren't a brainless doll. He'd favored her with friendship, and she'd adored him for that. But she'd been an idealistic child of seventeen when he'd bought his colors and rode away. She wasn't that child any longer.

She was a grown woman, and her head was still spinning over his angry declaration. She supposed she wouldn't be human if she wasn't just a tiny bit thrilled to be *wanted* by a handsome, courageous man, even if he only meant as a friend. That an honest soldier was willing to stand up in this mockery for her sake was a definite thrill. If she thought too hard about it, her heart would pound, and she'd start blushing, and that would not do at all.

She concentrated on the possibility of being free from Freddy's bullying forever. Could she go home? Not without her new *husband*, she suspected. But that was all right. She'd bring her home here, where she was surrounded by understanding people who liked her for herself.

A maid rapped at the door to announce, "Mr. Oswald has arrived. The captain wants to know if he should bring up Mr. Turner now."

"They'd better duck him in a bath and put clean clothes on him," Clare said, sticking a final pin in the hem. "When he's ready, we'll be ready. See that Mr. Oswald has tea and whatever the kitchen can serve him."

"That won't be much," Elsa muttered. "They're all at sixes and sevens thinking this is real. Anne will no doubt undercook a goose in celebration."

"Hunt will spit it on his sword and roast it over the fire, if so. Marie will stay silent about her grandfather until your brother is on his way. After that, the staff will work it out for themselves. A hearty celebration, for now, won't be amiss. As you said, we couldn't do this if we weren't so isolated." Clare sat back to admire their handiwork while Lavender fussed over lace and details.

Elsa studied herself in the mirror and briefly wished she was truly walking down the aisle with Jack today. But that was selfish and silly. "If I'd known we were playing wedding charades, I would have brought my grandmother's pendant necklace, unless my mother gave it to Freddy."

"Your grandmother's portrait in the gallery shows her wearing a diamond necklace with a ruby pendant. Is that the one?" Lavender asked eagerly.

"I have only seen the ruby. The necklace in the portrait is much larger than mine. I think Wycliffe portioned the diamonds by taking the originals apart, or so my grand-mother said." Elsa touched the bare expanse of skin above her bodice.

It wasn't a real wedding. She didn't need jewels.

"We think the earl hid the gems he didn't dole out." Clare began picking up the scattering of lace and silk. "But no one has ever found them."

"Grandmother seemed to think he meant them to be distributed among his great-grandchildren, but I didn't pay much attention to the stories. I never expected to have chil-dren and didn't wear the jewels I had." Elsa nervously squeezed her feet into the high-heeled slippers they'd found in the wardrobe with the dress. They were tight, but she'd wear them anyway. Her own awful boots simply wouldn't do.

Clare hugged her. "One never knows, children might be in your future."

"Fake ones?" she asked dryly. "Could we have food sent up while they're putting Freddy in chains?"

JACK NERVOUSLY ADJUSTED HIS NEWLY PRESSED NECKCLOTH. "Do fake weddings really require fancy dress?"

"They would look fake if you didn't dress properly," Hunt intoned in his authoritative voice.

"You will dazzle the ladies in your tails and shiny shoes." Henri had delayed going into town to help with this humbug.

Well, he had only himself to blame for agreeing to it. Jack glanced down at the dress slippers and grimaced. "I haven't worn these in longer than I care to remember. I'm not sure why they were in my bags."

"You thought Wellington might hold a ball and dance his way to victory?" Hunt brushed off Jack's silk hat.

"An officer is a gentleman. One is required to keep up looks." Except he was no longer an officer and after this, possibly not much of a gentleman. Well, he'd never been much of one from the start—half the reason he and Elsa could never marry. An heiress deserved far better than him.

Jack settled the hat on his fashionably trimmed hair. "If I'm just to wait in the great hall for Elsa to come down, do I really need a hat?"

"One is required to keep up looks," Henri mocked. "Did you find anything to suit as a ring?"

"It's horrible, but it will have to suffice. Keep pouring whiskey down Freddy's throat, and he won't be able to see the nose on his face." He glanced at the one-eyed captain, who now paced restlessly. "Did you really have the smithy forge ankle chains?"

"I did. Mostly ceremonial. You can let him free when the formalities are over, and we'll pour him on his horse and send him on his way. If he's fortunate, he can reach Birmingham and apprise Mr. Smythe of the nuptials before night falls." Hunt headed for the door. "I'll see if Quincy and Arnaud have cleaned up the prisoner."

"I'm as ready as can be." Jack had only a shaving mirror

but leaned over to be certain his linen was straight. "Can't we partake of the whiskey too?"

"Not unless you want the lady's brother to think we had to make you drunk to marry her." Henri straightened from leaning against the mantel. "Did you mean what you said last night, that'd you have her without a dowry?"

Jack wasn't entirely certain what he'd said last night. He'd been in a rage. "I made a vow long ago that I would never marry unless I could support my wife without needing her money. Right now, I can't do that, but yes, I meant it. I could not aspire to any woman better than Elsa."

"And they say we French are the romantics." Henri snorted. "Let us see if the wedding feast is being laid out."

Jack was almost as nervous as if he were attending his real wedding. He still couldn't believe Elsa had agreed to the chicanery. He thought perhaps this new family of hers was a bad influence, but he'd agreed to go along, so he couldn't complain. It was just a damned good thing they weren't in Scotland, or they'd end up married in truth.

Not that he'd object to having Elsa in his bed. . .

That was not a path he should take.

But when he entered the dining chamber to find a hastily cleaned-up Freddy in ankle chains, imbibing Hunt's fine brandy, Jack found another direction for his jackrabbit thoughts. Picking up pickled beets and bread from the sparse buffet, he straddled a dining chair and admired the morose prisoner drinking his dinner.

A man had been murdered. Jack didn't think it coincidental that the fop had been on the road leading to Elsa.

"Elsa despised Basil Culpepper. How did you plan on using him?" Jack dipped his bread in beet juice.

Freddy glared. "Ain't got no use for the lying bastard."

"He carried a banknote in your name. Any notion why?" Aware that Hunt's cousins had entered the room, Jack paid them no heed. The Frenchmen knew nothing of London society.

Freddy shrugged. "Culpepper was in hock up to his ear lobes. Don't know how he came by any notes at all. The clod-poll had gone all about in his upper story. He had some bee in his bonnet about Smythe's banknotes being bad. Now why would Croesus forge notes? You tell me that."

Jack hid his surprise. "The question at hand is, *why would Culpepper come to see Elsa?* I can think of no other reason for him to ride in this direction."

Freddy shrugged. "I figured the cove wanted to pull one over on Smythe, beat him to the altar and the money. Mother must have told him how to find Elsa."

Now that, Jack almost believed. Elsa's mother was a ninnyhammer who liked her creature comforts. As one of the heirs, she would have known about the manor, even if she'd dismissed it as not worth her time. "So your mother knew Elsa had come here? And sent Culpepper, why?"

"Doubt she knew. They don't talk. Who knows what Culpepper told her," Freddy replied truculently, pouring another glass. "He may have let her think he'd marry Elsa, and she mentioned the manor in exchange for some portion of the settlements."

"Only Culpepper ended up with a bullet through his skull, and you were the one with an arrangement with Smythe," Jack suggested.

"Culpepper had so many debts, it's a wonder his family didn't put a period to his existence. Smythe has funds to spare." Freddy glared at Jack, not grasping his implication at all. "Did you even negotiate with her solicitors? I could have cut a better deal."

Jack sipped the ale Henri poured. "Elsa's money belongs to her. What did Smythe intend to do with it?"

"What does any man do with wealth? He'd make it

multiply better than you. The two of you will just waste a fortune on prancers." Freddy sulked and drank more.

"Smythe builds smoke-belching factories and would turn the tenants into serfs. Elsa and I will leave the land to the use for which it was intended. How does a Cit like Smythe know Culpepper?"

"Why do you care?" Freddy leaned back, looking belligerent.

The two Frenchmen took chairs on either side of the prisoner and began twirling daggers between their fingers. Where the devil had they learned to do that? With their hooded dark eyes and unfashionably long hair, they appeared the part of sansculottes, not aristocrats. But their great-aunt had married an English viscount, and there was a comte on her family tree, so they were genuine.

"We care." Henri leaned forward and spoke in an ominously low voice. "Did Mr. Smythe give Culpepper the funds to pay you and Mr. Hill with hundred-pound notes to aid his conquest of the lady?"

Although a seemingly even-tempered artist, Arnaud was larger and more dangerous looking than his brother as he leaned back and silently cleaned his nails with his knife.

Hunt's cousins were effective at intimidation, far more so than Jack was. He'd always been more farmer than soldier, which was why he'd taken the position in India. His horses were safer hunting gems.

Freddy looked a trifle confused. "Why would he use Culpepper? Smythe promised to pay me, but it didn't happen, did it?"

"I suppose Smythe uses the Liverpool Bank as Elsa does?" Jack was on firmer ground here.

Freddy shrugged. "It's a provincial bank. I think he owns it."

Smythe *owned* the bank, not just controlled it? Smythe held

166

Elsa's funds? Confirmation of the rumor ground like glass in his gut.

The imperturbable butler appeared in the doorway. "The ladies say they are ready to proceed, if the gentlemen will remove to the great hall."

Shaken by the puzzle pieces Freddy provided, Jack had almost forgotten to be nervous about his fake nuptials. Arnaud and Henri took Freddy by the arms and led the way down the corridor to the two-story great hall at the front of the manor. The hall's dark paneling was somewhat illuminated by the tall windows of the original priory chapel, but the forest outside blocked most of the sun. Someone had lit the chandelier and the massive fireplace. At the far end of the chamber, candles burned on the makeshift altar.

Altar. They'd created an altar out of a bookstand and tables in the area where the original sanctuary might have been. On the high wall above the altar, ancient ancestors in ruffs glared down.

Jonquils, bluebells, and budding tree branches filled ribbon-adorned vases on the altar and around the enormous chamber. Sofas and chairs had been turned to face what might have been the sanctuary. No country church could have provided better. The women had been entertaining themselves.

A gray-haired, wrinkled man of diminutive height stood at the makeshift altar, garbed in loose black cloth. He kept uncomfortably adjusting a stiff white collar. He frowned at the Frenchmen leading Freddy in his ankle chains to a chair.

Hunt arrived through a door on the far side of the fireplace. This block of a house hid more exits and entrances than ought to be allowed. Wearing his best dinner jacket and a freshly pressed neckcloth, the captain glanced impatiently in his direction. Jack assumed Hunt was meant to be his best man.

Trying to be casual, he strolled down the aisle between gilded, satin chairs. He greeted his host, then studied the documents Hunt's efficient steward handed over. They were damned good-looking counterfeits. He'd never seen a special license or marriage certificate, but he wagered Freddy hadn't either.

Dressed in an apricot silk dinner dress, Clare entered and sat down at a spinet Jack had never noticed before. Knowing this lot, they'd stolen it just for the occasion. Or perhaps there was a music room tucked away somewhere. She ran the scales and only winced once at a bad key.

The guests in the form of the staff and the button makers from the gallery arrived, looking around in awe. When they seemed reluctant to sit, short, plump Mrs. Abrams ushered them into chairs. Damned if they weren't making a real production of this pretense.

Jack almost laughed as the beribboned adolescent seamstress leaned around the far door, holding her hand over her puppy's snout to keep it from yapping. She was wearing a bonnet with every frill known to mankind and had tied it with lace. She'd outshine the make-believe bride.

When Lavender signaled, Clare struck up a march of some sort. Jack's pulse unexpectedly picked up its pace in anticipation. This wasn't real. He wasn't actually marrying Lady Elspeth. But when she entered behind Lavender, he mightily regretted that he wasn't.

He'd given up any thought of marriage. He'd always imagined that land and horses were all he needed to be happy.

He was a damned fool.

He jiggled the ugly bit of ring in his pocket and wished he had better to offer.

Elsa was radiant. In the light from the window and chandelier, she gleamed in old satin and gold, her hair a tumble of curls and sparkles, her dark-lashed eyes pools of aqua. Her lush lips turned upward in mischief when she found him in the shadows of the enormous room. She knew this was a jest.

His heart didn't. Oddly, a musky, heavier fragrance replaced that of the spring blossoms. Jasmine?

Elsa glided to the music, handed her bouquet of violets to Lavender, and chuckled when Jack bowed over her hand as he wished he could have done all those years ago. She should have been courted like this, with gentlemen begging for her dance card.

"You are magnificent, my lady," he murmured, brushing his lips briefly near her ear. "I am jealous of any man who takes my place."

She blushed and turned to the fake vicar, who was clearing his throat as if he were a prudish clergyman and not the local postmaster.

The old gent read the service. When he came to the lines about objecting, Jack glared at Freddy, who shrank into his seat and said nothing.

When it came time for the ring, Jack produced the alabaster bauble he'd carried as a watch fob. The blacksmith had affixed it with prongs to an iron ring and adjusted to Elsa's glove size. The lad had done a good job, but it was not the delicate jewelry Jack would have given her had he the time to shop.

Elsa's eyes widened in delight that he'd even remembered. She was so wickedly easy to please, he dared a kiss when the final words of the ceremony were spoken.

Elsa's lush lips clung to his. As if the guests distributed a barrel of potpourri, the scent of jasmine spilled around them. After this bliss, he'd never be able to enjoy another woman again. He had to fight to prevent his arms from circling her in front of all her friends and family. She felt so right. . .

Hunt coughed. Freddy drunkenly demanded his chains be removed. And Walker shoved the fake documents under their noses, making certain everyone signed.

Elsa laughed a little breathlessly when Jack had to step away to take the pen offered.

"Stupid female," Freddy muttered as he was unchained. "You could have done better than a penniless soldier."

Jack clenched his fists, but Elsa tapped his chest and spoke before he could. "Pennies are worthless without character. I have chosen a man rich in integrity. You have signed the paper as a witness, Freddy, now go away. Tell your poor bride that we'll have you transported if you ever attempt to interfere again."

Jack slid his arm reassuringly around her waist. She felt good at his side, leaning into him with her head against his shoulder. He glared at her stepbrother. "Tell all the world she's mine. Maybe, if you behave yourself for a year or so, we'll grant you an allowance."

Elsa elbowed him. He laughed and asked Clare if she could play a waltz.

She obliged. While servants escorted a drunken Freddy to the door, Jack danced his fake bride down the aisle.

EIGHTEEN

BOTH BREATHLESS AND RESTLESS FROM THE IMPROMPTU DANCE party Jack had instigated, Elsa clung to his arm up the marble stairs. It was early yet. She hadn't fixed dinner. But her head wasn't in the kitchen as usual. Her pounding heart had replaced her wits by the time they reached the door to her new bedchamber.

A gentleman as tall, handsome, and honorable as Jack had held her as if she were precious. And he wasn't just any gentleman, but Jack, the horse-mad man she'd adored all her life.

"A pity this is not really our wedding night." He murmured the words she was thinking, sending her heart careening from her chest. He brushed a kiss across her cheek. "You make a beautiful bride."

"You're sozzled, Jack," she said with a nervous laugh, not daring to believe he meant that. But because she'd had a little too much bubbly wine, she boldly countered, "If I'm never to know a real wedding night, shouldn't we take advantage of this excuse?"

His arms wrapped tighter, and he ran his broad hand down her spine while kissing her hair, apparently not as appalled at her directness as she was. "I'd like to say I'm sozzled enough to accept, but I cannot do that to you. You deserve better than an ex-soldier with no prospects."

Logic popped her bubble. She hit his shoulder. "And you deserve better than a fubsy squab. That is not the point, Jack. This is embarrassing, but I know you're too honorable to say what I've been thinking all evening. If you meant what you said about *wanting* me, then I'm admitting the same. I believe. It's not as if I have much experience. I'd like some, though."

Blissfully, his arms closed tighter, and his mouth pressed hard onto hers, greedily taking what she offered. She gasped as his broad hand caressed her posterior, almost making her feel small. Taking advantage, he parted her lips and teased her with his tongue. Just as she thought she might expire of desire, he pulled back, studying her in the poor light of a single sconce.

"I want you," he admitted. "I've wanted you since we were both too young to do anything about it. You were always this radiant sunshine beaming into my dull gray life. I grew up in a dark cottage without a mother and only the company of two scholars who expected me to sit and study as they did. You'd ride up and lure me out like a laughing golden siren. How could I help but fall in love?"

She wrapped her arms around him and drank deeply of the masculine scent that was just him, sandalwood, and brandy. She wanted to lick him all over, to sip and taste his lips. . . and more, if she were honest. "I was a bold hussy."

He chuckled. "You were probably eight years old that first time you rode over. And you were barely seventeen and on the brink of being presented to all the glittering wealth of London when I left. I expected you to make a glorious marriage to a duke or prince. You are that lovely, Elsa, inside and out."

"You are the only one who sees it," she complained. "A few stolen kisses have made me an outcast to all society without even considering my irascible nature, unladylike habits, and peasant looks."

He laughed. "Irascible! If pounding the skulls of nitwits makes you irascible, then what am I? And any fool who doesn't see your beauty or chooses to believe Culpepper ruined you doesn't deserve the honor of your presence. It is not what society thinks that matters, you realize."

He made her heart as tipsy as her head. If she could only believe his flattery. . ."Well, if you won't act on what you say, then I cannot believe you."

He tilted her chin up and planted kisses all over her face. "I cannot treat you like a mistress. If I take you as I would a bride, we may create a child. I will not take a chance of leaving any child of ours fatherless, like poor Lavender. I want you, Elsa." He pressed her hips close to his so she could feel the hard ridge behind his placket. "And I would like nothing more than to be your husband in truth. But unless we say real vows in front of all society so the world knows my claim is official, we cannot act on pretend ones."

She was just drunk enough to lean into him and whisper, "Is that a proposal, Jack?"

He sighed and rested his chin on the top of her head. "Most likely. I just hope you have more sense than to accept one from a near-penniless soldier."

She giggled, then hiccupped. "You're so romantic. I'm keeping your pretty ring as a promise. Do not marry anyone else until I've had time to think about it."

He kissed her again, with a passion that almost had her saying *yes* right there in the heat of a drunken moment.

But he was right. She did deserve at least a modicum of respect from one who professed to love her, even if she couldn't offer herself the same. When he opened her door, she reluctantly entered her room without him.

She was definitely not bringing her disapproving lady's

maid down here to report her scandalous behavior. Kissing had been her downfall before. Drinking and kisses. . .

She touched her fingers to her lips, lifted her satin skirt, and swirled across the room.

~

AFTER THE WEDDING PARTY BROKE UP AND THE FAKE newlyweds vanished, ostensibly to dispose of their fancy dress, Hunt couldn't settle his mind to work. Dancing with Clare to Lavender's rather decent music—if his limping steps could be called dancing—had left him restive as a stallion.

Only, after everyone else departed to their rooms, Clare still scurried about, ordering staff to rearrange furniture and prepare a light supper. He knew her too well. She'd clung to him during their dance as if she belonged in his arms. So now, she was avoiding him and the attraction between them. Or so he liked to imagine.

Finally, she headed for the marble stairs. He stepped out of the shadows, caught her waist, and swept her into his study. Breathlessly, she rested her hands on his chest and gazed up at him with what he hoped were starry eyes. Jasmine filled his nostrils. Had she taken up his grandmother's favorite scent? But no, he could still smell her usual lilies and rose. He was more drunk than he'd realized.

"I want that for us," he declared. Knowing he didn't possess romantic words, especially when his brain was fuzzed, he applied his mouth to better purposes. He kissed her with intent, cradling her against him. When she responded with all the heat he felt, he used tongue and hands to physically persuade.

Boldly, he cradled her breast and rubbed at the nub beneath her silk. She gasped and went weak-kneed. Holding her up, he relented, brushing kisses against her cheek. "I don't know how to make promises when the future is so uncertain."

"Neither do I," she whispered back. "Which is why we shouldn't do this."

"I know, but it becomes harder each day to stay away. I'm a man. Action is all I know. I like to think I'm honorable, but you're tearing me apart. Tell me, if I manage to keep this manor out of the bank's hands, will you stay here with me?"

He knew that hadn't come out right when she chuckled and pushed away.

"I think I might like that, but I am not a wanton woman. You may wish to rethink your question when you're ready to ask it." She slipped from his arms and darted off.

Hunt closed his eyes and cursed. Of course. She was a lady. She expected bended knee and rings and declarations of hearts and flowers or whatever. He wasn't even certain he could bend his knee.

But she hadn't said she was leaving forever. He had time to practice.

But not enough time or money to cover the unpaid mortgage.

He strode off in search of his cousins and Walker. If he couldn't have the action he wanted, he'd settle for a different sort.

The men were all in the breakfast room, inhaling the light dinner the staff had scrambled together after the impromptu celebration. Hunt filled a plate before it all disappeared, then took a seat to settle his aching leg. "If Aloysius Smythe is desperate enough to send Elsa's brother to abduct her, who else might he send?"

That stopped any frivolous chatter. All three men took chairs, although if the ladies had seen their positions, they would have smacked them upside their heads. Hunt thought they probably should open the billiard room in the new wing for these sorts of gatherings, but food was food.

"You think *Culpepper* might have been sent to abduct her?" Walker asked, following Hunt's thoughts. Too aware of his precarious position in society, he seldom relaxed, although he leaned his elbows on the table now and pulled his chicken apart with his fingers. "That would almost say Jack learned about the plot and shot him."

That possibility always lingered, especially after watching their guest's ferocity in defending the lady.

Henri tilted his chair back, sipped his ale, and provided a different perspective. "From what I heard, there was no love lost between Frederick and Culpepper. He thought Culpepper went off his noggin after learning the bank notes were forged. And then Freddy wondered why Croesus would forge notes. Sounds as if Culpepper accused Smythe of forgery."

Hunt chewed his bread and thought about it. "Then why would Culpepper come this way? Aside from no one knowing Elsa's whereabouts, why would he even look for her? She's the only one he knew here. What other reason did he have in Gravesyde?"

None, and they all knew it.

"How would a city fop even know a provincial banker?" Arnaud straddled his chair, presumably so he could reach behind him to take food from the buffet without standing up.

"The banknotes Culpepper carried were drawn on Liverpool Bank, which Smythe is said to control." Hunt spoke his thoughts to focus them. "A London man would have drawn notes on the Bank of England, not a provincial bank on the other side of the country. So how did he come by the notes—unless he was given them for some purpose?"

"Which may mean Smythe asked for his help in looking for Elsa. But why Culpepper?" Walker broke up his bread and dipped it in juice from the chicken.

"Culpepper needed funds. Smythe is wealthy. They both knew Elsa's brother, who also needs money. If an abduction and elopement were planned, as indicated by the note in Culpepper's boot, then he may have agreed to some part in it. We need Jack down here." Hunt stood to help himself to boiled eggs and pickles.

"Ten pounds says we won't see our fake groom for the rest of the evening." Henri leaned forward to clean his plate.

"Don't take that bet. He overheard Clare order a light supper sent upstairs to the blue salon. The lovebirds are probably up there." Arnaud finished off his brother's ale rather than stand to pour more.

"Forged notes, gentlemen," Walker reminded them. "If our murder victim was running errands for a wealthy merchant, why was he carrying forged notes? I don't think he meant to entice Elsa from safety with them."

Hunt nibbled at his bread, trying to fit the puzzle pieces together. But men who had no reason to know each other or any reason to forge notes did not fit together.

"Could Smythe have planned on paying the abductors with counterfeit notes? That would make Reginald Hill and Freddy, as well as Culpepper, parties to kidnapping." Arnaud stabbed a hunk of cheese. "England has no need of blood-thirsty revolutionaries when they have skullduggery merchants."

Arnaud's English was colorful, if not always grammatically correct. Hunt returned to what he knew best, machines. Counterfeit notes required a printing press. Birmingham had more machines than any place on earth, as far as he could tell. They'd have presses. And cheap paper.

"I should inquire who produces bank notes," Henri said, as if reading Hunt's mind. "If Smythe controls the Liverpool bank, then he'd have access to better notes than those we saw."

Hunt cut up a piece of cheese while he worked out his thoughts. "Banks must have some safeguards on real notes, correct?"

Walker shrugged. "No notion. Banks don't deal with the likes of me." He pushed back from the table. "Let me fetch Gentleman Jack. If the man isn't enjoying his nuptials, we need to put him to work."

Hunt hated disturbing the fake newlyweds, but after this morning, he had a sense of urgency in discovering Culpepper's killer. There were too many connections to Elsa, and thus, to his household.

Henri bit into a biscuit and chewed thoughtfully. After washing down the bite, he added, "I don't deal with banks much since they quit handing out gold. I'm about to quit taking paper money if it's so easily copied. I surmise that provincial banks have very little control of their notes now that they're using them as currency."

"But anyone *printing* fake notes for anyone less than a bank had to know they were fake, wouldn't they?" Hunt knew more about printing than banks. "There would be a danger that the printer might announce it to the world."

At the sound of boots pounding down the marble stairs, they waited until Walker and Jack appeared. The faux groom had stripped off his tailed coat and wore only his waistcoat over his trousers. He strode to the buffet and poured a brandy. "The ladies were only serving sherry. Walker says you are discussing counterfeit notes?"

"How do banks safeguard their notes? Wouldn't it be easier to steal genuine notes than to fake them?" Hunt tapped his knee impatiently. They were going in circles and guessing. He wanted real evidence.

"Ideally, the bank would number the notes and keep a ledger. But these new small notes they're passing out instead of coins. . . I don't know." Jack straddled a chair much as Arnaud had done.

"Might the bank just order a supply of notes from a printer?" Henri asked.

"And someone intercept them? Or the printer makes some

of his own?" Jack shrugged. "The printing plates would have to be kept at the bank, but any good printer could create his own. Or possibly make a few extra notes for himself."

"The question becomes, why would a man who owns a bank bother counterfeiting notes if they're that simple to obtain?" Hunt demanded.

Jack took a sip of his brandy before replying. "One, he didn't want anyone at the bank to know how he was spending the money. He couldn't just fill out a few notes to himself and stick them in his pocket. The cashier has to sign them. Two, he didn't want to spend his own money, like any thief."

"Which leads one to wonder if Smythe is as wealthy as proclaimed," Hunt said sourly. "Or if someone else is behind all this. We've jumped to conclusions."

Henri shoved back his chair. "I'll start tomorrow morning in Birmingham, asking who prints bank notes. And while I'm at it, I'll talk about banks and the safest ones for my money."

"You're likely to be taken for a wealthy man and get conked on the head," Arnaud said gloomily.

Henri wadded a bit of leftover bread and threw it at his brother.

Before a food fight could ensue, Hunt shoved back his chair as well. "If you can discover who makes and pays for the bank's printing orders, that's a start. We also need to find out who those other people are on the notes and determine where everyone was the day Culpepper died. I don't give a damn about counterfeiters, but I don't want killers on the loose."

Having the manor turned into a battlefield today had roused his protective instincts. Men who abducted heiresses weren't just filth but dangerous villains. That their banker had traveled with the scoundrels was a warning drum Hunt couldn't ignore any longer.

He needed to ask how he might go about removing the

manor's trust from Bosworth's bank—not a great way to influence the fellow who practically owned the roof over their heads. He'd probably have to remove the executors of the trust as well.

It might be easier to dam the Mississippi.

NINETEEN

MAY 6, SATURDAY

THE DAY AFTER THE FAKE WEDDING AND HUNT'S IMPROPER declaration, Clare forced herself off the cloud she'd slept on all night. She knew the captain meant well. She was fairly certain it had been a proposal of sorts. And foolish romantic that she was, she was actually considering her answer, even if he hadn't really asked.

At twenty-five, she was on the shelf. Her grandmother's trust containing the old townhouse wasn't hers to use as dowry, except as a life estate. Given her lack of family and reduced circumstances, she had no means of easily meeting gentlemen. She was no beauty and possessed nothing most men wanted. Her novel writing would place her beyond the pale were it known. She'd have to tell Hunt what she did to earn money before she dreamed too much.

She'd long ago given up hope of love and marriage. She had always been much too aware that men might complicate her life instead of easing it, so she'd been wary.

And she'd been right—Hunt certainly complicated her

life, but not in bad ways, which confused her. She knew he had family in America and might return there any time. She couldn't selfishly tear Oliver from his family and place in society to follow him. But if they waited. . . the problem might go away. Did she want to wait?

Would her family allow her to wait? They'd be breathing fire down her back if she didn't tell them where she was enrolling Oliver. They might object if she did not return him to London by autumn.

So she organized her day to keep busy and not think too hard. First thing Saturday morning, she chased Walker and Elsa into the library where Walker could dictate the letters Elsa resisted writing.

"I would rather watch what they're doing to my oven," Elsa complained, settling into a chair.

The fake bride had taken pains with her hair, Clare noted. And instead of wearing a drab uniform, wore a normal dark blue morning gown—with a fancy apron over it. Fake marriage must be good for her.

"Your estate steward needs his orders in *your* handwriting, unless you wish to travel home to instruct him," Walker reminded her. "I can write them for you, but will he accept just your signature?"

Clare was merely here as chaperone and to keep the two of them from butting heads. Alarmed that her dangerous suitor might own the bank where she kept her funds, Elsa had said she wanted to move them, except she didn't seem to like dealing with business.

Walker had explained that moving her bank account needed to be done by the estate's solicitors. Elsa had to not only write her steward, but the solicitors, and her brother the earl, as well, warning them about Smythe and Freddy.

Being an heiress required a great deal of responsibility, Clare concluded.

They were dithering over whether to have the funds transferred to the Bank of England in London, or the Birmingham bank that was easier for Elsa to access, when a bell clamored in the main corridor.

Walker muttered under his breath. Clare shrugged at Elsa's questioning look. "Hunt repaired the bellpull at the entrance. We now all must jump like servants."

"I may pull out the bell in the kitchen." Elsa turned back to her writing. "He needs to install it somewhere I can't hear it."

The engineer was unlikely to remodel what he had repaired to the satisfaction of his methodical mind. If they wanted repairs, they needed to bite their tongues on complaints of what Hunt did of his own accord. She simply waited for Quincy to appear with his silver salver.

The butler bowed and held the card for her to take. "He says he is here about the tutoring position."

A *tutor*? Already? Finally! Excitement almost paralyzed her. Did she meet him in here? The study? Did she call for Hunt? Where was Hunt anyway?

"Which of the two tutors responded?" Walker asked, bringing her back to earth.

Clare glanced at the card. "Mr. Terrence Birdwhistle, the younger one who taught a merchant's son. He is not so experienced, but he's been to Oxford. Should I interview him here? Should I call Oliver?" Now that she had a tutor at the door, she vacillated. And her horrible imagination struck—what if he were a spy sent by Elsa's predators?

"If he is to live here, then perhaps we should all meet him," Elsa suggested, oblivious to suspicion. "I imagine Oliver will show up if he's interested."

"You are just putting off writing the letters," Walker argued.

"No, she's right. He needs to learn we do things differently here." She couldn't live in fear. Clare nodded at the butler. "Offer Mr. Birdwhistle a place to freshen up, then please bring him back and send for tea."

"This is why towns have inns," Walker said gloomily. "We shouldn't have to be a rest stop for weary travelers."

"Unless we charge them. I think Hunt is keen on that idea." Clare nervously took the tutor's letter from the drawer of the table and re-read it. Why had she thought this young man would be suitable for Oliver? Just because he didn't mention corporal punishment or strict discipline. . .

Oliver slipped in and settled under the table with a book. Fine then. Why not give a seven-year-old an opinion as well?

Clare tried to remember what she liked about her governesses, but they were a blur. Bea had always demanded all the attention. Clare had simply practiced her letters and her reading and later, idled her time writing stories and poems for which she was praised. Being quiet had been all that was necessary.

Being quiet hadn't served her well after everyone died, leaving her alone with Oliver. She should have berated his father's grieving family and demanded assistance, but she'd been too shattered to do more than accept her circumstances.

Quincy returned with a young man—much younger than she'd imagined. She studied the fresh-faced Mr. Birdwhistle as he bowed without expression upon being introduced to a black steward and a lady cook, as well as to Clare. She supposed his features were even and not unpleasant. He was more Walker's slender height than Hunt's massive one. His clothes had probably been pressed before he set out. If he'd ridden from Birmingham, they'd only wrinkled slightly. They certainly weren't of the best quality, but they were of the modest sort a tutor might afford, just a simple black waist-coat, a blue broadcloth jacket, and moleskin pantaloons tucked into worn boots. He seemed genuine.

"Mr. Birdwhistle, please have a seat." Clare gestured at a chair across from her. "Excuse our informality. We have just reopened the manor and aren't anywhere near full staff. I'm sure your prior position was more comfortable."

The tutor replied in measured tones. "City homes, of necessity, are smaller than country manors. I am comfortable with a roof that does not leak."

"We can provide that and more, I'm sure. We do not have a schoolroom, as such. We've been using this library." She gestured at the walls of shelves that continued around the corner. "The books are old, I fear."

"Would I be given an allowance for ordering new books as needed? Science changes almost daily. I have my own small library of Latin, Greek, and mathematical texts, although I daresay a child as young as your nephew will not be prepared for them yet. May I meet him?"

Clare did mental calculations on both paying a tutor *and* buying books and shuddered. She kept smiling. "When he's ready. You do understand from my letter that Oliver can be non-talkative? He reads remarkably well for his age, however, and is eager to learn Latin so that he may study the text in the scientific books he's discovered. He is unlikely to respond aloud unless he has something pertinent to say. It takes time to build his trust."

"I understand." The tutor twisted his hat. "I have a younger brother who is just the opposite. He speaks well but has great difficulty in reading. We have discovered that he memorizes and recites what is read to him, but he does not actually recognize the words on the page. It has been a challenge to teach him, but we have carved wooden letters that he can touch and manipulate, and that seems to be helping. Every child learns differently."

Clare almost expired of relief. Had her mother and Lavender had such understanding families. . . They hadn't, which was why Clare resisted listening to her family about Oliver's education. "I was hoping you might say that. Oliver is almost entirely self-taught. He likes to explore, and books are his hunting ground. Directing his inquiring mind is a challenge."

Mr. Birdwhistle beamed. "An inquiring mind is the most important part of education. If he is willing to accept me as his guide, we shall go along famously."

"What books?" a suspicious voice asked from under the table.

The tutor looked briefly startled, then scooted back so he could lean under the table. "What textbooks?" Apparently receiving an affirmative response, he listed several texts that meant nothing to Clare.

They meant something to Oliver. He crawled out on her side of the table, nodded approval, and darted off.

It seemed they had hired a tutor. How much did textbooks cost?

And how did one determine if he might be a danger to their heiress?

JACK WOULD RATHER BE ANYWHERE THAN IN HIS DULL CHAMBER, working over codes. But he needed to stay away from Elsa in the kitchen. Since Elsa's groom had the horses in hand, he had little else with which to occupy himself. Perhaps he should have gone with Henri to the city to make inquiries about printing presses and banks, but he disliked leaving Elsa unguarded.

While he pushed numbers and letters about, he pondered improbable futures. Hunt didn't know if he could keep this manor. It had become little more than a hunting box, in any event, with little arable land attached.

Jack needed pastures to raise horses. His father's income was dependent on leasing out the lands of his small estate, and Jack's brother would inherit it, so he could not rely on their help. He needed his own land to make his dreams come true.

Aside from her wealthy dowry and allowance, Elsa held only life interest in her home, one of her late father's lesser properties. Villiers probably wouldn't object if Jack rented the Newchurch pastures and stable. Elsa certainly wouldn't.

He let the knowledge that Elsa wanted him the way he wanted her warm his otherwise cold thoughts. He hoped he hadn't misunderstood. She might just be bored, and she certainly had few men for comparison.

He found he didn't care. He was a practical man, not a romantic one. They were both old enough to know their minds. He'd known he wanted Elsa for ten years or more. That would never change. He thought Elsa had the integrity to honor marriage vows even if she didn't love him.

Only, he had little to offer beyond his pride. He simply could not accept living off her wealth. He had money enough to buy land or horses, not both. She owned both plus whatever dowry her father had left her. She didn't need him.

If Smythe was after her dowry, it had to be substantial. Jack couldn't live with his conscience if he took so much with so little in return. She could do much better than him.

Which was why he was concentrating on the code related to her grandmother's portrait, hoping he could at least be useful. The dowager possessed the ruby pendant, but the painting also depicted a glittering diamond necklace, earrings, and tiara, interspersed with garnets. From the size of the diamonds alone, the set would be worth a land grant or two.

If the earl hadn't disbursed the gems prior to his death, Jack assumed they would be part of the overall inheritance to be distributed like the manor, should they be found.

He glared at the scribbles on his paper. He couldn't fit the code into any directional words he knew. Perhaps they had some significance to the language in the deeds or the map, although if the damned earl had buried the jewels in the orchard he'd planted, they were as good as lost.

In hopes of disproving that theory, Jack took the codes downstairs to the library where Hunt had set out the survey map of the property. He was surprised to find Oliver and a stranger in there, poring over textbooks. He hoped the man was known to the captain. They didn't need more of Smythe's minions spying on them, learning the wedding was false.

The library stacks continued around the corner, so he rolled up the map and took it to the windowed area overlooking the wild forested side of the hill. Bushes had overgrown the windows so the light was meager, but there was another table he could work on.

Given the size of the manor's library, perhaps the code referred to a place on the shelves? The index with its large bookstand had been moved to this back wall after Hunt had set up his magnifying lamp on the other table. Jack flipped through the index pages, looking for a combination of numbers and letters that might match the code.

Clare slipped in from the connecting door to the study. She held a finger to her lips and hid around the corner from the main stacks, watching Oliver and the stranger at work. She sighed in evident frustration and came to look over his shoulder. "The tutor must communicate as silently as Oliver. I never hear them talking. Are you looking for a particular volume?"

He showed her the combination of letters and numbers he worked on. "I am working on the painting codes. I thought perhaps if the earl was such a reader that he collected this immense library, he might have used it as the base for his code. But I'm not sure I even know where to start."

She frowned at the index. "A letter could mean an author or a subject or almost anything. The numbers could be a page or a shelf or. . ." She waved her hand helplessly. "Why would anyone go to all this work to hide what they evidently wanted to pass on?"

Jack turned to the subject index under E. "From what little I've gathered, Lady Reid had access to the family jewels directly after she married the viscount, but she left them behind when she ran off to France, correct?"

"That's what her journals lead us to believe. We think she warned the earl that his dissolute son meant to sell or pawn the jewels and told him where she hid them. We have only her word for this. When she returned from France with an illegitimate daughter, her husband was dead, and the earl cut her off, so she had no access to the jewels. After he died, she was selling her pearls to keep a roof over her head, so we assume they were no longer available."

"The viscount mortgaged this property for funds after she ran off, which says he no longer had access to the jewels, or he'd have pawned them. So either she hid them well or the earl collected them and stuck them in a vault." Jack counted down the lines corresponding with the numbers in the code under the E subject header, read the title, and went in search of the shelf.

"I don't think Lady Reid had those codes scratched into the paintings. She never mentioned doing so." Clare frowned. "It sounds more like the action of a troubled man, not a woman desperate for her marriage and subsequently, her life."

"I've given little thought to their mental states." Jack pulled down a volume, flipped through it, and shrugged. "No hidden letters or carved-out pages."

"You're a man. If you were the earl, your only heir died, and you'd just released the entail on a fortune in jewels and property, what would you do? I need to return to work instead of spying on Oliver. Let me know if you hear anything unusual, will you?" She retreated through the study door, leaving Jack to his boring work.

If only that had been Elsa. . . he wouldn't have got a bit of work done. With a sigh, Jack returned to the index to look up authors under E. Or maybe the numbers indicated shelves and not the index.

Who had commissioned the index? Most likely the earl. Chances were good that when the earl sold off or gave away all his properties, he moved their libraries to these shelves. Had the library always been designed this way? Or had he built the wall that now cut off the study and offices from any windows, so he could expand the library shelves for his collection?

Jack wasn't much of a reader, but he worked his way through several shelves in different locations. It didn't take a lot of looking to see the newer volumes had been purchased during the earl's lifetime. The older ones may have belonged to previous earls. What did that tell him? Nothing, except that no one had bought books since the earl's death. Even if the viscountess was a reader, she'd been French and poor. Books in English would not be her choice of entertainment.

Of course, believing the code led to the library could be just a wild hare leading him astray. He still needed to study the survey map.

He counted down the lines under authors with names beginning with E, found the title, and checked that shelf. Still nothing.

He ought to install his father in here. Jack simply didn't have the patience for playing word games.

Glancing out the vine-covered windows, he decided the uncleared area left the manor open to risk. An army could ride up that forested hill and who would know? If he meant to protect Elsa. . . He set aside the books and went in search of a means to clear the undergrowth.

Maybe later, he'd ask around a bit about pasture land. He was dreaming, he knew, but it gave his head a better use than banging it against bookshelves.

TWENTY

AFTER WRITING TO VILLIERS AND HIS SOLICITORS ASKING TO MOVE her accounts out of Smythe's bank, Elsa took out her frustrations on dough. She'd like to check on her horses, but the manor's kitchen staff was still too new to be reliable. She needed to train her young assistant, Anne, as she had the one on her estate.

Of course, that would take a decent stove. She wondered if Hunt had spoken to the blacksmith about replacing the cracked top. Or if she'd have to go without until he designed some fancy thing she'd have to learn how to use like the Rumford.

She carefully instructed Anne on how to present the cold luncheon on the buffet. Then, determined to learn about the stove, she took off her apron and left Lavender's grandmother to oversee proceedings. The old lady didn't get up much from the table, but she knew when a pot boiled or a sloppy job was done.

The new staff was learning to work together. Perhaps, in a few weeks, she might leave them for longer periods. Of course, should she ever find a cook who could cook, she might pretend to be the heiress she was and play all day.

That didn't sound very appealing. Climbing the service stairs, intent on changing into riding clothes, she wondered exactly what she would do if she wasn't cooking. Nursemaids took care of children. Grooms took care of horses. Ladies were singularly useless. What did Clare do all day? She was always scribbling in her office. Spending the day writing letters was not appealing.

When Elsa reached the ground floor hall at the back of the house, Meera called to her from her infirmary. She stopped in to see what she needed.

The apothecary was shorter than her, but with her dramatic black hair stacked on top of her head, and wearing a swirl of colorful shawls and gown, she seemed to stand taller.

"I've ordered a few ingredients that I cannot grow here." Meera stood behind her work table. "I'd like to begin creating solutions that require mixing over heat. A fire can't be regulated in the same way as a stove. Is there any chance that I might use yours in the evening, after dinner? After Hunt rebuilds, of course."

"We should talk to Hunt about what we need. My Rumford would have enough space for anything, including bottling, but the stove that caught on fire. . . Might not be as useful as you imagine."

Meera frowned. "I've never had more than a small coal stove. Perhaps I could find one and. . ." She glanced back at her coal grate. "It might heat the room a little better."

"We should ask the captain. It would be nice to know when I can cook decent meals again. Do you know where he is?" Elsa lifted her skirt, prepared to hunt him down.

Meera grimaced. "Probably under the house, building his coal retort. Since it's difficult for him to see in the dark with his one eye, he's determined to give us lighting."

"Then why don't you talk to Walker and have him pin down the captain? I was planning on riding into the village.

Perhaps I could talk to the blacksmith and see if he has any ideas."

Meera brightened. "Since I don't earn my keep around here, I didn't want to ask. But if you want to know, also, then I won't feel as if I'm demanding it for myself."

"You saved Jack! A physician is *invaluable*. Do not say you don't earn your keep. Demand a fancy stove of your own!" Elsa hurried off to change clothes, her purpose more defined. If Hunt wasn't working on a stove, then the blacksmith must be.

The village market was unlikely to have much left at this hour. The mail had already been taken to town. She was foolish going to the trouble of taking out her horse, but if a lady couldn't do as she wished, what was the point of everyone recognizing her as a lady? She might as well be a servant.

She hadn't minded being a servant, hiding in the kitchen when it had meant she was safe and well occupied. But now. . . she had Jack and this small family of friends, and she was no longer alone and frightened. She ought to see how an heiress lived.

With a chaperone, of course, she realized as she called for her horse, and her groom saddled up as well. Learning Jack had taken out her stallion, she tried to persuade Hank that she didn't need company, but the captain had laid down strict orders. She'd have to have a word with him.

Although, she ought to be grateful that he was looking after her as her own family had not. She simply wasn't used to being held to propriety.

Or, given circumstances, the captain might simply fear another abduction attempt. If so, she was grateful for his thoughtfulness and supposed she ought to rein in her impulsiveness and learn caution so she didn't add to his burden. Only, with Freddy and Smythe out of the way, she wanted to experience true freedom.

The hilly manor drive was too rutted and steep to let the mare have her head. She should learn what lands belonged to the manor so she could have a good gallop one of these days. She'd seen a lot of unplanted fields when she'd come in from the west.

She assumed the lane going east would eventually take her to the London highway. That had been the direction from which Jack had arrived. She was tempted to ride that way to see if there was pasture, but her groom would protest. With a sigh, she turned west toward the village and the blacksmith's shop. This had all been priory land and belonged to the earls once, the captain had said. The bank now claimed the village belonged to them.

The manor at the top of the forested hill on her right was invisible from the road. Even if trees and undergrowth were removed, the rocky incline would never be pasture.

What looked like various vegetable gardens straggled through the field on her left. Perhaps she could learn who owned those and buy her vegetables directly rather than wait for market days.

Just as she reined in to examine the garden rows, a shot rang from the hill. Her groom shouted, and the mare startled. Elsa instinctively ducked against her horse's neck, holding the reins and kicking into a gallop. The explosive percussion of a second shot rang past her head. The shooter was good, if she was his target. If she hadn't halted when she had. . . Two weapons? Or two people? They'd need to reload.

She didn't wait for her groom's pony to catch up. The woods flashed by as she raced toward the village. Spotting her stallion near the blacksmith's shop, she aimed for the run-down stable beside it. Jack came running out of the shop just as she dropped to the ground.

"What the hell, Elsa?" He grabbed her in both arms, and she realized she was shaking like a willow leaf.

"Shooter." Rather than melt into his arms, she clutched his

muscled strength and tried to peer over his shoulder. "My groom!"

Grimly, he shoved her behind the stable wall and ran out into the yard just as she heard the pony riding up. No more shots were fired.

No more hiding. Furious, she lifted her skirt, peered into the yard, and seeing the lad holding his shoulder and barely controlling his pony, she dashed out, mouthing the curses she'd learned at her stepfather's knee.

"'Tis only a graze, my lady," the groom insisted, resisting Jack's offer to help him out of the saddle. "We need go back and look for the rogue."

Elsa glanced up at the forested hill looming over the village and shuddered. Had someone come down from the *manor* to shoot at her? Or had it just been a poacher? Now that it was over, she was reluctant to believe anyone would deliberately aim at her. But two shots. . .

Jack all but lifted the poor lad from the saddle. "Neither of you are going anywhere. The scoundrels have had time to reload. We need to bandage you up and return you to the manor where Meera can take a look at the wound."

He already had his handkerchief out and glanced over his shoulder at Elsa. "Stay in that stable," he shouted.

In his tall boots and form-fitting, tailed jacket, wearing his top hat, Jack towered taller than tall. She could imagine him in scarlet, shouting orders and wielding a musket and bayonet. But this was Jack. He didn't scare her.

She produced her handkerchief and added it to the one he was using to staunch the flow of blood. The boy had grown pale and wobbled unsteadily. "Not until you carry Tim into the stable too. He needs to sit down."

"That could have been you!" Jack shouted. "I heard the shots, but I had no idea—"

"He was a-shootin' at my lady, sir. Ain't nothin' flyin'

overhead to shoot at." The groom reluctantly took the weath-
ered bench inside the stable.

The shots had come from up the hill, of course. A poacher
would have been aiming at creatures on the ground, not over
the road, unless he was shooting geese. Elsa didn't know
whether to weep or look for a weapon. Helplessness was not
her strong suit.

"Rifle and pistol." She removed her neck scarf and handed
it to Jack.

His eyes widened a trifle at the flesh she revealed, then he
respectfully looked away to tie the bandage to the groom's
shoulder. "Explain how you know," he said gruffly.

Jack had seen far more of her when they were young. Not
embarrassed, Elsa adjusted her riding coat to cover more of
her shirt. "If I was his target, the degree of accuracy was too
close for a fowling piece or musket."

"Not a poacher." With the bandage secured, Jack reached
for her again, holding her close. "Bastards. Why you? It
makes no sense."

She buried her face in the smooth fabric of his coat. "They
may come for you next, if they believe we're married in truth.
I had no idea I'd—"

He shook her a little. "We don't know anything. We need
to fetch help, but I can't leave you alone. They could still be
out there. I didn't hear a horse."

"Let me ride back, sir," the groom said. "I ain't hurt that
bad. I can ride, but I can't fight."

Jack shook his head, then gave it a second thought. "The
road is dangerous. Take the back door and run up the path,
it's shorter. They can't watch the road and the path at the
same time."

The boy nodded, and looking almost as grim as Jack,
slipped out the back of the stable, and into the woods. Meera
would tend him, so there was one person safe. Elsa slumped
on the bench, mind racing with no conclusions.

The sound of hammering in the shop stopped, and a moment later, the young blacksmith emerged from the forge, wiping his hands. "Summat wrong, sir? I've got the bit done you wanted."

Jack waved him back to his shop. "A poacher. We've sent a lad up to the house. Stay inside until we're sure he's gone."

The young man nodded, frowning, but returned to pounding on his anvil. Elsa supposed there was very little a blacksmith could do unless the shooter revealed himself.

She started back out to fetch her stallion, until Jack caught her arm, glared, and strode out to do the same. The horses were too valuable to be left as targets for roaming shooters. She'd simply never had any man place her above himself.

Refusing to give in to her fluttering heart, Elsa set about calming her mare while Jack brought the stallion inside. The familiar action of rubbing down the mare's coat gave her thoughts time to catch up with her fury.

"First, they tried to abduct me, and now that they think I'm married, they want to kill me? Does that make sense?" she asked as Jack calmed the stallion.

She didn't think she'd angered anyone enough to have them actually shoot her. Shout at, mayhap, but *shoot*?

"Unless someone just thought to use any passerby as target practice, then we must assume it has to do with you— or your wealth," Jack reluctantly acknowledged. "I'd have thought they'd aim at me, though."

Elsa grimaced and rested her brow against the mare's neck while she processed that. "Since you know we're not legally married, I can assume you're not shooting at me for my inheritance. That rather leaves Freddy, doesn't it? Surely he's not foolish enough to believe I left him anything?" Despising herself for it, she wiped at a tear.

He didn't reject or accept that possibility. "One assumes Villiers doesn't need your funds badly enough to kill you for them. Would your mother inherit any of the trust?"

197

"The trust is all mine to do with as I choose, with the trustees' approval, of course. I had to make a will and every-thing. If I die, the funds simply pass as I instructed. They insisted I have a clause about spouse and children, but other-wise, it all goes to charity. Villiers has never been in need of funds, and my mother has her own." Elsa clung to the mare as her knees threatened to give out under her.

Someone meant to kill her? Why? It wouldn't benefit anyone, would it?

She gasped and caught Jack's coat. "I left a rather large sum to the village church, but no one should know that, should they?"

The vicar knew where she was.

~

AT WALKER'S SHOUT, HUNT CLIMBED OUT OF THE CELLAR. Emerging into the gray day, he saw Arnaud galloping away—not a good sign. Walker had his horse saddled and a rifle in hand. Definitely bad news. Hunt slammed the makeshift door over the cellar entrance before Walker even spoke.

"Shooters shot one of the grooms. Meera is with him now. The boy claims the lady was the target, and the culprit or culprits are in the woods below, near the village. He left Lady Elsa and Jack hunkered down at the blacksmith's shop." Walker nodded in the direction of the drive. "Arnaud's gone down to stand guard until we know the shooter is gone."

Cursing, Hunt scrubbed his filthy hands on his trousers. "Go down with him, please. If Jack's there, anyone trying to reach the lady will think twice about going through the three of you. Are we certain she's the target?"

"Lad thinks so. He's pretty descriptive." Walker swung into the saddle and rode off.

Walker hated horses and shooting, but he knew how to do it.

Clare hated shooting worse. Hunt hurried across the yard to reassure her that bandits wouldn't storm the house.

In full terror mode, his co-general paced the entry, holding a fire iron. Was it a good thing that this insane asylum was teaching a proper lady to defend herself?

Quincy stoically waited with her, not another soul in sight.

"We thought the gallery windows might be dangerous. We've sent everyone to the kitchens for tea." Clare wrung the poker anxiously. "How do we catch a madman?"

"*You* don't." Taking the poker away and handing it to Quincy, Hunt wrapped her in his arms, despite the dirt and spiderwebs he sported. "I'll need to talk with the groom, but this isn't a mad housekeeper we're dealing with this time. If Jack sent for help, then it's a situation he can't handle on his own. The shooter is probably already gone, but let's not take chances. Go down to the kitchen and keep everyone calm. Sing songs, eat luncheon, anything. Just don't let anyone outside until we tell you the danger is past."

He winced at an additional thought. "Is your new tutor with them?"

She nodded against his shoulder, then pushed back, still looking terrified. "Mr. Birdwhistle and Oliver are in the kitchen, but the grooms are saddling up. They mean to provide an army for your disposal."

Of course, they did, an army of young boys and grizzled old men who wielded whips. Brushing a kiss across her hair, Hunt limped for his study shouting, "Quincy, Adam, guard the main doors."

He kept his thoughts to himself—he'd have to count heads to be certain none of Elsa's army of grooms was the shooter.

He opened the armory cabinet and offered weapons to the two large guards Clare had appointed as butler and footman. They declined firearms and produced bludgeons from inside their coats. They left for their posts, silent and dependable.

Rather than the ancient hunting equipment in the cabinet,

he loaded his own rifle and pistol and added a pouch of ammunition to his pocket before heading to the stable yard. As he feared, he found the grooms arming themselves with whips, pitchforks, shovels, and any tool they could find. Some were already on their ponies, but there weren't enough mounts.

None of them appeared to be carrying firearms and none appeared to be missing.

Hunt directed the grooms with ponies toward the main drive. "Station yourselves far enough apart to cover the drive. Shoot a warning if anyone approaches."

As they raced off, he turned to the others milling in the yard. "We'll do the same on foot along the path. If the shooter is still in the woods, he has to escape one way or the other, and we'll have him."

Hunt signaled Ned, the deaf-mute boy he'd first hired, and directed him to a station between the drive and path. He gave him a musket to fire in the air as a signal.

While the ponies vanished down the drive, he led his foot soldiers to the walking path. It was rough and steep and fit only for excellent riders. But desperate men did desperate things. Hunt didn't want to believe anyone from the house had walked down here to shoot at Elsa, which meant he had to assume both man and horse hid among the new spring leaves and undergrowth.

He positioned the lads nearest the house and took the rest of the path to the village himself, knowing the road was the best escape route. He kept his eyes and ears attuned to horses hidden in the overgrown vegetation. Walker and Arnaud would safeguard Jack and Elsa and have the sense to ask in the village about strangers. They'd alert him if anyone rode off.

Until then, Hunt had to assume he had a potential killer on his grounds. He'd ask questions later. For now, he was pure soldier, scouting the woods as he'd learned to do.

Instead of staying on the path, he slipped into the shadows of the trees, grasping tree trunks to keep his limping steps light.

The widest area between walking path and carriage drive was at the bottom, near the lane, over half a mile of babbling brook, scrub, and decades of untouched forest. Whoever had originally landscaped the manor grounds must be turning over in their graves.

Landscaping had been the last thing on his task list. He might have to rethink that if thieves and killers took up residence.

There, in the bushes, a hint of silver and restless movement. Hunt whistled, a high-pitched bird call that Walker would recognize.

Stepping quietly with a bad knee had its difficulties, and he was a large man. He couldn't avoid brushing branches as he approached the horse. He could see movement that indicated it tossed its head.

A moment later, he heard a low curse and crashing through the undergrowth. He readied his rifle. With one eye, he wouldn't have an accurate shot unless he was in close range. "Halt or I'll shoot!" he shouted.

A ball rang wildly over his head. Hunt raised his weapon in that direction. When a horse tore through the whipping evergreens, Hunt shot high, fearing his one-eyed aim might harm the animal. He heard a grunt and curse, but he was too far away to shoot again. The animal wasn't a thoroughbred by any means. He could only glimpse a gray tail and the rider's brown coat before they vanished down the footpath.

Shouts echoed up from the village, but he couldn't run fast enough to lead the action. Instead, he limped back to the path. He sent the first groom dashing back to let everyone know the shooter was gone. There was nothing else they could do. He turned toward the village to learn what he could.

He could hope Arnaud or Walker might have set out after

the scoundrel, but they weren't soldiers, and their task was to guard the lady.

As Hunt reached the footbridge he'd rebuilt a few weeks ago, Jack raced past on Elsa's powerful stallion. They must have heard his whistle and been ready. Jack was far behind the shooter but had the better horse. Hunt didn't allow himself much hope. Jack didn't know the countryside. The other man might.

Would someone *hire* a killer? Why?

The manor path emerged halfway between the general store and the smithy. Mr. Oswald, postmaster, shopkeeper, and fake vicar, emerged from his doorway at sight of Hunt. "You be hunting your dinner, captain?"

"No, but someone else may have been. Did you see who just rode out?" Hunt was grateful he no longer needed a cane to stay upright, but his damned knee ached like blue hell. And his inability to hit a target as he once had irked. He might have been curter than he should have been.

Oswald didn't take umbrage. "Gray palfrey. Wasn't a gentleman. Old coat and hat, shabby boots. Poacher, no doubt, but in the clear light of day? Bold, sir."

Not if the poacher's quarry only came out in day. Hunt nodded and set out to the smithy. Arnaud and Walker emerged from the shadows of the stable, leading their mounts, waiting for orders.

It almost made him feel as if he were back in the army again. Who knew that commanding troops led to protecting estates?

"Take the grooms and search the woods. Make certain he left no one behind," Hunt ordered as he approached. "How is the lady?"

"Telling the blacksmith how to mend the stove," Arnaud said dryly. "It was the only way to prevent her from taking our rifles and going after the culprit herself."

"One female who takes the defense, the other the offense.

Heaven forfend, that women ever form their own military. Is it safe to escort the lady back to the house while I placate the smith?" Hunt needed to see what was being done anyway.

Lady Elsa emerged from the smithy wiping her hands on a rag. "I should have gone with Jack. He's not had time to build up his stamina, and I know my horse better."

Hunt tried not to laugh. The top of her head didn't reach his shoulder. She wore a bulky split skirt, and no doubt rode side saddle. He settled for a more polite reply. "What weapon would you use?"

"I'd scream the reprobate off his damned horse." Without an ounce of ladylike grace, Elsa pulled herself up on the thoroughbred Arnaud led out and flung her leg over the saddle horn, quite an acrobatic feat for a small woman. "I'll go into London tomorrow, be out of your hair. If Freddy is behind this, I'm shoving him into the Thames."

"That wasn't your brother. And we don't know for certain that you're the target. And if you'll consent to stay inside until we understand what's happening, you'll be far safer with us. So quit being ridiculous. Tell the lads to bring down the pony cart so we can haul your stove up to the manor. Plot a good dinner." Hunt had spoken to the blacksmith earlier. Except for a few fine details, the stove ought to be ready.

The lady cook looked momentarily lost and uncertain, then turned her mare to the drive where Walker was instructing a small army of grooms. Arnaud rode behind, rifle in his arms.

An artist shouldn't have to bear arms, but Hunt knew his cousin had in defense of his estate and his country. A man did what he had to do.

Instead of building bridges for armies, Hunt had to load a stove into a cart, then climb that miserable hill on a bad knee. But Clare would be waiting for him, so he had an incentive to hurry.

TWENTY-ONE

MAY 7, SUNDAY

"SUNDAY SHOULD BE A DAY OF REST," CLARE MUTTERED THE DAY after the shooting incident.

After their morning prayer reading, she'd ushered Elsa into her office to discuss what meals might be best served on the staff's half day off.

They'd all been shaken by yesterday's violence and needed time to sort themselves out. Particularly Elsa, which was why Clare had asked her in here. Since Hunt and the blacksmith had taken over the kitchen with the stove installation, this was a quiet escape.

"Should we ever have sufficient help and organize ourselves, the scheduling won't be quite so bad." Unusually quiet, their lady cook scribbled another idea on her menu list. She'd garbed herself in a cap and enormous apron again, blending in with the staff.

Clare now understood the uniform was a type of self-protection. How horrible to have to have lived that way most of one's life!

"You will be staying?" she had to ask. She was coming to rely on this distant cousin but understood Elsa had a thousand reasons to be anywhere else except here.

Elsa sighed and dipped her pen in the ink. "I want to, but I don't want to endanger anyone. If only I understood *why*. . . I was so hoping the pretend wedding would stop the problem."

"We cannot even know if the shooter recognized you! All we know for certain is that the shooter rode a gray palfrey and vanished between here and the city. He may have been a madman who shoots people for fun or a thief who wanted your horse. How is Jack feeling after yesterday's bruising chase? He hasn't harmed his health, has he?" Clare jotted notes of supplies.

"Meera gave him some strengthening potion. Maybe it would be better if she hadn't, and he had to take to his bed." Elsa slashed at an item on her list and wrote another. "He is furious that he lost the scoundrel and won't sit still. He's examining all the horses to be certain they didn't come to harm, as if Hank and the grooms couldn't do it."

"Jack strikes me as a man who would rather be doing anything than sitting still. Is he still thinking of joining Wellington? Surely he's done enough for his country and should be considering his own future."

"Men are a mystery," Elsa said grumpily. "He has always wanted to raise horses for the carriage trade. I have no understanding of why except that he loves the animals and is good with them. I've offered my land, but he insists he must do it himself. So my estate is operated by men I don't know and adds coin to the earldom's coffers, as if Villiers doesn't have enough funds to waste."

"Men don't want to be like women, reliant on others for our welfare. I can't say I blame them." Clare glanced up at the ringing of the front doorbell. "Who would be traveling on a Sunday? I've had no correspondence from any of our family."

She and Hunt had both sent letters to everyone on the family tree announcing that the manor belonged to all. Very few had responded.

Oliver darted past the door with Lavender's puppy on his heels. The tutor had agreed to keep him in hand as much as possible, but her nephew had a mind of his own.

The color departing her cheeks, Elsa rose. After yesterday's events, she had a right to be fearful of visitors.

"I think I'll see how the stove progresses. Even if it isn't ready, I believe we should be able to put together dinner." She left down the back hall, away from any arriving guests.

Clare ran over a mental list of people who knew how to find the manor and couldn't think of one who might be arriving on a Sunday. Surely bankers and lawyers and the like took the day off?

With Hunt in the nearly inaccessible crypt, Quincy inevitably turned to her. After picking up the card on the salver, Clare wished she could dash down to hide with Hunt or Elsa. But this was definitely her guest.

How had her Aunt Martha and Uncle George found them out here? They lived in Hertfordshire, didn't they?

Worse, *why* were they here?

"Take them into the great hall, please," she told Quincy, hastily rising. "Have Mr. Birdwhistle find Oliver and clean him up."

Quincy looked dubious, rightfully so given Oliver's habits. "Yes, madam. Shall I have tea sent up?"

"If it can be managed without a stove." Clare called up some of Meera's curse words. They wouldn't have decent biscuits or anything else prepared. She could only offer the remains of the cold luncheon. Her aunt would be proved correct in her condemnation of Clare's ability to care for Oliver.

For Oliver's sake, she needed to prove to her father's family that she was a proper lady, raising the only heir in a

THE MYSTERY OF THE MISSING HEIRESS

proper household. She glanced down at her ink-stained fingers and grimaced. At least, she was wearing her Sunday best.

Courage, she told herself, sailing down the dark corridor. She understood why Hunt wanted lighting through these halls. With no windows, the flickering oil sconces provided little illumination, even at full noon. She pondered the difference in oil cost versus coal just to keep from fleeing in terror.

She stopped in the family parlor to check her hair in the mirror over the fireplace, tucking a few pins in place, and adjusting her fichu. She pinched her cheeks and bit her lips to give them color and wished Hunt were upstairs. Or maybe not. One glance at his piratical features, and her aunt might fly away.

That's when she halted in mid-step. Her countrified, unsophisticated relations might have an aristocratic heritage, but they would gape in horror at almost *everyone* in this household. Even Arnaud, who was a comte, would have them worrying about French spies and degenerate artists. Her father's family possessed limited world experience, which was why they seldom visited the city. The unfamiliar frightened them.

Clare had to turn her fear around and consider her guests instead of herself. This didn't have to be war. She could simply reassure her family that Oliver was receiving the very best attention, in the very best of circumstances.

Right. Because she was so very persuasive and convincing.

Judging from the voices down the corridor, Lavender had already discovered the guests and had set out to entertain them, like the good hostess she aspired to be. At least Clare's relations didn't realize the girl was the illegitimate daughter of a maid and the late earl's grandson.

With its lofty cathedral ceiling, the formal great hall could not be adequately heated unless it was packed with people.

Adam had set the fire alight and pulled back the draperies to allow in the meager sun.

Tea hadn't arrived. Her aunt and uncle sat stiffly on the brocade sofa while Lavender occupied a side chair. Her uncle stood up at Clare's entrance. A stout man, still sporting a full head of graying hair, he was the younger son of Hertfordshire nobility and dressed formally, if not in the latest fashion.

Plump, with streaks of gray in her dark hair, Aunt Martha had not been blessed with children of her own and seemed always to wear a sour expression.

"Uncle George, Aunt Martha, what a pleasant surprise!" Clare tried to imagine herself as heiress to an earl's grand estate—which she was, even if it was only a small share—and conducted herself accordingly. "However did you find us amid our rural grandeur?" She offered her hand to her uncle and kissed her aunt's cheek, remaining relentlessly cheerful.

"I have told them all about how our modern new stove is being installed, and that we are on meager rations until then." Lavender grinned impishly, knowing she was whitewashing the truth. "Perhaps if Lady Elsa cares to join us, the staff will work faster."

Clare hid her grin. In her expensive boarding school, the adolescent had walked a fine line between her wealthy, entitled fellow students and her uncertain background. She knew how to embellish and disguise and distract.

"Lady Elsa is busy at the moment. Let me have a nice coze with my family. It's been ever so long." Clare took another wing chair near the sofa and waited expectantly for her aunt or uncle to answer her question about how they had found her.

Her uncle merely looked stern. Her aunt eyed Clare's best dress critically. Lavender had added ruching to bring it into fashion. The bodice was a trifle daring for the country and the silk was an extravagance for day wear, but it was Sunday, the one day of the week she dressed as a lady should. The staff expected it of her for the meager prayer services she offered, and they dressed in their best as well. They needed their own chapel and clergyman.

"Your solicitors had to tell us you were no longer in town," Aunt Martha finally said coldly. "We stopped to visit, and strangers occupied your mother's house."

"My house, now," Clare gently reminded her. "Had you written to tell us of your visit, I could have warned you. Since you have not visited since my father's death, I had no notion that our whereabouts concerned you. My apologies."

Tea arrived. Clare held her breath as clumsy Betsy rattled the silver tray and china in lowering them to the table. Betsy was more creative than graceful, but she'd been practicing. She dipped a curtsy without falling over and managed to depart without a comment on the guests or the fact that it was her day off.

As Clare poured the tea, hoping the ritual lessened any uneasiness, she continued. "I do hope all is well, and this is just a friendly visit."

Uncle George cleared his throat. "We would like to see Oliver."

"Of course! I have already sent a message to his tutor." Oh, how she loved saying that. The shocked expressions on her aunt and uncle's faces fed her courage. "But lesson plans on Sunday usually involve the outdoors. Have you come all the way from London just to see him?"

And not her, she noted, wondering once again why they were suddenly so interested in his education. She'd spent these last years attempting to engage both Oliver's families in his upbringing, without success.

"As I wrote to you, it is time he began school," Aunt Martha said stiffly. "He is heir to several family fortunes. He needs to make the connections that will put him ahead in the world."

Clare sipped her tea and, rather than say what she was thinking, tried to read between the lines.

Lavender scooped up her puppy and fed him a biscuit. "Oliver is only a little boy! Do you know how awful those boarding schools are?"

Clare didn't know whether to bless the girl or send her out of the room. Reluctantly, she chose the latter. "Miss Marlowe, why don't you see if you can help Quincy locate Master Oliver?"

Using their formal designations instead of the informal ones they'd adopted served as warning. Lavender's eyes widened. But ever adaptable, she rose and curtsied. "It was a pleasure to meet you, Mr. and Mrs. Knightley."

She swept out in a rustle of crinoline, looking more lady-like than Clare ever would.

"A lovely young lady," her aunt said grudgingly. "Your solicitors said that all the earl's family inherited?"

"Very strange," Uncle George said, picking up a biscuit. "An American saying females can inherit. Suspicious, if you ask me. You shouldn't be here."

Ah, another inkling of their purpose. Clare nodded politely. "I assure you, my father's solicitors have gone over all the documents thoroughly. I have spoken with Lady Spalding and Lady Lavinia, the late earl's granddaughter and daughter, who have also had their heirs and solicitors verify the earl's decision. It is strange, admittedly, but legal."

"We don't know these people," her aunt whispered. "Why could you not stay in town where you belong? Renting your mother's house out to strangers, indeed!"

"My house," she reminded her aunt again. "And the rent pays for Oliver's tutor."

"The Wycliffe Sapphire was intended for Oliver's education! Your mother mentioned it specifically for that purpose. Girls do not need school, but Oliver does." Aunt Martha set her empty cup down with a crash. "Since it is apparent that you will have no daughter to wear it, it seems reasonable to sell it now."

That was a cruel thrust. Her family had firmly placed her on the shelf. Clare attempted to keep a pleasant expression while wondering why the subject had come up at all. "The sapphire was part of my mother's dowry. Father refused to sell it. I would like to treasure it by keeping it in the family for as long as possible. Oliver's father left him very little to call his own." Except for a hoard of raw gems, but she refrained from mentioning that.

Aunt Martha looked triumphant. "Viscount Owen has agreed to pay for Oliver's schooling provided he performs well and that *we* oversee his education."

The viscount, Oliver's great uncle on his father's side. Clare didn't have time to process this before her nephew arrived, polished and tidy, in the company of Mr. Birdwhistle.

Her aunt exclaimed over Oliver while her uncle remained stiff—and a little uncomfortable? Clare couldn't help but fear there were undercurrents she was missing. But then, her mind was a fertile field for imagining trouble when there was none.

Oliver bowed politely and didn't dive for the biscuits. When asked what he was studying, he glanced at his tutor, then rattled off the name of textbooks. Their visitors could only gape and nod knowingly. The titles were well beyond anything Clare had studied.

Surely they could not complain about his education now?

Before Oliver could crawl under a table or hide behind a drapery, Clare passed the biscuits and sent Oliver and his tutor on their way. She almost closed her eyes in relief that this part of the visit had gone so well. The tutor's arrival couldn't have been more timely.

That was why she was caught completely unprepared when her uncle announced, "We are setting Oliver up as my heir and requesting that his guardianship be transferred to us.

Lord Owen has agreed that it would be in the best interests of all."

A gaping maw opened in Clare's midsection. They wanted to steal Oliver? How could she possibly fight all the men in his family?

And then her imagination kicked her cowardice out the door. *Or did they want the Wycliffe Sapphire?*

TWENTY-TWO

MAY 8, MONDAY

ARNAUD SET THE PORTRAIT OF CLARE'S GRANDMOTHER ON AN easel in front of the gallery windows so Jack might study the sapphire.

Clare's relations had spent the night and departed without ceremony this morning. Clare had immediately threatened to pack up Oliver and hide. Hunt had insisted there were better solutions. Jack didn't know what they were, but he did know a little about gems. He'd halted the shouting match by dragging Clare in to study the portrait. Hunt, of course, had followed.

"It would be better if I could see the sapphire rather than trust an artist's eye," he explained. "Where do you keep it?"

"I've only seen it once, when my sister was presented. Grandmother Clarice always kept it in a bank vault with some smaller jewelry I never have occasion to wear." Clare paced up and down, pretending to look at the other oils Arnaud had been working on.

Jack studied the gallery lined with portraits of Reid ances-

213

tors. Clarice? Clare was named after her grandmother. Didn't he remember Elsa once telling him the eldest daughters were all given similar names? Elsa's mother was Elena. He strained to remember—he thought her grandmother was Eleanor. Interesting but not relevant.

In the portrait, Clare's grandmother appeared delicately built, like Clare—average height but slender-boned. Jack gauged the size of the gem by picturing it on Clare. He shook his head at the number he arrived at and shaved it down a little. The sapphire was still huge.

"You might want to consider having it cut down into smaller stones," Jack suggested. "If the artist accurately represents the size and color, then my guess is that this is a coveted Ceylon sapphire. It may have once adorned the crown of a king. The size is rare and adds to its value, but wearing an egg around your neck might be backbreaking, and finding someone willing to pay the price. . ." He let that thought dangle.

Clare returned to study the gem. "I haven't seen the jewel in years. It seemed enormous when Bea wore it, and she was larger than I am. I doubt that I could gain an audience with royalty to see if they'd be interested."

"Neither would your relations," Hunt reminded her. "If they're after the jewel, how do they plan to sell it? Would anyone in your family have access to royalty?"

"Royalty couldn't afford it," Jack warned. "They'd confiscate it. Your instinct to keep it for the sake of your nephew's heritage is sound. There might be a duke or two who might be interested in buying it, if they'd like to attract attention to themselves, but why should they? With a war going on, you're unlikely to find foreign buyers. You would have to advertise it in an exhibition, have the news sheets write it up, and generate greed. I suppose you might write a few wealthy people to see if there's interest before you do anything drastic."

"Why would your aunt and uncle suddenly be interested in a gem now when they showed no interest before? Especially when it does not belong to them?" Elsa had just slipped into the room to study the portrait.

Jack tried not to be distracted, but she wasn't wearing her servant's uniform this morning, and her fichu could not completely hide her generous cleavage. He had to focus on the painting and force his body not to react, rendering him incapable of speaking.

"I think you might want to have your solicitors make a few discreet inquiries, Clare." Hunt was already heading out of the gallery. "If your uncle's income is primarily agricultural, he may be having monetary difficulties."

"If we could find the pearls that make the necklace in the portrait, we might sell those and help them out." Fortunately, Clare didn't sound serious.

"Anyone who places money over a child's well-being doesn't deserve a ha'penny. I'm glad the porridge was cold when they finally came down this morning." Elsa swung around to follow Hunt out.

Leaving Jack with nothing to do again but figure out the painting's code and hope to find the pearls.

"Jack," Hunt called before he exited. "The hounds arrived this morning. Would you be interested in taking a look at them? I don't have a trainer yet."

"I can do that." Relieved to have a purpose, Jack left Clare glaring at the painting. Tired of being treated as an invalid and still furious with his inability to stop a shooter, he gladly aimed for the stable.

He felt like a damned flat for letting a palfrey beat him, but the rider must have known the land. He'd almost caught up with his quarry until the palfrey had galloped around a curve and vanished. The area around the river was a wilderness of rocky cliffs and sheep pasture crisscrossed with deer paths, weedy lanes, and no discernible habitation. The shooter could have been hiding in the brush, laughing at him as he raced past.

Unfortunately, the few villagers who had seen the stranger hadn't recognized him.

He ought to just join Wellington as he'd planned, but he couldn't leave while Elsa was in danger. The dogs gave him some small purpose. If he could train them to follow human scent. . .

Outside, he studied the pack enclosed in a stall. He knew horse flesh better than dogs, but he understood animal training. If the animals were to be another layer of protection around Elsa, they needed to be brought up to the mark quickly. Studying the six-month-old puppies, Jack whistled at the enormity of the task.

Hank, Elsa's head groom, ambled up. "Pretty, ain't they? The captain plannin' on running a hunt?"

"Elsa might if foxes go after her chickens, but no, I think the captain intends them to guard the estate. I can probably teach them to heel and stay, but we'll need to find someone capable of teaching them to flush out intruders." Jack crouched down to scratch behind long ears, dodging whipping tails and puppy claws.

"Heard of a fellow over toward Stourbridge might be lookin' for a place, but he's not likely to come cheap." Hank scratched at his grizzled jaw.

"We can ask the captain if the maintenance budget allows for security measures. Just feeding this pack won't be cheap. And they'll need their own kennel." Jack snapped a lead on the little fellow climbing up his leg.

"Teach 'em to hunt rabbit," Hank suggested. "They feed theyselves."

Jack feared the ladies might object to that suggestion, but what they didn't know. . .

He had taken the puppy on a circuitous route of the gardens and drive and was debating asking Elsa if she knew any recipes for dog treats when Henri's cart wobbled into the stable yard.

The Frenchman had the staff trained. By the time the peddler jumped down from the seat, grooms poured from the stable, and servants emerged from the house to help him unload. At sight of Jack and the hound, Henri grinned and came over to introduce himself to the dog.

"You name her yet?" He rubbed the puppy's ears and had her wiggling in delight.

"There's half a dozen of them. We can call them Girl One and Girl Two and so forth." Jack was privately naming them after women and officers he'd known but assumed that wouldn't be acceptable.

"Better than Le Beetch One and Two." Henri laughed, following Jack's thoughts. "Don't let the ladies make pets of them if they're to be guard dogs."

"I'd rather have a good wolfhound to terrify intruders, but foxhounds are apparently cheaper." Jack crouched down to pet the pup. "Did you bring back any news?"

Henri glanced at the servants unloading the cart and nodded at the manor. "Let us talk with Hunt."

That sounded more ominous than hopeful. Jack took Girl One back to her pack, brushed himself off, and entered the manor through the garden door. Elsa was hurriedly emerging from the kitchen stairwell, still wearing her apron and cap.

"How's the new stove?" Jack offered his arm, hoping to entice her closer, if only for a moment.

She raised her eyebrows at the formality but accepted his offer. "It is a thing of great beauty. Instead of just repairing the old stove top, they've added extra space for two pots that can be lowered into the fire to cook faster, and a smaller oven next to the large one. I am experimenting."

Jack drank in her scent of vanilla and lavender and allowed himself the brief joy of having her brush against his side as they hurried toward the library. He didn't know how much longer he could torture himself like this, knowing she might accept his proposal but unable to work out how to support her.

If he faced a lifetime without her, he may as well succumb to temptation for a while longer. A jasmine scent floated briefly around them, as it often did. The maids must use the tropical fragrance for their polishing cloths.

Clare was settling Oliver and the tutor into her sitting room/office as they passed, apparently having removed them from the library.

"This must be serious," he murmured as she joined them in the hall.

"Not necessarily. We're all just nosy." Clare clipped along at a good pace, forcing Jack and Elsa to hurry. "And we need to start working out how we pay ourselves for all the work we're doing. Henri makes a small profit on the supplies he brings, but his time and effort should be worth more, Walker says."

Half the household appeared to be carrying in boxes and crates, cooing over the contents or digging through them for supplies. They didn't seem interested in a meeting.

"The budget is large enough to pay Henri?" Jack couldn't imagine servants' wages would be enough to live on— although the manor provided free room and board.

They arrived in the library before Clare could answer. Hunt was already seated, reading documents with his magnifier. He didn't bother standing as the ladies entered. They didn't object. Jack settled Clare and Elsa together.

Jack wasn't an heir and didn't belong here, but no one objected to his presence, so he stayed. Instead of sitting, though, he moved the library index to the end of the table where he could listen and work on the code at the same time. He had started hunting with Elsa's code, but after the contretemps with Clare's family, he'd switched to the code in her grandmother's painting to see if it gave him any new ideas.

"We should probably start with Henri's information, since I assume that's the only reason any of you bothered to stop what you're doing for a meeting." Hunt set aside his paperwork and dryly studied them with his one good eye.

"It doesn't mean much to us," Henri warned. "But I'm afraid it means a lot to Lady Elsa."

Jack wished he'd sat beside her. Her long turquoise eyes widened, her lips tightened, and he knew she was squeezing her hands together under the table.

When she said nothing, Henri continued. "I made inquiries about Aloysius Smythe and his bank, as well as about any counterfeit notes circulating, and so forth. I talked mostly to factory buyers and the like, not the gentlemen owners."

He waited a moment, giving Elsa time to question if she wished. Jack respected that, but he wished the Frenchman would just spit it out.

"Keeping in mind that rumor and gossip mean nothing without evidence. . . Word is that Smythe is nearly insolvent. His creditors are circling." The genial peddler looked uncomfortable repeating this.

"He needed to marry me for my money," Elsa concluded for him. "I always assumed that. Surely there are other wealthy women more eager for marriage than I."

"Should I call in Walker?" Hunt asked abruptly. "Is this a financial discussion?"

"Ultimately, I fear so, but I doubt Walker can elaborate on rumor." Henri waited as a maid hurried in with a tea tray.

Jack didn't want tea. He wanted to know what Henri didn't want to say. But he didn't have the right to speak up, so he silently worked his way through the index, using the letters in the code and tracking them to the shelves. The code on Clare's painting contained a C and an S. The code on Elsa's contained an E and an R.

Something clicked, and he stared at the codes as Henri continued.

"Word is that counterfeit notes are circulating on the Liverpool bank. We've seen them for ourselves. Since these are not small notes, men have been demanding payment from the bank, only to be told they're not legal tender." Henri sipped his tea.

That distracted Jack from the code. He thought thunderous curses and couldn't resist expressing what Henri appeared reluctant to say. "So if the rumor is that Smythe is bankrupt and Smythe controls the Liverpool bank, then they are assuming the bank is insolvent also."

Elsa gasped. "My funds may be gone?"

TWENTY-THREE

ELSA HAD NEVER SWOONED IN HER LIFE, BUT SHE FELT PERILOUSLY close now. She dug her fingers into the table to hold herself upright. *Her trust was in the Liverpool bank.* Her grandmother had been friends with the owner and no doubt helped him establish it. She had never for a moment. . .

Jack deserted his search to place a steadying hand on her shoulder, and she took a deep breath. It couldn't all be gone. Her steward would have said something, surely.

"If the bank is foundering, Smythe would want control of your funds so you wouldn't be aware of the state of affairs," Jack said coldly. "I'll shoot the bastard for that alone. But it doesn't necessarily mean the funds are gone, just that he didn't want you to do what you've ordered your solicitors to do. Yours is most likely the largest account. If you pull your funds, the bank may collapse."

Henri nodded. "There have already been a few attempts to withdraw large sums. They've been refused, which encourages the rumors. It might only be a temporary problem. Smythe has enemies who might be encouraging the rumors. But it does not appear to be a nest you want all your eggs in."

"If Bosworth and Smythe are working together, must we fear the manor's trust is in jeopardy?" Hunt asked.

Elsa clutched her hands. It was only money, she told herself. She had a home. She didn't need much. But the manor. . . She took another deep breath and stayed silent. Panic and impulse did not serve her well on practical matters.

"If solicitors are in control of the manor's trust, might they be persuaded to move the funds given this information? The economy isn't strong. Dividing up the monies might be wise." Jack sounded far more rational than Elsa felt.

She took courage in that. Next to her, Clare was nearly crushing her teacup. She had her nephew to worry about. Elsa only had her horses.

Hunt tapped a pencil on the table as he thought aloud. "The funds aren't all in cash. I know they're mostly invested in local companies. Smythe's various businesses may be among them. The solicitors and Bosworth will object to losing control of those investments. I will write to Lord Spalding, ask if he will speak as our representative in requesting that the trust be moved."

At Elsa's look of puzzlement, the captain explained, "My aunt, the dowager marchioness of Spalding, owns a share of the manor. Her stepson, the current marquess, assists us in some matters."

Ah, bringing in the authorities, she understood. She had never been interested in money so much as what she could do with it. Ask her about the church roof or feed for her horses, and she was fine. Investments, not so much.

Jack squeezed her shoulder and walked away. She wished he wouldn't. But she knew what he expected. "I've already asked Villiers to have my funds removed from Liverpool. He has an interest in those. I'm not sure how much interest he will take in this manor, since he's not an heir, but I can ask."

Returning to his end of the table, Jack pinned his gaze on Henri. "Elsa had someone shoot at her on Saturday. Might

Smythe be desperate enough to keep her accounts by having her killed?"

Everyone gasped at his bluntness, including Elsa, even though she had reason to believe that money was the only reason she was of interest to anyone.

Henri blanched and stared across the table at her. "Someone *shot* at you? While I was in town?"

She couldn't go to her kitchen and bake a cake to sweeten the mood. Instead, she got up and pushed open the door to Hunt's study, where she knew he kept his brandy decanter. She returned with the bottle and added a sip to her tea, then pushed the bottle across the table to Henri, who reached for it.

"Jack, you're driving the lady to drink," the captain complained over his coffee. "Perhaps we ought to let the ladies return to their pursuits."

"Balderdash," Elsa said, taking a fortifying sip while sorting out her thoughts. Retreating to her kitchen was no longer an option. She couldn't hide any longer. "Smythe is too stout and lazy to shoot me. If we have a killer in the woods. . . Henri, did you ask about the whereabouts of all the suspects in Mr. Culpepper's death? It's far more likely there is something nefarious happening with those bank notes."

Henri appeared almost relieved at the change of topic. "I did. Since Culpepper's body was found on a Tuesday two weeks ago, we're assuming he died on that Monday at the latest, judging by his condition." He glanced at her apologetically.

Elsa waved that away. "I've seen dead animals. I know about decay. Asking the whereabouts of people two weeks ago is a problem, I understand."

"Except you English have a strange holiday called St. George's Day, and it was that Sunday." Henri pulled a notebook from his pocket and sketched out a calendar.

"That's right." Ever restless, Jack looked over his shoulder.

"I left London after the holiday, stayed the night on the road Monday night, and found Culpepper on Tuesday."

"People remember where they were on a holiday. And remember who wasn't there when they should be." Henri flipped the page in his notebook.

Elsa held her breath. Would the same person who shot Culpepper also have shot at her? It had to be related to the bank funds, didn't it?

"I couldn't go all the way to Newchurch," Henri explained, "but I spoke to a merchant from there who was in town buying supplies. He said your stepbrother, Mr. Turner, celebrated the holiday at your estate but left shortly after, since you weren't home."

"Freddy was nosing around? I disappeared for a *month*, and he was just finding out?" *Two weeks ago.* The vicar hadn't found her until Friday. Her brother had arrived on the following Monday, more than a week after St. George's Day.

So even though Culpepper carried a banknote with her brother's name on it, he had *not* told Freddy of her whereabouts. The vicar most likely had. He'd been traveling to Bath. Freddy's new home was in that area.

"If Freddy was in Newchurch on St. George's Day, he was most likely too far away to have murdered Culpepper here— unless he knew where to find him and rode directly to meet him after the celebrations." Jack frowned at that possibility.

Henri continued. "The merchant mentioned that the vicar was in Newchurch for services Sunday morning, but he was also called away from the celebrations that afternoon. He was gone for a week or more after."

"He didn't show up here until Friday of that week," Clare said, frowning. "I remember because that was the day I. . ." She hesitated, then added defiantly, "The day I received a cheque."

Elsa wondered why that was a memorable occasion and why Clare might be defiant about it, but now was not the time to question. "The vicar said he'd been hunting for me, most likely because Freddy had set him on it. But if they didn't know where I am, why would either of them ride all night to shoot Mr. Culpepper, then not show up here until a week later?"

"If one of them was in on the plot to abduct you, they may have arranged a meeting with Culpepper for after the holiday." Jack had returned to examining bookshelves, pulling down volumes to flip pages, then shoving them back. "If Freddy was part of the plot, he must have been shocked to discover that you had flown the coop when he traveled to Newchurch to grace you with his presence."

Elsa winced. She would scarcely believe anyone wished to abduct her. . . except Freddy had tried. And he was far more likely to have known citified Culpepper than the rural vicar, who no doubt sincerely believed he was doing a good deed by looking for her.

Freddy must have been in a right panic. How much was he in debt to the bank? "And where was Mr. Smythe?"

"He was in Newchurch for the holiday but was gone by Monday. His assistant, Mr. Hill, was not with him over the holiday. Neither of them was at the factories on the Monday Culpepper was killed." Henri tucked his notebook back in his pocket.

Searching for her in panic at her absence? That must have been most upsetting to their abduction plans.

"They may very well have been at the inn on the way to Liverpool, waiting for Culpepper to produce an heiress," Hunt suggested. "But they all should have realized by then that Elsa had vanished."

"Except Mr. Culpepper learned where she was," Clare reminded them.

"And that got him killed? That doesn't make sense if he was part of the kidnapping plot. Nor does the counterfeit banknotes hidden in his saddle." Jack pulled another book

225

from the shelf but glanced at Henri. "I don't suppose you saw any of our suspects in Birmingham on Saturday, while Elsa was being shot at here?"

"According to all reports, Smythe has been in Liverpool lately, dealing with the bank situation. Hill was running the factory in Birmingham. Elsa's brother and the vicar don't normally frequent Birmingham, so I'm unaware of their situations. Is there anyone else?" Henri finished his tea.

"Bosworth," Hunt suggested. "He generally manages to stay the night here when he travels to town. But if he's shooting at Elsa, one assumes he wouldn't dare stop."

"I visited the Birmingham bank, but I doubt I would have seen him if he were there. I don't imagine we frequent the same places. Oh, I asked the bank about printing presses and talked to their printer," Henri recalled. "The Birmingham bank uses the same one as the Liverpool bank. I showed the printer one of the counterfeit banknotes, and he said he'd be ashamed to produce such poor quality. He suggested a press that was just starting up, but there was no one there the two times I stopped by."

"This detection business isn't very satisfying," Hunt complained, pushing back from the table. "Birmingham is too large. I wouldn't even know where to start asking for physicians who may have treated our shooter."

In the process of rising, Henri stopped. "Treated the shooter? The one who shot at Elsa? He was injured?"

That was the first Elsa had heard of it as well. She wished to return to her kitchen to think about all this, but if Hunt had shot her assailant. . .

"I think I at least grazed him. My aim is bad, but I thought I heard him grunt after I shot. Apparently not enough to keep him from riding away." Hunt spoke with disgruntlement as he stood up. "There was a time when I'd have knocked him off the horse."

"When I inquired at the factory, Reginald Hill was

wearing one arm in a sling wrapped around his chest, as if he had shoulder trouble," Henri stated flatly.

"Is there a way to find out if he rides a gray palfrey?" Jack demanded, slamming a book back on the shelf and looking ready to murder.

"The vicar does," Elsa said, wanting no more than to lay her head down on the table and weep. "He keeps a small horse for visiting. It's not quite gray but close enough."

"We need *evidence*," Hunt roared. "I can't throw anyone in the dungeon because of their choice of horse or drunken stumbles."

He stalked out. Clare hurried after him.

TWENTY-FOUR

"Bankrupt!" Hunt paced his study in a fury. "Bloody damned bankers bleeding the country dry. . . And using helpless women to cover it up!"

Clare had followed Hunt into his study. She took a chair in hopes he might sit and rest his leg. The world as she knew it was spinning. Once, she would have turned to Meera for sensibility, but her friend would be as devastated by the loss of the manor as Clare. Carrying a child meant Meera shouldn't be fretting over whether bankers might steal their home.

Hunt was a rock they could rely on, she prayed. "My uncle is suing to have Oliver's guardianship taken from me. I had hoped living here, with family and a tutor and men like you would influence the court in my favor. But if we cannot even count on the trust. . ."

She didn't dare finish. She didn't know how she could hide Oliver if she lost the suit.

Hunt offered a strained smile. "If all it takes is a man to convince the court, then you have me. But without the manor and the trust, I'm not much of a bargain."

He'd made a similar offer after the fake wedding, but she

wasn't a foolish romantic child any longer, hearing wedding bells in every pleasantry. She reacted only to the part she knew he meant.

"You are a far better man than my uncle will ever be! I do wish you'd appreciate your talent and intelligence more. But I am fully aware that it's our unexpected inheritance, meager as it is, providing this harbor of safety. If you leave. . ." Her mind was in too much turmoil to contemplate it.

"I would take you and Oliver with me if you would agree, but therein lies the rub, doesn't it?" Hunt leaned back in his chair, crossing his strong, capable hands over his broad chest. "I think you'd find your uncle's estate better for Oliver than my parents' small home. I have no place to call my own."

Clare forced down her concern to stare at him. "You'd take us with you? To America? Why? If you have no place of your own, you don't need a co-general."

He chuckled and his smile seemed almost fond. "And you think I underestimate myself? You are far more than a bossy housekeeper. Had I any right to do so, I'd happily make you my wife. I thought I'd made that clear."

Oh. Clare rubbed a blush forming on her cheek. "I don't know how I could have missed such a romantic proposal."

She didn't react well to surprises. The faint scent of jasmine she associated with the countess wafted around them, distracting her enough to continue more reasonably. "Did I not know you so well, I'd send you away with a flea in your ear for your unromantic offer. But I know you're not after my home or meager trust or even my family's connections, because I don't think you're even aware that they exist as more than a nuisance."

He shrugged. "I know you have family because we share the same ancestral connections, even if the bloodlines don't match, for which I thank the heavens. I am not much impressed by earls and viscounts, however. And I suspect your tiny townhouse would seem even tinier with me in it.

Add Walker and Meera, because they rely on us even if they won't admit it, and your walls might explode."

She nodded, relieved that he understood. They *needed* the manor. Whether or not they needed each other was a topic for another day. "As do your cousins and Lavender. We cannot lose this place. Just think of all the staff we've hired with promises of a home!"

But that brought them right back to the problem of Oliver's guardianship.

Before Hunt could speak, a light knock interrupted and the door burst open.

Frowning, Elsa held a packet of mail and waved an open letter. "I don't know what to make of this. It's from my mother."

Hunt sorted through the mail she placed on his desk. Donning her spectacles, Clare took the letter Elsa handed to her. The stationery was expensive and scented. The scrawl still crisscrossed to avoid extra postage. She tried to find any relevant passages but her eyes almost crossed with the words.

Elsa grabbed it back. "Sorry, she abbreviates to cram in words she doesn't need if she'd bother editing her thoughts." She skimmed until she found the passage that apparently had her concerned and read it aloud.

Oh my dear, Freddy just told me about C. so sorry. C. came to me with an urgent message for you, so I fear I told him about the manor. Naughty girl, running away like that. He was trying to mend his ways.

"I'm fairly certain by C, she means Culpepper." Elsa shoved the paper into her pocket. "What do you make of it? Culpepper was trying to mend his ways? How?"

"An urgent message for you?" Hunt wrinkled his forehead and rubbed his temple. "Wouldn't that have been important enough to relate?"

Elsa threw up her hands. "No one tells my mother anything they don't want shared with the entirety of civiliza-

tion. The part about *mending his ways* seems of more importance. Culpepper gambled. He took wagers on any ridiculous
thing. Kissing fat Lady Elspeth at her first ball was one of
them that he won. But if he gave up gambling, what would
that have to do with me?"

"He wanted to apologize?" Clare asked in doubt, putting
her spectacles back in her pocket. "Although that is scarcely
urgent." Then she got angry. "*Fat* Elspeth? I do wish someone
had coshed him over his fat head. It is a shame that ladies
cannot demand satisfaction and shoot the insulter. Your
brother should have."

Elsa shrugged. "De Villiers is ten years older than I. We
shared a father, but we were never close. He was newly
married at the time and had no part in my coming out, other
than providing the funds. He is far too sensible to do
anything so foolish as to fight a duel."

"A young gambling man wanted to carry an urgent
message to you." Hunt interrupted their gossip. "It seems
your mother is telling us Culpepper asked for your direction.
That does not necessarily mean he knew you'd vanished, just
that he wished to speak with you. He had fraudulent
banknotes in his saddle and a message about a possible
abduction in his boot. How does this sound like a man who
wanted to make *amends*?"

"But remember, someone shot him on his way here," Clare
added. "He may have been coming to warn Elsa and the
kidnappers found out."

"How would they have found out?" Hunt demanded. "Do
we need to call in Jack?"

Jack had been in London at the same time as Culpepper.
But that was the only connection Clare could see.

"He's still working in the library." Elsa pushed open the
panel connecting the rooms. "Jack, did you speak to anyone
in London who might have known anything about me? Or
who may have known Culpepper?"

Jack entered carrying a slim volume. "I had to consult Clare's solicitor to find her direction. I stopped to see my tailor. I stayed at my club. I may have mentioned heading to Newchurch to visit my father, but I doubt anyone present connected that with you. I would most likely have planted Culpepper a facer had we met. Why?"

Elsa handed him the letter. "Because Culpepper left London at about the same time as you, presumably with a message for me. Hunt thinks he meant to abduct me. Clare thinks he may have wanted to warn me about Smythe, and that was why he was killed. My mother may have guessed my whereabouts, but that does not explain Culpepper's *urgent message.*"

Jack squinted at the letter, turning it around to read the crosshatching. "I never saw him and heard no rumors about any urgent matters. If anything, I expected to find you in Newchurch when I visited my father, after I stopped here to give Oliver his inheritance. I may have mentioned visiting Newchurch, and I asked directions for Gravesyde, but I cannot see how that relates to Culpepper."

Hunt glowered and bounced a magnifying glass. "The question remains, *why* was Culpepper seeking Elsa? It seems central to the motive for his demise."

Impatiently, Clare interceded. "Take it one step at a time. One, Culpepper learned from Elsa's mother that she might be at the manor. Two, the manor is only a slight detour on the way to Newchurch, where the note in his boot indicates the assignation was to take place. Three, he was carrying counterfeit banknotes made out to himself, Elsa's stepbrother, Reginald Hill, and unknown rogues, drawn on the Liverpool Bank. Four, after Mr. Culpepper's death, Mr. Hill and Freddy came here personally to abduct Elsa, claiming she was affianced to Smythe. Five, Smythe might be in financial trouble and Elsa's funds might be involved."

She held up her hand before anyone could jump in. "Ergo,

if Culpepper had an urgent message for Elsa, it most likely had to do with the abduction and notes drawn on a bank she's known to use. He may have come to abduct her or to *warn* her. If we are to believe this letter, that might be how he was mending his ways."

"And someone shot him." Jack flung the letter back to the desk. "We laughed at his parents claiming he was a good man, but he might have been trying to make amends. If we accept that theory, who knew that he was about to expose the plot?"

That left them no closer to uncovering a killer. It only made Clare sorry they'd not treated Mr. Culpepper's grave with more respect.

While Elsa folded up her letter again, Jack held up the book he'd brought in. "I might have a clue to part of the code. I was just about to look for Walker or Arnaud."

~

THE ARMY WAS SIMPLER, HUNT MUTTERED TO HIMSELF AS HIS troops scattered in search of Walker and Arnaud.

He'd just proposed to Clare. He thought that's what he'd done. She hadn't run screaming from the room. She hadn't accepted either. But then, he probably hadn't posed it as a question. Maybe there was a book in the library about romance.

Apparently, there was a book about codes. He'd rather have one on how to convict criminals and transport them anywhere but here.

While the others chased a dream of treasures, Hunt considered going back to the cellar to pound on the coal retort. Using his hands didn't require straining his one eye. It was work he understood and could finish to enjoy the result. Eventually. He still needed to run gas lines.

Grumpily, he slit the seals from the letters Elsa had

brought in, starting with the one on the stiffest paper. He was unfamiliar with the escutcheons of nobility and couldn't differentiate them from any other seal. He had to glance at the signature to determine the writer.

Lord Villiers, Elsa's half-brother. She must have been so distracted by her mother's letter that she hadn't noticed since it wasn't addressed to her.

The note was brief and alarming only in that it might mean they'd lose their excellent cook. The earl meant to stop to see his sister on his way to visit their estate. Why? Elsa had said they weren't close. *Damn.* Hunt doubted the visit was a good thing, but he'd at least be able to speak to the man directly about Elsa's situation.

If the earl was a man of business and not an arrogant fop, Hunt might even discuss the lack of law in an exclave so distant from the seat of power.

Which meant he ought to at least apprise himself of what books on law might be at hand. If nothing else, he could learn about guardianships for Clare's sake.

He'd like to have some notion of how to deal with a shooter should they ever catch him. He'd ask the earl about that. Might as well make use of the turmoil the arrival of nobility would create once the women found out.

Oliver and his tutor had returned to the library while the adults conferred over Jack's notes on jewels. Hunt removed the index to the back table overlooking the rocky hillside on the west side.

Someone had cleared the vines and shrubbery off two of the windows. Lo and behold, he had light. He could see down the forested hill.

The highway to the city was about a mile downhill on this side, across a river at the bottom. It was a good defensible position for the original priory. Did monks need forts? Presumably, since King Henry must have had the priory sacked.

Hunt appreciated the brighter light as he worked his way around the shelves.

The library's organization was fairly decent. He found all the law books in one section. In school, he'd studied with Walker, but their interests had taken divergent paths. Walker preferred dollars and cents, pounds and shillings. Hunt preferred practical applications of geometry and calculus.

Law had little to do with mathematics of any sort. He'd have to ask Walker if he was interested, but he had a notion that Walker's spare time was being spent with Meera and learning measurements for her potions.

The books were old, but Hunt assumed the law did not move with any great speed. He'd ask Mr. Birdwhistle the best place for buying newer volumes. He settled into an old leather chair by the window, put his lame leg up on a stool, and began flipping pages.

He didn't notice when Oliver and his tutor left the library. He did notice when they appeared outside the window, traversing the narrow cleared space between the manor and the woods. The early May day was bright, and they had availed themselves of the luncheon buffet because they carried knapsacks.

Hunt felt his stomach gnawing and set aside his book to see if Elsa had had time to create anything interesting. Since they had no formal luncheon hour, the meal was generally cold. Cold foods didn't give a cook a large palette to create with.

He could tell the buffet had already been raided. He put together a plate of ham, cheese, bread, and an assortment of relishes and what appeared to be chopped cabbage mixed with a sauce. English food tended to be bland, but Elsa usually produced at least one spicy dish for his sake.

He'd prefer to be sharing his meal with Clare. What would it be like to spend the rest of his life with a woman of her character? Not simple, assuredly, but he enjoyed a challenge.

Walker and Meera wandered in before he'd finished. Hunt didn't comment when Walker assisted Meera into a seat and filled a plate for her. She babbled on about some experiment she was working on, while Walker listened as if she held the secrets of the universe. His valuable steward would be learning to be a pharmacist next.

Hunt supposed it was inevitable that someday their interests would divide, but he missed having someone to bounce his ideas off of.

Meera finally wound down and turned her attention to Hunt. "If they find the jewels, might their value be applied to the manor's mortgage as a way of dividing them up between the heirs?"

Hunt hadn't given the fantasy much thought. "I'd vote for that. I'm not sure all the heirs would. Or the executors. They may insist the gems be included in the maintenance trust, which can't pay debts."

"He that finds, keeps, doesn't apply?" Walker asked. "Jack and Arnaud are working hard at decoding those portraits. They'd deserve some reward."

"I'm fairly certain that old proverbs don't apply to English law," Hunt said dryly, pouring a cup of coffee from the cooling pot. "Although. . . since there was no specific reference to jewels in the late earl's will, we might play fast and loose with anything we find. I didn't report that diamond the maids swept up when our previous butler shot a vase. Jack said he'd look into selling it. I was just intending to put any monies in the household account."

"What if. . ." Meera hesitated and gestured deprecatingly. "I know I'm coming from the perspective of someone pursued for a valuable book. But what if the rumors about the jewels are leading others here to search for them? Perhaps thieves thought Elsa knew something and that is why she's hiding here?"

"Why would an heiress need jewels?" Walker scoffed. "Now, if the *tutor* thought we knew something. . ."

"Or the shooter thought they could hold her hostage until we handed over a treasure?" Even Meera sounded dubious.

"You've all been talking to Clare." Hunt finished his coffee and stood up. "Speculation is useless. Catch the shooter. Then we'll have the answer."

But the idle discussion left Hunt uneasy. The tutor had arrived the day of the shooting. Oliver was with him now, climbing down a hill that led to a highway.

Hunt wasn't imaginative and didn't waste time conjuring trouble, but he went in search of the boy anyway.

TWENTY-FIVE

JACK WAS IN THE GALLERY, CROUCHED DOWN IN FRONT OF ancestral oils, comparing notes with Arnaud, when Oliver burst in shouting, "Soldiers!"

The quiet boy actually yelling startled him more than what he shouted about. It wasn't as if Napoleon might invade rural nowhere for a picnic in the woods.

Arnaud startled more. Having been imprisoned in some of France's worst dungeons, he didn't hold soldiers in high regard.

The slight tutor entered with less fanfare. "Master Owen, explain more clearly, please."

Now that he had the attention of a roomful of people, Oliver settled down to more cautious speech. "Soldiers in our woods."

He beat a hasty retreat, leaving the new tutor to explain to an audience of seamstresses and artists. They waited with interest.

"We were studying geology and botany on the western hillside," Mr. Birdwhistle said, almost apologetically. "I am unaware of the manor's boundaries and was about to turn around when Master Owen's sharp ears heard movement on the other side of a ridge."

Jack pictured the landscape out the library window. He'd been staring at it more than the code books, thinking he ought to explore. Except exploring wasn't productive—or so he'd thought. But his brain kicked in now. Soldiers in the woods. . . men who knew how to shoot. . . required investigation.

"To the north?" he asked. "On lower ground, near the highway?"

The tutor thought about it. "Yes, I believe we were angling northward, where the slope is less steep. I'm unsure of the highway. We only took a quick look. We saw tents, a few men around a campfire."

"Uniforms?" Jack asked, already heading for the door.

"I'm unfamiliar with the various regiments," the tutor admitted. "We saw a few scarlet coats, but they did not seem to be in full military dress."

"Discharged," Jack said curtly. "Not everyone returned for a second bout with Boney."

Not everyone could.

He understood soldiers far better than books and paintings and codes. He glanced around at the unsurprised workers. "Anyone else aware of the camp?"

One of the seamstresses shrugged. "We get beggars, poor souls. Didn't know where they was from."

When no one else added to his knowledge, Jack strode out. Gathering up his hat and gloves, he headed for the stable, then hesitated.

As far as he was aware, no bridge crossed the river on the west side of the property. But it had been past that curve in the highway where the river and highway parted ways that he'd lost the shooter.

A camp needed water.

He met Hunt coming around the kitchen garden and heading for the stable, rifle in hand.

"Oliver told you about the camp?" Jack asked.

Hunt nodded grumpily. "I was headed down on foot when I realized I should follow the river and not break a leg climbing over cliffs."

"I suspect they're discharged soldiers with no place to go. The military makes amputees and alcoholics but doesn't provide for them. I thought I'd climb down the hill, see how far they are from the manor."

Hunt grimaced but nodded agreement. "Probably the shortest route. I'll take a couple of the grooms and a few hounds, explore from below. I need to learn the property lines now that the weather has improved."

"The hounds are a good idea. I'll take one too. Elsa left some biscuits in the stable we can use for rewards." Jack didn't like carrying firearms if the men were simply homeless, but with a shooter on the loose. . . He went back inside and armed himself before setting out.

Keeping the hound on a leash, Jack let it sniff for a path on the rocky hillside. Girl One instantly located a faint deer trail. He suspected over the years the manor sat empty, poachers had depleted the game population. He could scarcely blame a man for feeding his family, and the earl hadn't been too concerned if he never fenced in the estate or hired a bailiff.

Jack had a good sense of direction, but he wanted to scout the layout of the terrain. Once he reached an observation point, he tied the hound to a limb and climbed a pine. Discerning the direction of the river where it diverted from the highway, he decided the slope was navigable. He saw no evidence of trespassers.

He'd studied the survey map and knew the estate ended at the river on the west side, the village in the south, and at the creek on the east. But this northern back part with the gradual slope and distant river had no clear physical delineation like a wall. He couldn't declare trespass without a marked boundary.

Climbing down, he unhooked the hound and scrambled through the bushes on the downhill slope.

He caught sight of the camp's sentry at the same time the man saw him. They both lifted their weapons to their shoulders in an armed position and watched each other warily. The dog yapped and waggled his tail.

"Heel," Jack crisply ordered. The hound sat. That worked.

Jack studied the sentry's coat facings. Judging from the camp's location, he lowered his weapon and took a stab in the dark. "Herefordshire, 36th?"

Warily, the shaggy sentry loosened his grip. "Second battalion."

Jack nodded, summoning memory of the peninsula war. "They retired after Toulouse? I was in India, but I knew a sergeant who told me he'd been discharged." He lowered his weapon as well.

The man looked half starved, almost as bad as Arnaud, who'd had rations since reaching the manor. Jack suspected this man lived off game and little else.

"Wore us down, threw us out," the soldier said wearily. "Are ye here to do the same?"

"Not my place." Jack shrugged. "We've had a bit of trouble over by Gravesyde Priory, someone who knows weapons. The owner of the manor is rightfully concerned. I'm Jack, by the way." He held out his hand.

Still cautious, the ex-soldier shook it. "William. You're welcome to come down and talk to any willing to do so, if ye're not here to tell us to move on."

"To be truthful, I'm not certain whose land it is. Since the captain's not using it, I doubt he minds. But he does mind having his guests shot at. I fear if he doesn't catch the bad apple, he'll have to arrange to move everyone out." That's what Jack would do, anyway. Hunt might have other ideas.

"We know how to defend ourselves. Come along, talk to the lads, ye'll see." William led the way down the hillside.

Jack held the dog's leash as they clambered downhill. The irregular troop had found a grassy hollow between a jagged ridge and the forest. More trees provided concealment on the shallow slope down to the river.

As expected, they were a motley lot. Some had attempted to stay clean. Others had not. Trimming hair and beard required effort when living rough. Jack noted stumps where limbs should be on many, not all. He kept a sharp eye for anyone with all four limbs and weapons at hand.

Chances were good these were all enlisted men. He didn't introduce himself as an officer, although his speech probably gave him away. "I'm Jack, a guest at the manor. We were unaware anyone lived out here. The ladies are rightfully concerned about a shooter who has murdered once and tried again. If he is not found, the owners may have to ask you to leave."

"You and what army gonna make us?" A whiskered older man with a sergeant's markings on his coat whittled at a solid piece of wood.

Jack's hound emitted a mournful howl, which was immediately echoed by another below. Timing. Hunt must be riding along the road below. He nodded in the direction of the highway. "We *have* an army. We're all old soldiers. We have horses, hounds, weapons, and ammunition. But that's not why I'm here. All I want to do is find the shooter. He has a gray palfrey and all his limbs. He rode this way when I chased him. If you have a killer in your midst, you need to tie him up and send him to us."

Evidently assigned as company spokesman, the sergeant glanced down the rocky hill. "Reckon your horses will have a time of it. You got any food you can spare? It's been a long winter."

The hounds exchanged greetings again. The distant one was coming up the hill. Jack had a notion that Hunt's sturdy gelding would have no difficulty in this terrain.

"Again, not mine to say, but I can ask. The manor has been empty for a long time, so there are few provisions stored except what's needed for the household. I believe that's the captain approaching now. You can ask him. He's in charge." Jack circled the campsite and stood on the lower ridge so Hunt knew where to find him.

A shot fired from below. An explosion of pain blossomed in Jack's shoulder. Another shot fired, grazing his head as he dropped to his knees. The hound tore from his loosened grip and bounded off as Jack tumbled down the slope.

Dying on a hill to nowhere, helping no one, hadn't been in his plans.

～

"No, no, no, no, no, not Jack." Elsa tore off her apron and raced upstairs after the maid who'd brought the news. "Please, not Jack."

She stumbled on the last step and wiped angrily at her tears before running down the corridor toward the infirmary. Hunt blocked the door, his coat covered in blood. She could hear Meera shouting for boiling water. Elsa nearly fell to her knees. Water. They needed boiling water.

Jack couldn't be dead. She raced back the way she came to fetch hot water. She sent the maid to pump more to set over Meera's grate. She had no idea how much water was needed, but this was something she knew how to do.

By the time she lugged up a pot of boiling water, others had gathered in the hall. Hunt kept everyone out. He took the heavy pot and handed it inside.

"Linens," the apothecary shouted. "Fresh linens."

So pale she resembled a ghost, Clare dashed off in search of those.

Walker emerged from the infirmary and shoved Hunt

toward the garden door. "Let's round them up. Someone has to talk."

There were *shooters* out there. Feeling murderous and helpless, Elsa hoped the men shot them all and burned their weapons. *Why Jack?* Who would shoot Jack?

Freddy? Would her stepbrother be desperate enough to shoot the man he thought was her husband? No, she couldn't think that way. Her universe had become the man bleeding in the infirmary. Elsa took over Hunt's command position before the hovering servants could push her aside.

She could only see the colorful apothecary hovering over a cot in the back, behind the fire screen. Elsa knew nothing of treating wounds, but this was Jack. He'd always been the happy part of her. She had the decided notion that her life ended if his did. She couldn't bear it. She would not cry. She would be strong and so would Jack.

Not knowing what else to do, she wanted to don her boots and ride out with the men. She was a bruising rider and a good shot. She wanted to rip off heads. . .

But this was *Jack.* He needed her more than the men did. She might ride and shoot, but she was useless at being a lady who knew how to do anything domestic. She didn't want to simply stand here and wring her hands.

What would Clare do? Not stand here, dithering.

Inching inside, Elsa finally made herself known. "May I help?"

"Grab that tin with the gold label," Meera demanded. "Bring me scissors from my bag."

Relieved to have a task, Elsa gathered the requested materials and handed them around the fire screen.

Jack lay stripped to the waist, his muscular chest and proud brow soaked in blood, his eyes closed. Weak-kneed, Elsa forced herself closer. At Meera's gesture, she pressed the blood-soaked bandage against his powerful shoulder while Meera cut more linen.

Jack, her beautiful, courageous Jack. Oh, Lord, please, I'll never utter another foul word if you'll save him. She'd even marry Smythe and poison him if it meant Jack would be safe. She should have faced her enemy long ago instead of hiding like the coward she was. And now, look what she'd done.

TWENTY-SIX

TUESDAY MORNING, HAVING HASTILY SWALLOWED RUNNY EGGS and limp bacon, Hunt was on the way out to continue the search for the soldiers who had scattered yesterday, when a haggard Lady Elsa halted him.

"How's the patient?" he asked in concern.

Hunt could tell from the fare that the lady hadn't been in the kitchen. She must have spent the night watching over Jack so Meera could rest. It was an upside-down world when the daughter of an earl was waiting on a humble chemist.

It was an insane world when unknown men shot down a good man for doing nothing wrong. He knew war changed a man. He hated to think any of those homeless soldiers had thought Jack was the enemy, but he couldn't take chances. Had they done the same with Culpepper? Much as he hated being judge and jury, in this case, the killer had to go.

"Meera says he's lost a lot of blood." Elsa looked pale enough to claim the same. "She's removed the bullet. She gave him something to rest, but he's coming around." She glanced down at the burned toast. "I should prepare something more appetizing."

"He's a soldier. He's probably eaten boiled rat. He'll eat burnt toast. What you need to do is rest." Hunt was none too certain of his own appetite. The woods and fields were now teaming with armed and dangerous strangers, and it was up to him to keep the village and household safe.

He didn't want to be a soldier any longer. He wanted family. He wanted to fix and build, not destroy.

Life didn't always work the way one wanted.

The single thread of hope for Hunt's future entered after Elsa left. Clare's eyes were red-rimmed, as if she hadn't slept all night. Hunt detected streaks of tears that she'd ineffectively rubbed at. His gut stirred uneasily.

He knew it was bad when she voluntarily approached him and wrapped her arms around his waist and leaned against his shoulder. Given tacit permission, he held her and tried not to let his heart care too much.

"I can't do it," she whispered into his lapels. "I cannot risk Oliver for a dream. At least, in the city, he was safe. I. . . I just can't. . . Soldiers and guns and. . ." She shook her head, and he could feel her trembling.

She'd seen her sister blown to bits by terrorists, watched innocent bystanders shot by soldiers. Clare was a dreamer, raised to be a lady, not a battle-hardened warrior. He understood, but what remained of his soul crumbled knowing he hadn't the power to assure her that her nephew would be safe with him.

"How will you hold off your uncle?" he asked, because he cared about the boy.

She sobbed and shook her head again. "I can't. We'll have to go to him until my house is empty again. I will take Mr. Birdwhistle. Perhaps, as long as he is having his way, my uncle can be convinced that Oliver should wait before going off to school. If all he wants is the sapphire, he can have it. We won't tell him of the dinosaur eggs. They'll provide any future Oliver wants, if I can just keep him *safe*."

His sensible co-general had spent the night working this out. He couldn't argue with her. She was an intelligent woman who knew what was best for herself and the boy. Hunt had given her no reason to care about him or the vague future he'd planned. He'd wanted to be certain he could provide for her. He still didn't know if he could.

"I understand," he said reluctantly. "If you'll understand that I don't want it this way." He caressed her hair, duty calling but hating to leave her like this. This had been the reason he'd wanted to quit being a soldier and be the man of peace she needed.

He released her. "I have to go now. They're waiting for me to lead the search. Don't leave yet, please. It could be dangerous on the road. Stay a little longer, give me time to think?"

She sniffed, backed away, and produced a handkerchief to dry her eyes rather than look at him. "I'll try to keep Oliver upstairs. Please don't get shot."

Grimly thinking it might be better if he died now rather than being tortured later, Hunt caught her shoulders and kissed her. He tasted the salt of her tears, and rather than add his own, he let her free. The scent of jasmine withered with his hopes.

He couldn't die now. It would hurt her. So he'd have to live to die another day.

He crossed the corridor to load up his weapons from the cabinet in his study. Adam rushed in from the back hall, his young brow creased in worry.

"Sir, there are. . . men. . . coming up the back hill. Ned sent a warning." He darted a look toward the front of the house that his father guarded, but no hint of danger arose there.

"Patrol the back hall. Tell the staff to stay inside. Arnaud and Henri?" Grabbing his rifle and ammunition from the cabinet, with Adam in his wake, Hunt strode toward the side exit to the stable yard where Quincy patrolled. The butler needed to be warned.

"They're outside with Mr. Walker. The grooms are saddling up for the hunt. A few of the locals are there as well. Word spread about the soldiers, and they want to help." Adam stood irresolutely in the dark corridor. "If we lock all the doors, I could ride with you."

The young footman was large enough to crush two starving men with his bare hands, but he wasn't a soldier. Hunt doubted he'd ever been on a horse. "I'm trusting my family with you, lad. Take whatever weapon you're comfortable with and stand guard. If there's trouble, shoot in the air. Don't try to fight alone. I'll tell your dad the same."

Clare had chosen well in picking these two gentle giants to guard the interior. They were politer than most gentlemen, but they'd knock heads if anyone broke through the doors. She was also right to be afraid. Two men couldn't guard every window and door in this sprawling monstrosity of a house. He'd need an army.

Apparently, the army was in his fields.

Slamming on his hat, pocketing his gloves, Hunt threw open the side door, prepared to join his tiny band of friends and family. He wished Jack were here to lead the grooms.

The horror of carrying Jack's bleeding body back to the manor yesterday might be engraved upon his conscience for the rest of his life. The man didn't even belong here, but he'd stood by their sides in every fray.

Jack had been one of the despised British soldiers Hunt had fought against for years, but Jack had never held that against him.

The irony of American, French, and British soldiers defending the same fortress didn't escape Hunt. One defended one's home, wherever it was.

Stepping outside, Hunt nearly walked into a straggling

band of ragged scarecrows in the drive. Before he could react, they shoved a bound and gagged man in civilian clothes in his direction.

"This here's your assassin, my lord." A square, sturdy man wearing a sergeant's stripes on his folded coat sleeve nodded for his fellows to shove their prisoner forward. "He's got a right to fair trial, don't he? He's been done wrong like the lot of us, but we don't hold with killing innocents."

Keeping an eye on his surroundings with his limited vision, Hunt noted his own people circling behind the ragged ex-soldiers. With the perimeter secure, he turned to their captive. In a drab brown coat, wearing worn boots and an outdated gentleman's hat, the tall prisoner looked familiar. It took a moment to see past the unshaven jaw to the polished businessman he'd met last.

"Reginald Hill?" he asked, for verification. His mind was already spilling over with possibilities of why Smythe's assistant was shooting at Jack. And possibly Elsa—and *Culpepper*?

The man sneered and didn't reply. He'd taken off the sling Henri had mentioned, but his arms tied behind him revealed a bulge under his dirty shirt where a bandage remained. *This was the man who'd shot at Elsa?*

The sergeant continued as spokesman. "His brother was one of us, died in Corunna. His da lost the land back there to the bank. He told us no one cared if we camped there since the old earl let his da run his sheep up the hills, and the bank didn't know nothin'. I'm tellin' ya plain, my lord. We don' mean no harm. But me and my men ain't got nowhere else to go, and that campsite is a godsend. We hope you'll see straight to let us stay. We know we can't tell ya what to do with the boy here, but he did try to help us."

Hunt ran through every curse he'd ever heard in a lifetime. Judge and jury. . . He simply couldn't do it. He didn't have knowledge of the law required. But if Hill had shot Jack and at Elsa. . . He'd be transported at the very least, whether or not they could prove he'd cold-bloodedly killed Culpepper.

He gestured at his cousins to take Hill to the crypt. The clerk tried to fight them off, but with an injured shoulder and hands tied by what was most likely his neckcloth, he didn't have a chance.

Rubbing one hand over the scar at his temple, Hunt examined the filthy soldiers awaiting his decision. He was easier with this verdict. He'd been a soldier. He knew what happened when men lost an arm or a leg. . . or an eye. Despair, desolation, the knowledge that they could never be productive again, never be what their family needed, never be whole. . .

These men had fought for their country. They deserved better treatment.

"I thank you for your honesty," he said first. "I cannot say what will happen to Mr. Hill once he stands before a judge, but I am grateful you saved my friends and family from harm."

"The young gentleman Jack?" the sergeant asked with a frown. "Is he. . .?"

"He's recovering. We're all old soldiers. It takes a lot to kill us." Ideas boiled. Clare had taught him to think beyond the immediate. She'd envisioned a future that he would never have seen by encouraging the villagers to set up their tiny button factory in the gallery. She'd inspired Lavender to start her own seamstress shop, starting with uniforms paid from the manor's trust. She'd showed him how much they could accomplish. . .

If they kept the manor.

"I do not own this estate," he warned the wary men. "But for now, I am in charge. I haven't yet learned the boundaries, but if no one else in the vicinity objects, I see no reason you shouldn't keep your camp."

PATRICIA RICE

He watched the stiffness of their stances relax to a degree. He owed them much more than a camp, however, if Hill was found to be the culprit. "Understand that we've just moved in ourselves. We have no fields, no crops or herds, no funds to do more than maintain the roof over our heads. And right now, our cook is sitting beside Jack's bed, weeping, so we can't even offer much from the kitchen."

Hank, Elsa's head groom, spoke up. "We got a bath to the back of the stable, captain, sir. And Miss Lavender's been making us up old shirts and the like she's found in the wardrobes. She might be able to rustle up a few coats and trousers. Maybe, if they look a little less scary. . ."

Hunt bit back a laugh at the horrified expressions on the soldiers' faces. "The ladies are more likely to feed you if you don't terrify them."

He knew that clean clothes and shaven jaws wouldn't repair what was broken, but it was the very least they could offer.

TWENTY-SEVEN

THE DAY AFTER THEY'D THROWN HILL IN THE CELLAR DUNGEON, Clare stoically sat in her small office, writing letters to her family, while Lavender wept and protested.

It hurt to leave. She didn't want to go. But Oliver was only a little boy with his entire life ahead of him. She simply could not risk him in the lawless wilds with bands of dangerous criminals viewing the manor's occupants as a target to be taken.

At least, in London, they were safe behind their modest townhouse walls, where no one knew they existed. She wasn't as certain about her uncle's estate, but it was in a rather more civilized area not far from the city. Now that Oliver had a tutor, he didn't need to attend school until he was twelve or so, surely. And there were good schools in London and nearby. He could come home regularly.

Meera weighed on her mind though. They hadn't had time to talk. Her aunt and uncle would never accept her friendship with Meera. Clare hoped Meera would stay here until after her child was born, at least, and they could return to London together in the autumn as previously planned. Meera could take care of herself far better than Oliver could.

If it turned out that Meera and Walker had a future together, Clare would simply have to return to London alone.

"If you go, and Lady Elsa leaves, then what will *I* do?" Lavender cried. "I've just accepted orders from Lady Spalding for new uniforms for her maids. But she thinks you're here, keeping us respectable. I don't want to be in charge of telling the maids what to do. And if we have no cook. . . Even the men will leave. It will be awful!"

"No one says Elsa is leaving." Not that she was aware, anyway. This morning's breakfast had indicated that the lady was back in the kitchen. Jack must be awake and hungry. Clare stopped to polish a teardrop off her glasses.

"Why would she want to stay? She has a home of her own, just like you. I'm the only one who has nowhere to go!" Lavender sat by the grate, sniffing into her handkerchief.

"This manor is your home now." Unless the bank took it away. She shivered at that thought and tried to stay positive. "What you make of it is up to you." Clare knew she was being cruel to a homeless orphan, but she couldn't even help herself.

She was giving up this precious place where she could write and be happy, for a household where she'd be little more than a servant. She tried not to think in terms of giving up a man who was everything she could want. She'd given up dreams before.

Her aunt would be appalled if she discovered Clare's occupation, so she might have to give up writing as well. Perhaps she could work in her room at night, after everyone had gone to bed. Like Lavender, she had to make of circumstances what she could.

"You don't understand at all!" With a wail, the girl raced from the room, brushing past their footman, weeping.

Clare rather wanted to wail with her, but she was an adult, not a child any longer.

Tugging anxiously at the black lapels of his new uniform coat, Adam remained in the doorway. "Da says carriages are turning up the drive, miss, fancy ones. The captain is loading the prisoner into the cart. The soldiers have set up a tent in the yard, and Lady Elsa has everyone taking out food, and there won't be room. . ."

"More than one carriage?" That couldn't be good. Clare rose from her desk. "Send them around to the front. We're not expecting visitors, so the drivers can just let out their passengers. If they plan a lengthy stay, have the carriages continue down to the stable in the village."

This was why Hunt called her his co-general. She'd grown up on the fringe of the aristocracy and had learned how things were done. Or should be done. "Have Quincy take the visitors to the great hall. Let Lady Elsa know we may need tea. I'll be there directly."

Hunt had the villain in hand. She didn't have to worry about shooters, she hoped. If the visitors had come to take the manor away, fine, it was no longer her concern. She didn't have what it took to carry the burden of a household. She wasn't Bea. She'd never be her adventurous sister. She had never been more than a spinster, a convenient caretaker for her family. Hunt would be far better off finding a courageous lady to stand by his side, as he deserved.

But while she was here, she'd do the best she could. She ran upstairs, donned her best visiting gown, pinned her hair to respectability, and hid her reading glasses in her pocket. She didn't dare hope anyone had arrived offering help instead of more trouble.

After checking that Oliver and his tutor were in the blue salon studying an atlas, she descended the marble stairs, expecting to hear angry voices echoing in the ancient hall.

She hesitated in the odd silence. Even Quincy didn't

appear with his salver of visiting cards. Had the guests been insulted by her rather supercilious orders to send the carriages away? In her mind, arrogance deserved arrogance in return. Could she hope they'd left? Or shot each other on the drive. That might be more than she could hope for.

The butler emerged from his place beneath the stairs to indicate the side door. One could never tell from stoic Quincy whether the news was bad or good. One simply followed his expectations. She accepted a shawl and a bonnet and sailed off into the unknown.

Even prepared for chaos, she was a trifle taken aback by the spectacle invading their quiet side yard. Had a clown ridden in on a unicorn, she couldn't have been more shocked. Her first reaction was to write a scene that captured madness in all its glorious color and clamor.

Appearing as much part of the circus as the carriages and shouting men, Elsa approached her from the direction of the kitchen door. Wearing her apron and cap and swinging an empty, but greasy, iron skillet, she nodded at the drive. "The tall, scowling fellow in the huge collar points and stiff cravat stepping out of the barouche is Villiers, probably come to wring my neck. I don't believe I'm familiar with the gentleman prepared to strike him with his cane. . ."

"Bosworth," Clare said in barely concealed horror. "The manor's banker."

She tried to comprehend the argument between the gentlemen, but it appeared to be one of long standing. Only the combatants knew the grounds.

"I believe the lady shouting at them is the Dowager Marchioness of Spalding, Hunt's aunt." The plump lady wore an old-fashioned, black traveling gown and an enormous bonnet that billowed in the breeze. "Might the gentleman traveling with your brother be the marquess, then? We've never met, and I don't recognize the escutcheons on either carriage."

"I am not acquainted with Spalding. Shall I dive into the fray and escort them inside?" Elsa appeared amused at the thought. "I am dressed like a sheepherder and covered in flour, but I can threaten them with my skillet. It should be exciting."

Clare studied her with a frown. "I take it Jack is feeling better and you see no need to defend him from your brother?"

Elsa laughed. "Jack and Villiers talk horses. Meera has ordered him to sit still." She gestured toward the stable. "You see how well he does that."

And there, in the center of the chaos preventing the carriages from entering the yard, was a stack of hay bales. The patient, tousled dark hair falling over a bandage, coat sleeve hanging loose over his damaged shoulder, lounged on top, directing. . . A line of new stable hands? Soldiers?

"What is he *doing*?" Clare whispered, watching in awe as men scattered at Jack's command.

Some—the less scruffy ones—had tin plates and mugs and were crouched on the drive, listening to Jack. Others were lined up to enter a tent beside the stable. Grooms ran about, carrying pails and stoking a fire where they presumably heated water. Even as she watched, a soldier emerged from the tent, rubbing his bare face, wearing what suspiciously looked like a footman's blue pantaloons and shirt with his crumbling boots.

It wasn't until she looked past the tent and carriages that she saw the manor's old pony cart and mare tied up. Hunt's tall hat was barely visible as he presumably loaded the prisoner into the back.

"Oh dear," Elsa murmured as another carriage arrived. "That's Freddy with *Smythe*. I believe the captain meant to take Hill to a magistrate this morning? Has Smythe come to stop him?"

"And that's my aunt and uncle. I don't think this is fun

any longer." Clare turned to Quincy. "Escort the ladies and gentlemen inside, please. Cram tea cakes down their throats."

A shout rose from the far side of the carriages. To her horror, Hill had broken free and was running toward the gentlemen. . . or at least toward his employer. He'd torn the linen ties loose from his one wrist, but it still hung off the other. He stumbled on the length and righted himself.

Clare clasped her hands and strained to see Hunt. He was scolding one of the grooms while limping after his prisoner. He was fine and simply angry.

"Oh, goody, I've been longing to do this." Swinging her heavy skillet with the strength of a practiced cook, Elsa dashed into the fray—much to Clare's alarm.

Before the scoundrel clerk even noticed her approach, the lady slammed the skillet into his nose, knocking him backward. Blood gushed, and Hill screamed.

"One shouldn't torture prisoners," Walker murmured from behind Clare. "I've been ordered to haul Jack inside. Should I escort the lady instead?"

"Both of them," Clare said with a touch of acid. "They deserve each other if any two people ever did. Keep everyone distracted. I'm dragging in the captain before our noble guests realize the gentleman they've come to berate is no better than the rogues blocking the drive."

In one of his military coats, with the insignia stripped, tall boots, out-of-date hat, and khaki-colored breeches, with the black patch covering his eye, the captain looked exactly like one of the scruffy soldiers. He hadn't bothered trimming his hair recently either. He reached the carriages and unsympathetically hauled his bloodied prisoner to his feet.

Walker chuckled. "He does seem to blend in with the motley lot, doesn't he?"

No, he didn't, not if one knew how to look beyond appearance. But most people didn't even look beyond the eyepatch. She abandoned Walker to deal with cries of alarm and a triumphant Elsa and wound her way past soldiers and carriages to where Hunt thrust the weeping, protesting prisoner at Arnaud and Henri to tie up properly.

"I forgot Villiers said he was coming today," Hunt said in disgust as she approached. "Did he bring the whole blamed family?"

"And Bosworth and Smythe and Freddy although Freddy might count as family, sort of. You need to slip in the back door and change."

He glanced down at her fresh attire and raised a scarred eyebrow. "You look beautiful and gloriously aristocratic. I can't compete. Why don't you politely tell them all to go to hell? I'll stay out here where I belong."

She indelicately smacked his muscled arm. "Are you giving up? Those are the men who can help you make the manor ours."

He shrugged and skirted around the melee in the stable yard, heading toward the hedge concealing the garden door. "Your elegant nobles looked right past me as if I weren't there. What are the chances they'll listen to anything I say?"

"America must be a very strange place if you never needed to learn to blend in." Clare lifted her narrow skirt and hurried to keep up with his long strides. "They didn't notice you because you look as scruffy as those soldiers you're feeding. The soldiers pay attention to you because, right now, you look like them. Dress like a gentleman, and you'll be accepted into the herd of gentlemen. Then you can bare. . ."

"My fangs?" he asked in amusement.

"I meant to say your intelligence, but if you want to be the wolf in sheep's clothing, fine. There is a reason for that saying. Put on your stiffest collar and whitest cravat and finest waistcoat. Dangle a pocket watch. Look down your nose. Do not shoot bats over their heads."

He laughed aloud as they entered the back hall. "That reminds me. . . We found Culpepper's pocket watch on Hill.

259

He's a dangerous man, possibly deranged. Don't let his weeping persuade you otherwise."

~

IN HIS CHAMBERS, HUNT YANKED OFF A MUD-SPLATTERED BOOT and worked up a mental list of what he needed to demand from an earl, a marquess, and a banker. From the sounds of the argument echoing up the stairs, he needed to decide what to ask of whom before they killed each other. Smythe was not a quiet man.

A knock at the door intruded on his grim thoughts. *What now?*

Walker entered, leading one of the newly-scrubbed soldiers, one functioning on a wooden leg. "Says he used to be a batman for a general. I don't know one battalion or general from another, but if he can polish boots, you're one step ahead of where you are now."

Hunt snorted and stripped off the boot. "Name?"

"James, sir. I'll have them spit and shined in no time. I don't do no champagne baths like the city fellas, though," he said doubtfully.

"The only thing bubbly wine is good for is cleaning boots, but I don't require it. Can you tie a decent cravat? Press my coat?" He pried off the other boot and stood up, towering over the poor fellow. "I have an earl and a marquess waiting to take off my head, and my lady says I need to look like them before my execution."

The man lit up like a lantern. "I can do that. Let me see what you got." He limped off in the direction Hunt pointed, opening wardrobe doors and drawers and tut-tutting and muttering.

Walker cynically saluted. "Jack and I are taking notes of what the men can do. We've already found one who says he can hoe a garden with one hand, and another who claims he can train hounds. You're on your own with the fancy-dressed clowns downstairs."

"Thanks," Hunt hurled at his friend's departing back.

"Why ain't he your valet?" James asked, pronouncing it like *valette* while examining a meager assortment of starched cravats.

"Because Walker is a trained accountant and keeps books better than I do. Our butler is a prize fighter, our physician is female, and our cook is daughter of an earl, so you'll have to withhold judgment if you're to work here." Hunt started stripping off the clothes he'd thought suitable for meeting with whatever magistrate he had hoped to track down. Apparently, they weren't suitable enough for a marquess.

"My da was a valet for a gentleman. He said the gentleman and his friends weren't no better than the drunkards at cock fights. Money don't make a man. It's what he does with it that counts. I just ain't never seen no blackamoor do anything but scut work." James found a clothes brush and quickly cleaned off Hunt's best coat.

Hunt had a notion that valets did not speak to their employers in this manner, but he didn't much care as long as the man cleaned him up the way Clare expected.

When he was all decked out in knit pantaloons, long-tailed blue coat, a white embroidered vest, and sparkling white cravat neatly tied in some complicated knot Hunt would never attempt, he glared at himself in the mirror. "I look like I'm going to my own funeral."

"Nah, the embalmer would cut your hair. But from the sounds of it, I ain't got time to do that properly. You got an eye under that patch?"

Hunt lifted the patch, but his image in the mirror didn't improve by much. The jagged scar was no longer red but still ugly, although the meager light no longer stabbed into his brain. He supposed that could be called an improvement.

"Leave it off, sir. The eye looks fine from here, and the scar

261

reminds them that you're a war hero, like my limb here." James glanced down at his wooden stump.

After that, Hunt couldn't very well hide behind the patch. He threw it on the dresser.

The noise from below escalated, and the valet glanced nervously at the door. "You'd best go rescue the ladies, sir."

Hunt snorted. "If we're lucky, Lady Elsa is still carrying her deadly skillet." He strode out, barely limping. These past weeks of exertion had strengthened a few muscles, at least.

He took the marble stairs at a stiff-legged pace, but the loud voices had retreated into the great hall. The maids must have brought up the tea tray. Needing to collect his thoughts, he stopped in the family parlor to adjust the tight collar and check his ugly visage in the mirror over the mantel.

Jack lay sprawled on a chaise longue, his boots on the headrest and his head near the fire. He was using a pencil to check notes in a small notebook. At Hunt's entrance, he squinted an inspection of his attire. "Clean up fairly well, I see. Liked it better when you resembled a pirate."

Hunt growled at the gentleman. "Why aren't you in there defending Elsa? I assume Villiers is here because Freddy ran to him with tales of your purported marriage. He'll be demanding documents and hauling her off."

TWENTY-EIGHT

JACK CLOSED HIS NOTEBOOK AND TUCKED IT INTO HIS POCKET. With the scar emphasizing his square cheekbones, the tall captain in aristocratic attire was damned intimidating.

"I was ordered to keep my feet up and lie about like a vaporish female." In fact, he hurt enough in so many places that he wasn't particularly prompted to move. Or face consequences, if he wished to be honest. He wasn't up to killing Elsa's brothers as they deserved.

"Meera give you pain powder?" Hunt demanded, decidedly unsympathetic.

Jack rummaged around in his pocket and produced the packet. "But I don't want to sleep. If I hear Elsa shouting, I can at least stagger in."

Hunt rummaged in the cabinet and produced the sherry bottle. "Take the powders. Liquor isn't recommended, but I don't have time to call for tea. The powder works."

Jack snubbed the sherry and dumped the packet on his tongue, shuddering. At least the captain understood pain. If he said the powder worked. . .

"Now get up and make yourself useful," Hunt said callously. "You know them better than I do."

"To the lofty Villiers, I'm just a gadabout who knows horses," Jack protested, swinging his legs back to the floor. "He won't listen to me."

"All anyone sees right now is that you are a first-class prime idiot for deserting a woman who loves you. You don't think her brothers are better than you are, do you?" Hunt stalked out like an avenging Zeus.

Elsa *loved* him? She ought to know better.

Still, she had said she might marry him. . . And she'd been hovering over his bloody carcass when she'd had no business doing so.

She was the best woman he'd ever known, and she deserved to be treated like a princess. He couldn't afford to do so, but her brothers were piss-poor protectors. *That*, he could do.

"Oh well, put that way. . ." Jack checked the mirror, decided his bandages gave him excuse for his slovenly attire, and followed the captain into the fray.

He'd almost rather follow Wellington. Wellington was a calculating general, not a belligerent captain who stormed the front lines. A general would employ a pincer movement to surround the enemy. Well, Jack could arrange that.

Leaving Hunt to make a grand entrance through the double doors, Jack slipped into the library and slid open the panel at the far end of the great room just enough to see where everyone was.

He found Elsa instantly, his gaze drawn like a tack to lodestone. She was sitting next to Lavender and chatting with an over-dressed old lady with all the distinctive features of the earl's family.

His warrior Elsa wouldn't be intimidated by her shouting brothers—as long as Freddy didn't hit her. With Villiers watching, Freddy would behave.

Judging from the ladies' tranquil demeanors, the shouting

argument by the windows had nothing to do with them. Jack suspected their serenity was a façade.

Clare entertained her aunt and uncle near the fireplace. The unfashionably garbed rural couple appeared intimidated by the noble company. He didn't know why the devil they'd returned, and at this moment, didn't care.

At Hunt's grand entrance, Clare's eyes widened, and she froze, teacup in hand. The captain's striking appearance had the intended effect on the lady, at least.

Since Villiers and Spalding had never met the captain, their reactions were less interesting. A friend of Villiers's, the marquess had visited Newchurch a time or two. Jack had only been a puffed-up adolescent at the time, but he'd pointed out a few defects in a horse the marquess—a mere earl then—had been considering. In return, Spalding had helped Jack's reputation as a horseman when he'd arrived in London.

Villiers appeared to be taking Smythe apart, while the marquess worked on Bosworth. Bankers and nobles, the devil's partners. Jack wanted no part of their business. The lot of them straightened and cautiously acknowledged Hunt as he approached. Rather than wearing a welcoming expression, the captain appeared ready to mow them all down.

On his own, Freddy squirmed edgily, searching for the brandy even though it couldn't be more than noon. Jack's stomach rumbled to remind him of the hour.

He had the decided notion that if he entered now, he'd become target of all that tension. Did they need him? He knew nothing of banks and deeds or even how to transport villains. He was more comfortable with horses and soldiers—

As was Hunt. But the American captain had just introduced himself to a stiff-necked marquess as if he were Spalding's equal. Damn. His host had never asked anything of him —but Jack knew these men better than the American did. They were already looking down their aristocratic noses. The captain would punch those noses before he'd puff up his consequence—probably not the best option for their futures.

Jack slid the panel fully open, and despite his bandages and casual garb, strolled in as if he were the late earl lowering himself to speak with his unruly constituents.

At his appearance, Elsa beamed like the sun after a rainy day. There was worry in that little wrinkle between her eyes, but he winked, and the line melted away.

"So, this is where you're keeping the rations." He helped himself to a teacake. Wounded warriors could be rude.

Smythe stopped shouting to glare in Jack's direction. Most excellent. That meant the lout still thought him Elsa's husband. Jack bent over and planted a husbandly kiss on her brow. She pinched his thigh, dangerously near a sensitive location. He laughed. Elsa had seen stallions gelded. Her warning was quite clear. Why had he ever thought a docile miss would suit him?

Because he seriously misjudged himself, he decided. He might be naught more than a farmer, but here he was, prepared for war, despite all odds against him—including Elsa, most likely. And himself. He was his own worst enemy.

Why had he ever thought those aristocratic snobs better than him? Different, maybe. Wealthier, certainly. But *better*? Not for Elsa, as she'd made plain.

So, he was still good at puffing up his consequence. Who cared, if it made Elsa look at him as if he were her hero?

"De Sackville, I want a word with you," Villiers said ominously. He cut off his argument with Smythe to focus on Jack.

Jack shrugged, accepted the teacup Clare handed him, and took the offensive position before the earl could. "I apologize for not asking you first, but young Freddy needed convincing. You can still draw up the settlements if you like. Elsa will have your gizzard if you try to cheat us."

Elsa laughed while everyone else gasped or frowned at his

forwardness. He only needed to please Elsa. He might only have his name and small savings, but that meant he was obligated to no one. He was a free man and could say whatever he liked.

"The marriage is a sham," Smythe shouted. "There is no church, no vicar, nothing recorded anywhere. You are trying to cheat a lady and ruin me!"

Uh oh.

Elsa's muscles bunched, but Jack pressed her shoulder to indicate she stay seated. "As you tried to ruin the lady, Smythe? And when she outsmarted you and ran away, you hunted her down and tried to have her abducted."

Jack turned to Villiers before Smythe could sputter a response. "Have you inspected the estate accounts as we asked, my lord? Are they in order?"

"They are not," Villiers said flatly, scowling.

～

ELSA BRIEFLY CLOSED HER EYES AND LET JACK'S GENTLE TOUCH soothe her roiling tempers. With his tousled hair spilling over the bandage on his head, his movements hampered by the wound under his shirt, and his clothing barely respectable, Jack still managed to command the room. He was prepared to stand toe-to-toe with two peers of the realm and men wealthier than he'd ever be.

For her. She could not have loved him more if she tried.

She wanted to leap up and defend this good man, shout like a shrew at her brothers until they fled the room, and berate them all for their abandonment.

Unlike every other man who'd scarred her life, Jack did not need defending. He was his own man. He did not need her wealth or her fury or her defense. What did he need, then?

She looked across at Clare, who conversed serenely with

the aunt and uncle she feared, all the while behaving as if a tempest of roars didn't swirl around them. Any minute now, the men would produce weapons or fling fists, and the quiet spinster with a backbone of steel beneath her lace and muslin simply smiled.

Clare was a lady. Even though Elsa had been born as one, she had never set her sights on being a weak-willed creature. She had flung herself at life, cooking, eating, riding, and fighting as needed. She'd never had interest in smiling demurely and deferring to her so-called *betters*.

But when men behaved like animals. . . Elsa had retreated to the comfort of food. Perhaps she could learn to go into battle with a smile and a teacup like Clare.

With Jack at her side, did she dare command the respect a proper lady deserved? She would never be frail and dependent, but would simply playing that role make them listen? If nothing else, it might be amusing to see their reactions.

She rose, and instead of retreating to see how lunch was faring, she took Jack's arm. Using Clare as an example, she interrupted the male posturing with haughty chin lifted and voice modulated. "Gentlemen, we've had quite enough of this hullabaloo. Lunch will be in the dining room. If you cannot partake without uproar, then go outside and kick a tree." Well, perhaps a lady would not say that. Oh well. "Quincy and Adam will show the gentlemen where they might refresh themselves. My lady, madam, if you'll both follow Miss Marlowe, she can show you to the powder room."

Jack clasped her hand on his arm and regarded her with an impish gleam. "Dispersing the enemy, conquering the field, and charging ahead?"

Since the startled, surly men actually departed as ordered, she answered audaciously. "Preventing Meera from having to flatten you so you put your feet up, as ordered. Let us snatch some food while everyone else is washing and find a place where you can rest."

With the guests scattering, Clare and Hunt intruded on their escape.

"Strategic planning required," Hunt said bluntly. "Let us nab rations and retreat to my study."

"Jack is supposed to be lying down," Elsa answered defiantly. If this was her house, too, then she had an equal say in how business was conducted.

"Parlor, then. We'll lock all the doors. Food first." With their guests spreading out across the huge manor, they slipped into the main dining room.

The four of them stacked plates with the cold fare Elsa's assistant had produced and the bread Elsa had baked. Then they hurried into the shabby parlor they normally congregated in before dinner.

Hunt locked the doors while Jack took the lounge Elsa had seen him occupying earlier. She tucked a pillow under his poor bandaged head so he could reach his food easier. He grinned and rubbed the ring he'd given her, the one she wore like a wedding band.

"Let's run off to Scotland and marry," Jack whispered. "We'll find a little croft and raise sheep and never have to hear the word bank or money again."

"And let the villains abscond with your funds?" Hunt paced past the lounge chair. "I've never had more money than I needed to feed myself and my horse. I have no notion of how we remove funds from scoundrels and place them somewhere safe."

"Smythe fears that *all* his investments, including the Liverpool bank, will collapse if Else removes her funds." Jack explained one problem succinctly before biting into his cold meat pie.

"Elsa's half-brother wants to shake our prisoner until he coughs up the cash he's stolen from Smythe, but I've talked to

269

Hill. He's been paying Bosworth in an attempt to buy back his family's land." Hunt paced, tearing off hunks of bread and meat in between sentences. "Hill was only following his employer's example. If Smythe could hire men to abduct an heiress, then why not use fake banknotes to pay the black-guards and keep the real cash for himself? We're surrounded by villains."

Elsa sighed and picked at her food, settling into a chair she pulled closer to Jack, in case he needed any help. "I ought to give away all my money and become a nun."

Jack took her hand and kissed it. "Villiers won't allow it. We'd have to marry in truth so you're free to give it all away."

"Do we really need to run off to Scotland? The May flowers are just opening, and I'd love to see if the apple orchards will produce enough harvest to practice canning." Elsa concealed the joyous child bouncing inside her behind nonchalance. Did this mean Jack was no longer protesting about not marrying until he could support her?

Clare poured coffee and handed a cup to Hunt. "Shall we leave so you may make a more romantic proposal, Mr. de Sackville?" she asked acerbically.

"If we can remove all the financial quibbling, I might have a chance to talk to the earl and marquess about law." Hunt grabbed another handful of bread and cheese and glanced longingly at the door. "Why don't I leave bank talk to you, Jack?"

"I left Arnaud with my notes on the code to the jewels." Jack sipped tea with Elsa's aid. He was so seldom still that she took advantage to brush his hair back. "If he finds gems, you'll have to learn to discuss finances on your own or leave them to Walker. I might help with jewelers, but I've never had much dealing with legitimate financial institutions."

A fist banged against the locked door and Villiers's recog-nizable roar rang through the panel. "Elsa, I want to talk to you and that rapscallion de Sackville!"

Jack kissed her hand. "He won't shoot me while I'm down."

She remained where she was, holding Jack's hand, and nodded at the captain to open the door.

Her tall older brother stormed in, his high collar only slightly wilted from his ire. He was nearing forty, and a distinguished gray threaded his dark locks. He'd not allowed himself to run to fat, but he wasn't muscular like Hunt or Jack. He scowled when he saw her holding Jack's hand. She squeezed Jack's fingers and crossed the room to kiss her big brother's cheek.

"I am of age and sound mind. My decisions are mine alone to make," she said before he could start shouting again. "If I am forced to marry Smythe, I shall poison him. If Hill is not hauled off to assizes, I will bash his nose again and cut his throat. I *will not be bullied* anymore, understood?"

"I had not realized you were being bullied at all." Villiers glanced at Jack. "Do you know what she's talking about?"

Bless Jack's heart, he merely sipped his tea and nodded.

Before the earl could explode, Hunt stepped in. "I want to charge Hill with assault and murder. Once we have his story, we might have evidence to charge Smythe with abduction and fraud. I have no understanding of English law. How do we bring this about?"

To Elsa's relief, her straightlaced, practical earl of a brother immediately reverted to his authority. "Wycliffe Manor has manorial rights. You are effectively the law on your property, entitled to pass taxes and whatever a city might do. I recommend properly applying as a magistrate in the future. Until then, just for the looks of it, have the locals elect you to the position. Then you may take witness statements, hold court, and if found guilty, remit the defendant to assizes in Oxford."

"And then may I cut his throat?" Elsa purred.

TWENTY-NINE

Had it only been six weeks since Hunt had sat in his study, shooting at bats and hurling books at the fire? With fluttering butterflies in her middle, Clare admired the elegantly attired captain taking a position beside the enormous fireplace in the great hall, looking more magisterial than an earl and a marquess. Hands behind his back, legs akimbo, he played the part of master of all he surveyed well. And he'd *kissed* her. Her. As if he'd meant it.

She had to quit being a silly miss and think logically, but it was very hard when her thoughts whirled and her heart raced—and the scent of jasmine drifted in. She could almost swear the viscountess watched over her home.

Hunt waited for all the excited, whispering villagers and servants to gawk at a room they seldom glimpsed. The towering oak ceiling and ancient panels covered in aging oils of illustrious ancestors, their ships, their horses, and their jewels impressed as well as a courtroom. The company gradually silenced and turned its attention to the man standing military erect at the center of the room.

Tails and cravat might declare Hunt as part of the upper classes, but his accent was pure American. Most of the townspeople and servants knew him as a man willing to work a blacksmith's forge.

The knowledge that an earl, a marquess, and two bankers watched the proceedings had everyone squirming in their chairs.

Hunt introduced the subject of needing a magistrate. "The Village of Gravesyde Priory is hampered by a lack of clear land ownership, but we have an earl and marquess present to lend consequence to our decisions. They will report our choices to the Lord Lieutenant of Shropshire and any legalities may be ironed out then."

As Hunt led the proceedings, the manor's banker, Bosworth, looked as if he'd bitten into a sour apple. As the viscount's blood heir, did he imagine himself as lord of the manor in Hunt's place? But he hid his birth, preferring the pretense of legitimacy and wealth provided by the respectable banker who had adopted him.

As a direct descendant of the earl, Lady Spalding stood up. "I request that Captain Huntley, as heir to Wycliffe Manor, take my grandfather's place as magistrate."

The Marquess of Spalding stood. "I find my stepmother's request legal, since the late earl bequeathed his estate to females as well as males. The decision only requires a vote of the people who must accept Captain Huntley's rulings."

Clare was fairly certain not a soul in the room, outside of the nobility, had ever voted in their lives. Lavender's seamstresses whispered questions, and the girl happily stood up to face the family who had never recognized her. "The women of the village are not the earl's heirs and have never owned land. Are they allowed to vote?"

"I will assure the lord lieutenant that everyone present is acting as representative of all the heirs and landowners," Spalding intoned.

Clare was fairly certain the men had concocted that excuse on their own. They simply wanted a reason to haul

Hill and Smythe before a judge, and they needed the legal trappings.

After a few more uncertain questions, the town voted unanimously to make Hunt magistrate. Only Clare understood how much he resisted. This must all seem strange to his American ways, but apparently, voting was something he accepted. He graciously accepted their confidence in him— although he sounded more grumpy than grateful.

Clare sat with her aunt and uncle. She'd offered them a room where they might retreat, but the entertainment factor plus the possible interaction with nobility held them riveted. They did not even ask about Oliver, who was perched in a window seat behind the draperies. His tutor sat in a chair next to the draperies, apparently whispering explanations of the proceedings.

Oliver was a legitimate heir, just as she was, but probably too young to vote. Clare would have preferred her nephew not be exposed to the world's cruelty, but perhaps the future generation needed to be less naïve than she had been.

Arnaud and Henri hauled the prisoner in from the cellar, accompanied by a ripple of anger from the crowd. No one had attempted to clean up Hill. His clothes were bloodied from Elsa's nose slamming. His coat hung off his bandaged shoulder much as Jack's did. He'd apparently been living rough for several days since his hair was dirty and his face unshaven. Homelessness painted a picture of guilt before a trial even took place.

Looking like a polished gentleman, Smythe had attempted to leave earlier. Elsa's older half-brother, the earl, had practically tied the merchant to a chair to prevent it. The lady's younger stepbrother, Smythe's fellow conspirator, merely squirmed in discomfort.

The crowd shuffled restlessly while Hunt ran through a list of questions identifying the prisoner for the record. Walker, of course, took notes.

"We have witnesses to your assault on former Lieutenant de Sackville. What have you to say on your own behalf?" Hunt directed the question at the once refined clerk struggling against his bonds.

"Nothing," Hill muttered.

"Then we shall charge you with assault on the lieutenant and take statements from the witnesses to be read in the next assize court." Hunt waited for Walker to note that down, while Hill turned purple beneath his unshaven whiskers.

"De Sackville *stole* the lady," Hill shouted. "He *lied* to steal her funds and destroy the bank! Why isn't he on trial?"

"Because Mr. de Sackville, not you, had the lady's permission to act on her behalf. Why should you care what happens to the lady's funds?"

Clare could tell Hunt was uncomfortable questioning Hill. The captain was an engineer, not a lawyer. But he knew how to raise tempers, and that seemed to work.

"Women are fools! That's why they're not allowed to control their own funds. She's endangering the livelihoods of hundreds of people." Hill glared at the nobility seated not far from Hunt. "You lot were handed all this land and wealth. Men like me have to fight to keep a roof over our heads."

"You had employment. Unless your employer paid you to shoot the lieutenant, I fail to see your point," Hunt intoned ominously. "We will proceed to the next charge unless you have extenuating circumstances you wish to report."

Clare was fairly certain they had no evidence for any other charge. What did Hunt plan to do? Harass Hill's employer?

"If Smythe goes bankrupt, so do I!" Hill cried. "How am I to support my mother and sister? I did what I had to do— shot a thief."

"Did you also shoot at the lady?" Hunt asked. "Perhaps to stop her from removing her funds from your employer?"

Murmurs of disapproval rippled across the audience. Shooting ladies simply was not done.

Smythe uncomfortably glanced at the exit. The elegant earl planted himself nearby, discouraging escape.

Hill must have sensed the tide turning. He glared at his employer. "He was supposed to marry her and save the bank! But he didn't have the mettle to do it himself. So he hired sapskulls who bungled everything. They let a damned female get the better of them! Fortunes will be lost because of a dithering old maid!"

Oh, charming. Clare glanced at Elsa, who held Jack's hand and simply grinned.

"Did your employer ask you to arrange for these hired sapskulls?" Hunt proceeded without revealing a single emotion. He was good at that.

"He had permission of the lady's brother. I was just the messenger." Hill had apparently decided to bring everyone down with him. He glared at Freddy, who glared back.

Hunt continued. "To clarify, your employer, Mr. Aloysius Smythe, spoke with Mr. Frederick Turner, the lady's younger stepbrother?"

"Right. The swell needed the blunt. He rounded up some others what needed funds too." Hill's speech was rapidly deteriorating. "I was given a bit of ready to distribute once the lady was persuaded onto the yacht and on her way to her nuptials. That's all I did. The rest of them, they made a hash of it."

"Not quite all you did," Hunt said with a bit of acid. "You decided to pay the bunglers in counterfeit notes, did you not?"

Hill looked stunned, then squirmed and cast a glance at Smythe, who practically swelled with outrage.

"*You* made those notes?" Smythe shouted, unable to contain himself any longer. "You nearly ruined me!" He turned to Hunt. "How did you know? Can he be charged with counterfeiting? I want him hanged!"

Villiers focused his fury on Smythe. the factory owner.

276

"You do not deny that you arranged for this villain to *kidnap my sister*? I will see *you* hanged!"

The audience broke out in excited chatter as nobles and gentlemen leaped to their feet. Clare gasped and pointed at Freddy attempting to sneak out. Henri tripped him and placed a boot on his back.

Walker impassively handed a hammer to Hunt, who slammed it against a chunk of firewood set on the table for this purpose. Thoughtful of them not to damage a lovely Chippendale. Clare hoped they'd placed padding beneath the firewood.

"Sit down!" Hunt roared in his best carrying officer's voice.

The fair-haired Marquess of Spalding, older and not as physically imposing as Villiers, but every inch a regal aristocrat, took a stand behind Smythe, blocking his escape. The earl hauled Elsa's young stepbrother from beneath Henri's boot and pinned him into a chair.

"The notes, please," Hunt demanded as the uproar died down. "Did you or did you not counterfeit notes to give to these kidnappers?"

"I did," Hill admitted sullenly. "I needed the funds more than they did, and no one would believe any note the likes of them handed out was bad. I gave the lot to the fancy bloke to pay people as they earned it. I'd be cast in irons if I got caught holding one."

"Only, after all the careful planning, the lady vanished, didn't she?" Hunt asked.

"The sodding swells took too long! I could have done it myself in less time than it took them to decide on hiring horses and luring the lady away and finding an inn and all that. I'm surrounded by clodpolls that don't know which end to wipe."

To Clare's admiration, Jack stood up. Fury boiled beneath his cold question. "You met one of the conspirators at an inn halfway between Birmingham and London on St. George's Day, did you not?"

Weary and bewildered, Hill could only stare. "They botched it. The lady was gone. I wanted the notes back."

"What did Mr. Culpepper say when you demanded the money back? He refused, did he not?" Jack almost sounded reasonable, except his knuckles were white where they clutched the chair Elsa sat in. Elsa patted his hand.

"Bastard all fancied up in his nobby boots and watch called me a clod and ordered me to find the lady, like he had any right to tell me what to do!" Hill indignantly dug his own grave.

Hunt held up a timepiece. "Is this the watch he carried?"

Hill suddenly clamped his mouth shut.

"You followed him, didn't you?" Jack asked. "You wanted those notes back."

Hill refused to answer.

Hunt pounded his hammer on the wood as the noise began to rise again. "Let it be recorded that the watch in question is engraved to Basil Culpepper, a man found dead in the hedgerow with a bullet in his skull, a man who carried the counterfeit notes in his saddle. Let the prisoner be remanded to assizes for murder and counterfeiting as well as assault and attempted abduction."

Hill leaped up, overturning his chair, and screaming. "What about them?" He tried to go after Smythe and Freddy who were on their feet, looking for escape. "They're the kidnappers!"

"Attempted kidnappers," Hunt said wearily. "They'll be dealt with under manorial law. Arnaud, take the prisoner to the cellar, please."

Arbitrary law, Clare suspected. Hunt had no notion of what to do with failed kidnappers.

"You can't charge us," the merchant banker shouted, leaping up.

The Marquess of Spalding blithely spun Smythe back into his chair with a punch to the jaw. Villiers grabbed his protesting stepbrother by the collar and shook him until Freddy squealed.

Chaos reigned after that.

Clare stood and held out her hands to her wide-eyed aunt and uncle. "Come, let us retire to the parlor and have some tea. I've had quite enough excitement for the day."

She was becoming very practiced at concealing the turmoil of anxiety and love in her heart. How would she ever write a heroine gaining courage from love when all seemed hopeless—especially when love and courage led to way too much unsettling excitement?

If Hunt could do it, so must she.

THIRTY

"THIS IS ABSOLUTELY DREADFUL," AUNT MARTHA CRIED IN shock, dabbing at her eyes with her handkerchief as Clare led her into the family parlor. "We must take that poor child away from these terrible people immediately!"

"You would have to find said child first," Clare said dryly. She indicated where to set the tea tray a maid carried in. "Besides, the terrible people are the ones being taken away. Why have you returned before I could write you of my decision?"

"Villiers's estate runs near ours. We heard he was setting out to retrieve his sister, and we thought to apply to him on Oliver's behalf." Uncle George took several sandwich triangles from the tray and settled in disgruntlement in a wing chair by the unlit fire. "He told us of the shootings, and we turned right around to come back."

Aunt Martha took a scone. "You'll need to pack your things, too, as well as Oliver's. I can't be expected to run after a little boy. We don't have room for a tutor, but I suppose we could put him up somehow until Oliver starts school."

This was exactly what Clare had always wanted—safety, shelter from the slings and arrows of misfortune. For years, she'd longed for security: after her father died, leaving them near penniless; after Bea and her husband died, leaving her an infant to raise; after her mother's death left her all alone except for Meera. Five years ago, she would have trembled in gratitude for the shelter of family.

But these last months had taught her a lesson or two. Watching Hunt walk into the unknown to take command of an entire village, she realized action provided one's own safe haven. Every person in this manor had created their own home—because they took action and helped each other, as her real family hadn't. Here, she was no longer alone.

No one could protect her from life's complications. Security came from within first, with her own knowledge and choices. She might be uneducated and cowardly, but that did not make her useless or stupid. And when she could not handle a problem alone, she now had people who had shown that they would help her, as she did them.

She trusted Hunt and Elsa and all their friends in the manor to *listen*. She could not say the same of her aunt and uncle, who did not need or even want her.

"Oliver is too young to attend boarding school," Clare stated firmly. "He needs a tutor to prepare him, and he needs friends to teach him confidence. He needs time to grow into his size so he cannot be bullied. We will be staying here."

"That is ridiculous," her uncle sputtered. "I shall write Owen at once. The courts will give us guardianship."

"What is it you really want, Uncle?" Clare asked, masking her terror that he was right. "In all of Oliver's seven years, you have not once expressed interest in his welfare. And even now, you only wish to send him away. What does he have that you want?"

Her aunt and uncle stared at her as if she'd grown a second head. Perhaps she had—or at least grown a backbone.

Before they could reply, Hunt let himself in. Fatigue lined his face, but his square jaw was set in determination. In his fine clothes—Clare would have to thank Walker for finding that valet—he appeared the part of earl or comte that he might have been, had circumstances been otherwise. Her heart melted when he took the seat on the sofa beside her and allowed her to hand him a cup of hated tea.

His fine clothes made him no less intimidating than when he'd worn an eye patch.

"Mr. and Mrs. Whitestone, I know this is informal, but I prefer to speak with you in person rather than through correspondence." He sipped the tea, grimaced, and set it aside. "I would like your permission to speak with your niece about marriage. I will, of course, adopt Oliver as my own. We will reside here at Wycliffe, where I can provide for both of them, and Miss Knightley can have the advantage of her mother's family for support. I have spoken with my aunt, Lady Spalding, and she agrees that this will be the best arrangement for all."

Clare nearly spluttered her tea. He had *not* talked to the dowager marchioness. The old biddy scarcely knew Oliver existed. And permission to speak? When had he ever cared what he said to anyone? He was completely ignoring her desire to leave. . . Because he knew she didn't desire it.

Out of curiosity, she bit her tongue and waited for the reaction.

Her uncle's jaw worked, but no sound emerged. Her aunt smiled grimly and spoke for him. "There must be settlements. Clarissa is a distinguished young lady of fine family and possesses an excellent dowry. What do you bring to the marriage?"

Clare set her cup down with a sharp rap. She would not be discussed as if she were a shawl to be haggled over, with no part in the matter. "We bring ourselves. Captain Huntley is an excellent engineer, an honorable soldier, and a kind and caring man. My dowry is a townhouse that may earn the grand sum of fifty pounds a year and a sapphire that I mean for Oliver's education. I bring *nothing* to a marriage except a domestic education and a talent for words, which I daresay no one but the captain might appreciate. I repeat my earlier question, *what is it you wish from me?*"

Hunt raised his eyebrows. He'd question her later. Well, she'd question him too. Asking for her uncle's permission before he asked her, indeed!

She didn't allow her fluttery insides to deter her from her mission.

Uncle George looked uncomfortable. He tugged at his neckcloth. Aunt Martha reached for another scone. This time, she waited for him to reply.

"I do not have your father's head for investment," he finally admitted. "Owen has agreed to provide support for his nephew. We know of a school willing to accept him as a scholarship student. We can use the funds Owen provides to help with our current situation. It does not seem fair to lose our home while the boy lives in luxury."

Hunt squeezed her hand. This was not a problem his engineering head could solve.

The sapphire and her home belonged to her *mother's* family, not her father's or Oliver's father. Her father had kept his small family comfortably for years, until he, too, suffered a financial reversal, but he'd *never* sold her mother's family jewels.

She had kept Oliver in comfort, not luxury, these past years, through frugality and her grandmother's small trust. She owed these people nothing.

But they were family. Oliver might need them someday. And he was their heir.

She squeezed Hunt's broad, comforting hand, then released him to press her palms together as she made a painful decision. "I will *not* relinquish Oliver's guardianship. If Viscount Owens is willing to pay for his nephew's education, then I will use his funds for Oliver's tutor and be grateful for your intervention in the matter. In return, I will arrange to have the funds I meant for his tutor and school sent to you."

That meant sending them the townhouse rent, earnings from her books, and eventually, some of the proceeds from the sale of the sapphire if she fell short. But Oliver would be where he was happy.

She would not be able to return to London.

She stood, and Hunt rose with her. She might weep a little in her chamber later, but for now, they had guests, and she was their hostess.

And then she'd have to straighten out Hunt and his unromantic declaration.

～

AFTER LUNCH, THE CAVALCADE OF CARRIAGES ROLLED AWAY, bearing the prisoners with them. Jack didn't know what had been decided about Elsa's bank accounts, but he assumed an earl and a marquess were better situated to squeeze blood from stones. Or money from a merchant behind bars. Smythe might yet buy himself out of court.

Elsa would survive whether she was heiress to a fortune or not.

Except—her powerful noble brother would return after he verified their lack of marriage documentation. Jack's head would roll then. He and Elsa had decisions to make.

For now, he was satisfied that the earl was arranging for Freddy to be shipped off to the antipodes or the Caribbean, whichever ship came first. Smythe—well, the nobles would take care of him, too, one way or another. Even the courts might overlook his wealth under the weight of an earl's fury.

Having Elsa beside him in the library for a family meeting, holding his hand under the table, made him happier than he'd ever been. While Arnaud presented his findings on the codes, Elsa's hand kept Jack sitting still for a change.

"Upon Lieutenant de Sackville's suggestion, Henri and I chose the code in the oil of Miss Knightley's grandmother, Lady Clarice. The only letters in the code are C and S. He suggested that the C stood for Clarice and the S for sapphire. There seem to be corresponding initials in the other paintings. The painting for Lady Eleanor, Lady Elspeth's grandmother, for instance, contains the letters E and R, and the necklace is a ruby."

Since no rubies or diamonds littered the table, Jack assumed the jewels had yet to be located. Worse yet, they were most likely in different places if each code led to a different ancestor and necklace.

"Jack also suggested that the library was our strongest clue. The late earl went to a great deal of trouble to extend the library around the corner and bring in the volumes from all his estates. We verified that with Lord Spalding." Arnaud opened the huge library index. "If we cannot use the letters to search the index, we were left with using the numbers."

Arnaud was enjoying the attention, Jack decided. The big Frenchman might be a quiet artist most of the time, but he'd been born the heir to immense estates and raised to take command.

As a younger son of a minor baron, Jack had no desire for attention or command and no penchant for violence. He simply wanted his horses. If he could have those, Wellington would have to save Europe without him. Now that he might have a chance to have the woman of his dreams, he had no desire to sacrifice his life as cannon fodder. He'd always been a lousy soldier.

"We found a pattern in the numbers that led us to this volume." Arnaud held up an ancient, leather-bound book. Opened, it revealed antique typography. "It's one of many histories written by the earl's ancestors about the priory, the first earl, and his descendants. The volume itself might be valuable and could be the reason for the code. An appraiser might be hired to determine if more volumes ought to be in a vault for safekeeping."

Jack caressed Elsa's palm with one finger. He should probably ask his father to examine the library. The old man would be delighted. At the head of the table, Hunt did not seem much more interested than Jack. He and Clare were scribbling hasty notes back and forth. He suspected the notes had nothing to do with the topic of treasure.

More interestingly, Hunt kept borrowing Clare's spectacles to read the notes.

"Why that book?" Lavender asked. "It looks like all the others."

Jack hid a snort. His reaction exactly. Perhaps history books were apropos for Clare and Oliver. Oliver was most likely under the table studying one now.

But the rest of the manor's inhabitants, like Jack, had other interests. Meera and Walker and the tutor had elected to leave the family discussion to family. Smart. Jack should have done the same, except he'd been the one to break the code, and he was curious about what they'd found.

"This particular volume because the code led to it, and it contains this note." Arnaud triumphantly produced a yellowed piece of stationery. "It is signed by the last earl."

Everyone at the table sat up, shut up, and turned to Arnaud, eyes wide.

He gave the paper to Clare. "He addressed it to his daughter Clarice's descendants."

Wide-eyed in shock, Clare cleared her throat and read the shaky writing slowly.

I am here to attest that unearned wealth does not bring happiness. I appreciate that it might provide a safe roof over one's head. I suspect that only those without a safe roof will attempt the monumental task of searching for the family jewels. If you have come this far, then you are either desperate or very clever. I doubt I can hope that you are a historian and simply opened the book in the interest of research. Whichever it is, you deserve a reward and encouragement to continue searching.

Clare held up a second sheet of paper, then passed it around.

A map—of sorts. Mostly, it looked like a large square.

THIRTY-ONE

THURSDAY MORNING, WITH BREAKFAST SERVED, AND SOUP simmering for their mid-day meal, Elsa took off her apron and headed for the stable.

Last night, after all the excitement over the strange map, she and Jack hadn't had a moment to themselves. He hadn't come down to the kitchen this morning looking for her. Did that mean he'd learned not to invade her territory? She rather missed his invasions, if so.

More likely, it meant he was crawling through the attics with Hunt's cousins, trying to work out the meaning of the odd drawing. Men liked puzzles.

She needed to ride and unclutter her thoughts. Too much had happened these past weeks, and she was no longer so clear on what she wanted. She had her beloved kitchen and horses. Villiers had finally acknowledged her enough to drive off the bullies and villains. For all anyone knew, she might not be wealthy any longer. That should leave her safe enough to do as she wished—if only she knew what that was.

If she no longer had men bullying her, she could go home. Jack didn't need to pretend to be her husband. But she no longer had any interest in returning to an empty house with only servants to talk to. If even the vicar had thought she should marry Smythe—he had loaned his palfrey to Hill!— then there was no one in Newchurch she could rely on.

By the time she reached the stable, her stallion was already gone from his stall. The grooms disliked riding him. Only Jack would have him out at this hour. She smiled at his proprietary attitude. He'd helped her buy the thoroughbred when the horse was only a yearling. That made the stallion's welfare his concern.

Except the damned man was supposed to be lying flat and not risking his health for a *horse*.

She wasn't his mother. Or his wife. He was a grown man. She couldn't force him to behave.

She took her time, checking with the grooms about the mares in foal. She didn't want to move the mares again. But she'd have to take the others home unless she found larger pastures here. Would she have the funds to buy land?

She'd never had to worry about money. She wouldn't start now.

Unable to stand it any longer, she chose a restive bay and rode down the drive, fearing she'd find Jack's prostate body in the hedgerows. She took the lane through the village. Smoke swirled from a few chimneys. There were signs of a few roofs being rethatched. The manor was slowly having an effect on the abandoned cottages.

Before she had traveled far, her stallion raced from the opposite direction. Fool man would break his neck or someone else's. How was he even controlling the horse with that shoulder?

With his legs, of course. With one hand, he reined in instantly upon seeing her, his seat in the saddle as strong as hers. Devil take it, her stupid heart nearly leaped from her chest every time she saw him. And he'd be riding off to soldier any day.

"Just the person I want to see!" he called in excitement. "Come along. Let me show you."

With no reason to resist, she rode beside him. "Slow down, you madman! You're supposed to be swooning over the furniture for another week."

He shot her a look that boiled her blood, then defiantly spurred the stallion into a gallop.

Really, what was she thinking? Men were hopeless, marriage, ludicrous.

They raced nearly neck-in-neck, turning down a dirt path past the village. From the neat hedgerows, Elsa assumed this was not manor land. Someone had been tending the fields. They slowed down on the narrower path. Elsa admired the ivory-blooming hawthorn hedge, underlaid by a carpet of purple violets and the last of the yellow primroses.

"This is almost like home," she cried. "Isn't it marvelous? Are those blackberry brambles?"

"No idea." Jack turned in at a break in the hedge. An old wooden gate hung loosely from its post. "I've been talking to the locals. They say an elderly widow lives here. Her grandson has gone to work in town. She has no one to look after the property. She doesn't want to leave her home, but she can't keep it up."

"But she's done so well!" Elsa protested. "Look at the pasture. Does she have sheep? Goats?"

"She does, but she's having difficulty keeping them as well. Come along and meet her." He blithely rode down a stranger's drive.

Elsa rode ahead, blocking his path. "Why? *Why* are you showing me this?"

He blinked in surprise, as if it were royally obvious. He gestured at the pasture. "Your horses need land. You don't need a farmhouse. Did you not wish to stay at the manor?"

She opened her mouth, but nothing immediately came out. She didn't know what she wanted, did she?

Well, looking at Jack in all his broad-shouldered manliness, the mad soldier who kept looking after her for no good reason. . . Yes, she did know what she wanted. But he'd given very little evidence that he wanted to settle down.

Yes, he had, but he'd attached so many strings to how he wanted his life to be, that she assumed he wasn't serious.

"I cannot know if I have the funds to buy land." She could be as obtuse as he. The man needed to learn to explain himself.

He beamed. "That's just it! *I* can buy the land. Without the house and outbuildings, it is not worth a great deal. I'll even have enough funds left to buy a couple of carriage horses to breed. In time, I hope to restore the old stable."

"Jack, this is the outside of enough." She slipped her boot from the stirrup and threw her leg over the saddle to slide down. "Lack of blood has sapped your brain."

He was right there to catch her, probably ripping his wound open taking her hefty weight. He didn't even flinch. She ought to punch him for his stupidity. Instead, she threw a saddle blanket on a patch of grass and sat down, hoping to force him to do the same.

He didn't protest but obediently settled beside her, lying flat to admire the leaves of a crabapple that had grown up through the hedge. "All right, lecture me. Where have I gone wrong?"

She loved the fool man so much, she could cry. But she wasn't the crying sort. "You have left out a few steps. The last I heard, you meant to return to war. Now you're buying land for *my* horses? Why? I have more than enough land if I take them back to Newchurch."

He crossed his wide brown hands over his broad chest and frowned at the sky. "You want to go back to Villiers' dubious protection?"

She broke off a spindly elder branch and swatted him with it. "I do not."

He turned his head warily to watch her. "I am not very good at reading minds, especially female ones."

"As I am not very good at reading male minds! What are your intentions, Jack?" She couldn't be much plainer.

His eyes widened. She could almost see his thoughts whirling in his dense head. Without sitting up, he took her hand, the one bearing the alabaster ring, and rubbed the band. "I thought I'd made my intentions clear, my lady. But if I must get down on one knee, I wish to at least have a pearl in hand, not this piece of nothing. You deserve the best of every-thing, Elsa, and I am aware I am not it. But I'm hoping, if you see I can provide anything you need. . ."

"Dash it all, Jack! Will you quit being such a gentleman, forget that I'm supposed to be a lady, and understand that my needs have naught to do with wealth and pearls?" She leaned over and kissed him.

His arms instantly wrapped around her, hard, and she sprawled atop him while he explored places she hadn't known needed exploring.

"Finally, Jack, I thought you'd never ask," she murmured, laughing, as he rolled her over and tore open her shirt.

"I'll start hunting for a clergyman tomorrow," he murmured.

His hands and kisses transported her to a place without words.

∽

HUNT SCRATCHED AT HIS SCARRED EYE. IT NO LONGER HURT, SO he assumed it was as healed as it would ever be. Vague light and shadow would never be sufficient to shoot a pistol with any accuracy. Still, he was learning to read with one eye and. . . spectacles. He needed to have some made of his own.

Or perhaps just a single glass that he could slip in and out of his pocket so he did not appear entirely antiquated.

Recognizing that his good eye didn't have the best vision ended any hope he might have harbored of returning to surveying. But these days, his thoughts followed a vision of loveliness and warmth and led to a future of children romping in a ridiculously moldering old manor, through woods and orchards.

If he could keep the manor. . .

He'd find a way, if he could have Clare by his side. And in his bed. By not treating him as a cripple, she'd brought him out of his self-pity and returned him to living. He just didn't know what he had to offer her in return.

But he had to ask. Now that she'd chosen to stay, he couldn't keep living with her and not ask. After her amazing performance with her aunt and uncle, he knew she'd changed as much as he had. He didn't know if her new independence was good or bad for his plans, and there was only one way of knowing.

While the house was quiet, he knew she'd be sequestered in the little room she'd turned into an office of sorts. From there, all domestic matters seemed to be settled without need of his interference. He appreciated that more than he could say.

She always left the door slightly ajar so anyone might pop in. He hesitated in the hall, debating whether he ought to set a romantic scene. . . and remembered Walker had told him the trees were budding in the orchard. The sun was out.

She was scribbling furiously, and it took her a second or two before she even noticed his entrance. She blinked and hastily turned the paper over, then frowned, and set it right again. "Hunt! I thought you were pounding at the crypt ceiling."

"Drilling is next. I'll have to hire help for that. Would you care to take a walk? It's a lovely day, and I've been told the apple blossoms are almost ready to open." He felt like a dunce uttering such rubbish, but he'd been assured that women wanted romance.

She smiled, and he was certain mischief danced in her eyes. "The apple blossoms are very pretty, and Elsa is already plotting jams and sauce and butter. May I thank you for helping me with my family by suggesting that, instead of walking, you take a seat by the grate and simply talk to me as you might with Walker."

"You are worth taking the trouble to learn what you like," Hunt insisted, not immediately accepting the offered seat. "I've not known you even two months, and they've been rather harried. Would you prefer to go into the city and shop? See the sights? I'm negotiating for a carriage, but all I have at the moment is the cart."

"I like to *talk*." She sat back and waited for him to sit. "And perhaps now, with everything relatively quiet, is the time I should start this conversation."

That sounded ominous. He raised his eyebrows and took the chair. It was a lady's chair and didn't exactly welcome his bulk, but that wasn't where his thoughts fled. Was she about to say she was leaving after all? He thought they'd agreed. . .

She handed him a book. The gilded title was blurry, as was the name of the author when he opened the cover. It appeared to be a novel. "Have you discovered more hidden clues?"

She removed her spectacles and handed them to him. "No. I want there to be no secrets between us. I cannot tell another soul, so you must swear not to speak of this. I could lose Oliver if word got about."

Her glasses frame was too small for his big head, so he had to hold it in place. *The Monk's Spectre* by Charles Knight. He flipped the pages and found nothing of curiosity. He glanced up. She was twining a lock of golden hair around her finger and watching him intently. And that's when it struck

294

him. He glanced at the author's name again, back at Clare and her ever-present pen and paper, and a bell tolled in his dim brain.

"You are Charles Knight?" he suggested.

She smiled, not quite in relief. Worry crossed her expression. "Are you horrified?"

"That you can write an entire tome like this?" He held up the book in amazement. "I can barely sit to read an entire book, and you have *written* one? Just out of your head? And had it *published*?"

She nodded, still watching his reaction.

He sat back and began reading, despite the difficulty. The print was small. "No wonder you shouted at me that first night we met, when I was flinging books on the flames. You write the books I was destroying!"

"Well, not exactly," she said with a trace of amusement. "You were tearing up ledgers. They were unique and irreplaceable. Novels sell by the hundreds, so it's not quite the same."

He shook his head in disbelief, at his density, if nothing else. "They sell these in bookstores? Charles Knight is a known author? How do you manage this?"

She shrugged. "I do not make public appearances. My entire family, even those in the grave, would spin in their beds if they knew. Even my publisher does not know for certain. He sends funds and correspondence to my solicitor, who forwards them to me." She studied him carefully. "You do not mind? You do not think me terrible for exerting my poor female brain on such rubbish when I should be applying it to domestic concerns?"

"Rubbish?" He glanced up from the book and stared at her. "You wrote a *book*! How many men can claim that? Is this how you mean to pay your uncle?"

She nodded uncertainly. "I've written a second. The first one so far has earned almost as much as the rent on my townhouse for half a year. My publisher assures me it will sell more once the second is published. If I can continue writing my stories, I can hold my uncle off for a little while, perhaps until his financial difficulties have eased."

She brightened. "Of course, Arnaud and Henri might find treasure, and we will all be rich!"

Hunt snorted and set the book aside. He got up, shut the office door, and produced the box he'd been carrying with him this past week of uncertainty. He thought he detected a whiff of his grandmother's floral French perfume. Clare must be wearing some of the fripperies Lavender had scavenged from the wardrobes. The scent was arousing, giving him more courage to say what needed to be said—before he died of longing.

With some difficulty, he got down on bended knee and held up the ring. "I am in awe of your intelligence, your courage, and your character. I am aware that I need you more than you need me. But if you would do me the honor of being my wife, I promise to shower you with love and all that is in me to provide. I fear romantic declarations will not be frequent, but I can promise to tell you that I love you every day from here until eternity."

He thought she gasped, but all his senses reeled when she dropped to her knees in front of him and flung her arms around his neck. Thought didn't enter his head then. He sat down, hard, and pulled her into his lap, covering her face with kisses, until their mouths finally met.

Once she was curled in an unladylike ball in his lap, he chuckled and pulled back enough to study her expression. He thought she might be happy. Perhaps he had done it right, after all. "You have not answered me. Will you consider this unemployed, half-blind American for husband when you deserve so much better?"

"If you truly love me, you will quit disparaging yourself like that. I have never met a man as wonderful as you. My next book will have a hero who fixes things and notices people, including women and children. He will ride to the rescue of entire villages, because that is what heroes do. He shoulders the work that must be done without complaint. Well, maybe he shoots bats, but he won't fling books because they're too precious in medieval times. Do they have muskets in the fifteenth century?"

He laughed and held her before she could scramble away to search the library. "Give him a rapier and a cutlass. Now, will you marry me or not?"

"Of course, I will marry you!" She sat up and began adjusting the lace and fripperies he'd disturbed. "But we don't have a church or a clergyman, and I'm not at all certain a bishop will entertain an uncouth American who isn't Anglican, so a special license may not be easily attainable."

"I shall tell him we'll be living in sin unless he grants special dispensation, but we still need a clergyman to hear the vows." He rolled her on her back and leaned over her. "The sooner, the better. I shall have Walker start a letter-writing campaign. Surely one of our immense family can provide."

"As if any of them have spared us any interest," she scoffed.

He nuzzled her ear and drank in the sweet earthy scent of roses. "I will tell them we have found treasure. That should do it."

"Better, let us tell them we have found love and romance under the spell of your French grandmother. I swear, she is here. We should open an inn for would-be couples, advertise the presence of a romantic ghost. . ."

He covered her mouth with kisses before her creative mind conjured ghostly vicars, haunted chapels, and chanting monks as well.

Wycliffe Manor would be a home again. That was all that mattered now.

CHARACTERS

Captain Alistair Huntley—engineer US Army; great-grandson of Earl of Wycliffe

Clarissa (Clare) Knightley—spinster; great-granddaughter of Earl of Wycliffe

Oliver Knightley Owen—Clare's seven-year-old nephew

Daniel Walker—Hunt's friend, accountant, secretary

Arnaud Lavigne— Hunt's artist cousin, eldest son of Comte Lavigne

Henri Lavigne—peddler brother of Arnaud; younger son of Comte

Meera Abrams—druggist / apothecary; Clare's best friend

Lavender Marlowe—granddaughter of Lady Lavinia Marlowe (Wycliffe's daughter)

Lt. Honorable John (Jack) Cecil de Sackville—retired soldier, son of Baron de Sackville

Lady Elspeth (Elsa) Laurel Villiers (Lara Evans)—great-granddaughter of Earl of Wycliffe

Earl of Villiers—Elsa's half-brother

Frederick Turner—Elsa's stepbrother, newly married

Basil Culpepper—impoverished dandy

Geoffrey Garrett—vicar in Elsa's hometown

Aloysius Smythe—inherited factories in Birmingham, owns estate next to Elsa's

Reginald Hill—Smythe's factotum

Benedict Bosworth Jr.—banker for Wycliffe Manor Trust

Hank—Elsa's head groom

Aunt Martha—Clare's paternal aunt

Terrence Birdwhistle—tutor

James—Hunt's valet

Marquess of Spalding—stepson of Hunt's Aunt Elaine, dowager Lady Spalding

George Reid, Earl of Wycliffe—deceased, left manor to all his family

GRAVESYDE PRIORY MYSTERY

Secrets of Wycliffe Manor
Book #1

Be wary of what you wish for. . .

In Regency England:
The descendant of adventuring—dead—aristocrats, Clarissa Knightley supplements a modest inheritance by penning gothic novels that cost more than they earn. Upon learning that she has mysteriously inherited a share of an earl's estate, she rashly packs up her household. In remote Gravesyde Priory, she hopes to find a safe haven and family who will welcome her and her young nephew.

Instead, she discovers a drunken American army captain, his African servant, and ancient, surly caretakers. Terrified, prepared to flee, Clare is lured to linger by the prospect of secret diaries, hidden jewels, and an increasingly intriguing man. Then a killer strikes.

The crumbling manor's ominous and baffling history offers fascinating fodder for Clare's horror novels—if only she can survive real-life madmen and a spectral murderer who may seek the jewels at any price.

To Buy, Please Visit
https://patriciarice.com/books/the-secrets-of-wycliffe-manor/

The Mystery of the Missing Heiress
Patricia Rice

Published by Rice Enterprises, Dana Point, CA, an affiliate of Book View Café Publishing Cooperative

Book View Café
304 S. Jones Blvd. Suite #2906
Las Vegas NV 89107

BOOK VIEW CAFE

ALSO BY PATRICIA RICE

The World of Magic:

AMBER AFFAIRS

MOONSTONE SHADOWS

THE WEDDING GIFT

THE WEDDING QUESTION

THE WEDDING SURPRISE

School of Magic

LESSONS IN ENCHANTMENT

A BEWITCHING GOVERNESS

AN ILLUSION OF LOVE

THE LIBRARIAN'S SPELL

ENTRANCING THE EARL

CAPTIVATING THE COUNTESS

Psychic Solutions

THE INDIGO SOLUTION

THE GOLDEN PLAN

THE CRYSTAL KEY

THE RAINBOW RECIPE

THE AURA ANSWER

THE PRISM EFFECT

Historical Romance:

American Dream Series

MOON DREAMS

REBEL DREAMS

The Rebellious Sons

WICKED WYCKERLY

DEVILISH MONTAGUE

NOTORIOUS ATHERTON

FORMIDABLE LORD QUENTIN

The Regency Nobles Series

THE GENUINE ARTICLE

THE MARQUESS

ENGLISH HEIRESS

IRISH DUCHESS

Regency Love and Laughter Series

CROSSED IN LOVE

MAD MARIA'S DAUGHTER

ARTFUL DECEPTIONS

ALL A WOMAN WANTS

Rogues & Desperadoes Series

LORD ROGUE

MOONLIGHT AND MEMORIES

SHELTER FROM THE STORM

WAYWARD ANGEL

DENIM AND LACE

CHEYENNES LADY

Dark Lords and Dangerous Ladies Series

LOVE FOREVER AFTER

SILVER ENCHANTRESS

DEVIL'S LADY

DASH OF ENCHANTMENT

INDIGO MOON

Too Hard to Handle

TEXAS LILY

TEXAS ROSE

TEXAS TIGER

TEXAS MOON

Mystic Isle Series

MYSTIC ISLE

ABOUT BOOK VIEW CAFÉ

 *Book View Café* Publishing Cooperative (BVC) is an author-owned cooperative of professional writers, publishing in a variety of genres including fantasy, romance, mystery, and science fiction — with 90% of the proceeds going to the authors. Since its debut in 2008, BVC has gained a reputation for producing high-quality ebooks. BVC's ebooks are DRM-free and are distributed around the world. The cooperative is now bringing that same quality to its print editions.

BVC authors include New York Times and USA Today bestsellers as well as winners and nominees of many prestigious awards.